STOKESBY GRAVE

A DCI Tanner Mystery
- Book Twelve -

DAVID BLAKE

www.david-blake.com

Proofread by Jay G Arscott

Special thanks to Kath Middleton, Ann Studd, John Harrison,
Anna Burke, Emma Stubbs, and Jan Edge

First edition published by Black Oak Publishing Ltd
in Great Britain, 2024

Cover Photograph ID 82324917 © Leighton Collins | Dreamstime.com

ISBN: 978-1-7385418-1-2

DEDICATION

For Akiko, Akira and Kai.

DAVID BLAKE

THE DCI TANNER SERIES

"Beloved, never avenge yourselves, but leave it to the wrath of God, for it is written, 'Vengeance is mine, I will repay, says the Lord.'"
Romans 12:19

- PROLOGUE -

Friday, 8th July, 1994

VINCENT O'RILEY BROUGHT his dented, rusty old transit van creaking to a halt at the end of a narrow, potholed, country lane. Turning off the engine, he sat for a moment to draw in a series of nervous, shallow breaths. Directly ahead was Stokesby Church, silhouetted against the orange light of a steadily rising sun. Seventy miles beyond that was Lord Montgrave's sprawling stately home, where he'd been less than an hour before.

Peeling his sweating hands from off the grimy plastic steering wheel, he tugged on the handbrake to gaze around at the long, angular face of the man sitting next to him, his oldest and most trusted friend, Coby Morgan.

'I take it there's no one behind us?' came Coby's low, rasping voice, leaning forward to stare into the van's rectangular side mirror.

'There 'asn't been since we left.'

'Then we can relax, can't we?'

'Only if we stick to the plan,' Vincent replied, as Coby passed him one of two sawn-off shotguns that had been resting on his lap.

Opening the doors to climb out into the unsettling stillness of dawn's mist-shrouded air, they slunk quietly around to the back.

'Hey, Jake?' Coby called, banging his fist against one of the panels. 'Are you still in there?'

'Course I'm still in here!' came the muffled sound of another man's voice. 'Where else am I supposed to be?'

'I just thought you might 'ave fallen out, 'alfway down the M1,' Coby replied, grinning at Vincent as he did.

'Are you gonna let me out, or not?'

'Well, we would,' Coby replied, 'but Vincent's gone and lost the key.'

'Ha, ha. Very funny.'

'Sorry, Jakey-Boy,' Vincent chirped, doing his best to keep a straight face, 'but Coby's right. It must've fallen out of m' pocket when all those bloody dogs was chas'n us.'

'Tell you what, either you let me out, or I'll set fire to the money. The paintin', as well.'

'How's you gonna do that?' Coby queried, still grinning at Vincent. 'You ain't gotta a light. I know that, cus I've got yours here, in my pocket.'

'I'm gonna rub two fuck'n sticks together, that's how.'

'I didn't know you was a Boy Scout.'

'Are you gonna let me out, or am I gonna break down the fuck'n door?'

'Alright, alright! Keep your 'air on!' Coby laughed, taking the keys from Vincent to whisper, *'not that he's got any.'*

'I heard that!'

'I didn't say nuff'n,' Coby added, wriggling a key into the lock. 'Certainly nothing about your hair, *or lack of it.'*

Tugging open one of the doors, both Coby and Vincent peered inside to see a small, balding man, perched on a bench seat to the side, another sawn-off shotgun resting on his lap.

'Are you coming out, or not?' Coby asked, taking the second door off its latch to lever that one open as well.

Jake glared menacingly out at him. 'I assume no one followed us?' he asked, switching his gaze to Vincent.

'We've barely seen a car since we left.'

'And you didn't drive too fast?'

'I stuck to the speed limit, all the way back.'

'I told you to drive just over the speed limit!'

'That's what I did!'

'That's not what you said.'

'Well, that's what I meant.'

Jake craned his neck to stare cautiously down the shadow-filled lane behind them. 'Right, give me a hand with this lot, will you?' he eventually said, leaning forward to slide two of three large black holdalls over the metal floor towards them.

'Which one's got the paintin' in it?' questioned Vincent, as Coby hauled one out to place on the ground.

'This one,' Jake replied, grabbing hold of the one by his feet to climb slowly out. 'I divided the money equally between us during the trip,' he continued, jumping down. 'You can check, if you like.'

'We trust you,' muttered Coby. 'Besides, we know where you live.'

'I'll call the buyer I've lined up for the paintin' when I get home,' Jake continued. 'I'll give you a shout when he collects. Then you can come round to pick up your share, as agreed.'

'Are you sure you can trust him?' questioned Vincent.

'I'll let you know when the police come knock'n on my door, but as I've said before, the risk is mine.'

'Fair enough.'

'Which is why I'm changing the deal.'

As Jake's words were left to hang suspended in the air, Vincent and Coby exchanged a dubious frown.

'Sorry, Jake,' Vincent eventually continued, turning back, 'but for a minute there I thought you said you were changing the deal.'

'I'm taking my share now,' Jake continued, firmly holding onto the bag he'd carried out of the van.

'Er...' Vincent began, 'I thought we'd agreed to hide the money until the police stop lookin' for it?'

'Yeah, I know, but my circumstances 'ave changed, meaning that I can't wait that long.'

'So you're just going to take your share now, to start buying stuff with it?'

'Don't worry, I'm not going to spend it on anything stupid.'

'Knowing 'ow much you like your flash cars and fancy clothes, I find that very hard to believe.'

'Frankly, I don't give a shit if you believe me or not. I'm taking my share now.'

'And what 'appens when you get caught with all that cash stashed under your bed?'

'I'm not gonna keep it under my bed.'

'You know what I mean.'

'If I get caught, I get caught. It's my risk, not yours.'

'If you'd done the job on your own, then fair enough, but you didn't, though, did you?'

'You think I'd grass you up?'

'I don't *think* you would, I *know* you would. All they'd 'ave to do is offer you a reduced sentence, and you'd start singing like a bird, one that had just had its feet nailed to a tree.'

'I wouldn't – I promise!'

'Course you would. Anyone would, which is why we can't let you leave with that money.'

Jake glowered at Vincent for a moment longer before lifting the barrels of his shotgun to point directly at his accomplice's chest. 'Sorry, mate, but I don't see how you're gonna stop me.'

'You're not seriously threatening to shoot me?'

'I will if you don't let me go.'

'Well, I'm not, so you'd better get on with it.'

'I'm warning you!'

'Coby's not gonna let you leave either, not with all that money, are you, Coby?'

'Sorry, Jakey-Boy,' Coby replied, 'but Vincent's right. If you get caught with all that cash, we'll all go down.'

'Look, I promise, on my mum's grave, if I get caught – which I won't – but if I do, I'll keep my mouth shut.'

'You better tell your mate to put the bag down,' muttered Vincent, lifting the barrels of his own shotgun to point at Jake's bulging, over-sized stomach.

'Alright you two, just calm the fuck down!'

'I'm leaving with my share,' stated Jake, stepping back as his index finger rested against the first of two curving steel triggers.

'If you take one more step,' said Vincent, in a low, menacing voice, 'I *will* shoot you.'

With the two men staring at each other in antagonistic silence, Jake eventually lifted his fat, round, stubbly chin. 'Me first,' he grinned, pulling the trigger, only to hear the gun click harmlessly in his hands.

Gawping down at it, he pulled desperately back on

the second trigger, only for the exact same thing to happen.

'You didn't fink we'd be stupid enough to give you live cartridges, did you?' queried Vincent, taking careful aim at Jake's fat, bald, shiny round head.

'No – wait,' Jake spluttered, his eyes shifting between the gun and Vincent's ever-narrowing eyes. 'You're right,' he added, with a nervous laugh. 'We should all hide the money. I don't really need it. Not now, at least. I was only joking.'

'Too late, my friend,' Vincent replied, offering the short balding man a merciless smile. 'Too fuckn' late.'

As the shotgun went off in Vincent's hands, he watched with macabre satisfaction as Jake's head expanded into a halo of blood, leaving the body to topple to the ground like a demolished building.

With the blast echoing off into the distance, he turned to see Coby, staring at him with a look of incomprehensible disbelief.

'What 'ave you done?' Coby eventually demanded, his eyes blinking repeatedly, as if trying to make sense of what he'd just seen.

'Simple,' Vincent retorted, lowering the smoking barrels to the ground. 'Dramatically increased our share of the profits.'

'But – how're we going to sell the paintin' without him?'

'He's not the only person with connections. Besides, he was winding me up.'

Coby's eyes drifted down to what used to be Jake's pale, stupid-looking face, but now looked more like a plate of half-cooked mincemeat. 'OK, so, what do we do now?'

'Continue with the plan, as we should 'ave done before Jakey-Boy got greedy.'

'What about his body?'

Vincent shrugged with apathetic indifference. 'We'll just chuck him into the drainage ditch. I doubt if anyone will find him. Not here. Even if they do, I'm not sure how they'd be able to recognise him.'

'What about his fingerprints? You do know that the police 'ave got them on file, as with ours. If they find him, and identify him, they'll be knocking on our doors about five minutes later.'

'Then we'll just 'ave to cut his hands off and chuck them into the nearest river. It's no problem. I've got a hacksaw in the van.'

'Jesus Christ, Vincent. Are you some sort of deranged psychopathic lunatic?'

'I'm a man who gets things done, that's what I am! Now, are you gonna help me get rid of the body, or are you just gonna keep staring at me like some sort of gormless moron?'

The lights from a car's headlights, creeping into the lane they'd parked at the end of, had them turning nervously around.

'Shit,' Coby cursed, seeing a strip of blue lights along the top of its roof. 'It's the old bill. They must 'ave heard the gunshot. What the fuck are we gonna do now?'

'All right, there's no need to panic. All we 'ave to do is hide what's left of Jake's body,' Vincent replied, crouching down to take hold of the dead man's ankles.

'What about the guns – and the money?' Coby demanded, helping lift the body by its wrists.

Swinging it into the overgrown drainage ditch to watch it instantly disappear, Vincent glanced frantically about. 'Stick the guns in the bags,' he eventually continued, unzipping one of them to shove both his, as well as the one Jake had, inside.

'Then what?' Coby questioned, wrenching open

the one by his feet.

As a series of blue lights began ricocheting off the trees around them, Vincent grabbed a roll of tightly bound twenty-pound notes from inside the bag to stand slowly up. 'Just follow my lead,' he muttered, from the corner of his mouth, as he turned to face the approaching car.

When it eventually came to a halt, barely twenty feet away, he hoisted up a welcoming hand.

'Are you two alright?' came a young man's enquiring voice, as the outline of first a policeman, then a policewoman, came slowly into view.

'All good, thank you, officers.'

'We just happened to be driving through Stokesby, when we heard what sounded like a gunshot,' the policeman continued, turning on a powerful torch to shine into Vincent's squinting face.

'Yeah, sorry about that. It was my van misfiring. It doesn't seem to want to start.'

'I see,' the police officer continued, shining his torch around. 'May I ask where you're trying to get to?'

'We're on our way to work.'

The policeman raised the beam to take in Stokesby Church behind them.

'We were taking a shortcut,' Vincent replied, glancing around.

'A shortcut to where? From what I remember, this lane only goes to the church. Unless, of course, you work there, as choirboys, perhaps?'

'There's a track through the graveyard. It leads up to Filby Road, on the other side. I know we shouldn't, but it saves 'aving to drive through Stokesby.'

'Fair enough, I suppose,' the policeman continued, bringing the beam back to Vincent's chiselled, sun-bronzed face. 'Do you mind me asking your name?'

'O'Riley. Mr.'

'I take it you live around here, Mr O'Riley?'

'Not far.'

'Could you be a little more specific?'

'Tunstall.'

'And where are you going?'

'Potter Heigham. I own one of the boatyards up there.'

'What about your friend?' the policeman continued, directing his torch's beam into Coby's face.

Vincent glanced around to see his friend standing a few feet behind him. 'He's my business partner.'

'Does he have a name?'

Coby cleared his throat. 'Mason. Coby Mason.'

'And what's in all the bags, Mr Mason?'

'Just tools, and stuff.'

'So, why aren't they in the van?'

'We were – er – we took them out, when we were trying to get the van started.'

'You keep your tools in the engine bay, do you?'

'More to lighten the load,' Coby replied. 'We was about to push it up to the church carpark, before finding a phone to call the AA. Actually, now that you're here, perhaps you could give us a hand?'

'To push it, or to call the AA?'

'How about both?' Coby grinned.

'Tell you what, if you show us what's inside the bags, we'll give you a tow to the nearest garage, not that they'll be open, of course. Not at half-past six in the morning.'

Vincent exchanged an anxious glance with Coby, before offering the policeman a conniving smile. 'Perhaps we can come to some sort of an arrangement?'

'I thought that was the arrangement?'

'I was thinking more along the lines of us making a donation to the Norfolk Police Benevolent Fund,' Vincent continued, showing the policeman the rolled-up money he'd extracted from the bag earlier. 'Then maybe you and your colleague would be prepared to look the other way?'

A moment of contemplative silence fell over the group, as the police officer shifted his gaze to the attractive young policewoman, standing quietly on the other side of the squad car. 'How much are we talking about?' he eventually asked, turning back.

'How much do you want?'

'I see. So, you *are* trying to bribe us, then?'

'As I said, it would be more of a charitable donation. A generous one, at that.'

'I think it's time we looked inside those bags of yours, don't you?' the policeman continued, levering a truncheon out of his utility belt to step cautiously forward.

'It's just tools, officer, honest!' Vincent declared, crouching down to the bag at his feet. 'Look, I'll show you.'

'If you could stay where you are, please, Mr O'Riley.'

'Sorry – but – I thought you wanted to see what's inside?'

The policeman hesitated for a moment. 'OK, but do it slowly.'

'Honestly, I don't know what all the fuss is about,' Vincent muttered, in an affable, chatty tone.

Reaching inside the bag, Vincent stood slowly back up as a demonic grin spread out over his devilishly handsome face.

As the constable's gaze became transfixed by the barrels of the shotgun, pointing directly at his chest, he immediately began inching away. 'Now wait j-just a m-minute.'

'You know,' Vincent continued, his face adopting a more serious expression, 'fortunately for you, I'm not in the habit of murdering police officers, certainly not attractive girly-type ones, like your colleague. But if the two of you don't climb back into that little car of yours to fuck-off back to wherever it was that you came from, you'll leave me with little choice. Once you 'ave, if I find out that either of you has told someone, *anyone* about what you've seen here today, then I'm going to find you – both of you! And when I do, I'm not going to be quite so lenient.'

The sound of a distant siren, drifting through the air towards them, had Vincent turning to look at Coby with an anxious eye. The moment he did, he saw the young policeman dive into the squad car, just as Coby's shotgun exploded into life beside him.

As the hollow blast echoed away over the gently undulating landscape, Vincent turned to see his best mate, staring in wide-eyed horror at the ground in front of him.

Following his gaze, it took him a full moment to fully comprehend what Coby was looking at: the policewoman's small, fragile body, lying beside the squad car like a discarded doll.

Dragging his eyes off her pale, blood-splattered face, he turned to glare at Coby with a look of incomprehensible disbelief.

'It – it was an accident!' Coby declared, unable to look Vincent in the eye. 'The gun – it – it just went off in my hands!'

Hearing the churning sound of the squad car's engine being turned over in an effort to start it, Vincent glanced around to see the policeman behind the wheel, staring down at the key he was turning with a petrified grimace.

'Jesus fucking Christ,' he cursed. 'Now we're going to 'ave to kill both of them.'

Taking a deliberate step forward, he pointed the shotgun at the policeman's head to pull back on the trigger, only for it to click uselessly in his unshaking hands.

'For fuck's sake,' he cursed, pulling the gun away from his shoulder to glare down at it in disgust. 'Give me your gun,' he said to Coby, holding out a demanding hand. 'This one's fuck'n useless.'

'I'm sorry, Vincent, but I want nuff'n more to do with this,' came his mate's reticent reply. 'Nickin' stuff from rich people is one thing, but executin' police officers is somethin' completely different!'

'I wouldn't 'ave to if you hadn't been stupid enough to shoot one of them yourself. Now, give me your gun, or swear to God, you'll be next.'

'Sorry, mate, but you're on your own.'

With that, Vincent watched in raging disgust as the man who'd been his best mate since school, hoisted the bag up by his feet to sprint off towards the church.

Screaming a string of obscenities after him, he heard the sound of the squad car's engine finally rumble into life.

Expecting it to see it start reversing down the lane, he blinked in surprise when he heard the engine being revved hard instead.

It took only a glance at the policeman's pale, youthful face, glaring dementedly back at him from behind the wheel, to understand the driver's intention.

As the car lurched suddenly forward, its front wheels spinning on the lane's loose, dusty ground, Vincent was left with only two choices; to remain where he was, waiting for the squad car to slam first into him, then the van behind, or to take the more sensible option and run.

It took him less than a second to make up his mind.

- CHAPTER ONE -

Monday, 14th August, Present Day

S NEAKING OUT OF Westfield Police Station's small private office, the one that used to belong to the now retired DCI Philip Oakes, Tanner picked his way between various clusters of desks before making a beeline for reception.

Doing his best to avoid having to make eye contact with the various disgruntled police officers slouched behind them, he let out a sigh of relief as he stepped out into the building's empty reception area, only to find himself staring directly into the resentful face of the station's duty sergeant, perched behind a plastic security screen ahead.

Forcing a crooked smile at him before glancing awkwardly away, Tanner burst out through the building's main entrance to come to a breathless halt. There he stopped for a moment to take in Norfolk's broad, flat, tranquil horizon, before staring about for his car.

Remembering he'd left it in the carpark's furthest corner, as far away from everyone else's as he thought was possible, he made his way down the steps to hear the demanding sound of his phone, ringing from the depths of his threadbare sailing jacket.

Stopping briefly to dig it out, he answered it before continuing on.

'Good evening, Tanner, it's Forrester.'

'Yes, sir,' he replied, cursing under his breath for having forgotten to check the caller ID before answering. 'How may I help?'

'Are you on your way home?'

'That *was* the plan,' he replied, with dubious suspicion.

'From Westfield, or Wroxham?'

'Westfield,' Tanner replied, steeling a glance back at the building, half expecting to see the entire station's staff pressed up against the windows, sticking their fingers up at him.

'Dare I ask how it's been going?'

'Really well, sir. Thank you for asking.'

'What, seriously?'

'Yes, sir. The entire station's staff has thoroughly enjoyed spending the day being told, one at a time, that they wouldn't have a job by the end of the month, so much so that they all clubbed together to buy me a single Cadbury's Creme Egg, probably because that's all they felt they could afford.'

'Right, yes, I see. You're being sarcastic.'

'Not at all, sir. We've all been having a great time.'

'OK, Tanner, I get it.'

'Although, saying that, had I known that I was the one who was going to have to make them all redundant, I'm fairly sure I wouldn't have taken the job.'

'Yes, well, we did rather suspect as much, which was probably why we didn't tell you.'

Hearing Forrester laugh down the other end of the line, he pressed his phone to his ear. 'I'm struggling to see how it's funny, sir.'

'No, of course,' the superintendent replied. 'It isn't. And I'm sorry for having had to ask you to do it. Also for all the people you've had to let go. Dare I ask how they've been taking it?'

'Some better than others.'

'Have you had a chance to tell Cooper?'

'I did that on Friday.'

'And Haverstock's happy to stay?'

'It would appear so. He lives in Taverham, about halfway between the two offices, so he said it wouldn't have much of an impact.'

'Well, that's something, I suppose.'

With the line falling silent, Tanner pulled in a breath to ask, 'Was there anything else, sir?'

'Only if you don't mind.'

'Only if I don't mind... what?'

'Doing me a quick favour.'

Tanner rolled his eyes. 'Well, sir, I had hoped to be going home for the night,' he continued, glancing down at his watch, 'especially given the fact that it's going to take me a least twice as long to get there.'

'Don't worry. This shouldn't take long.'

'I don't suppose you'd mind telling me what it is *before* I agree?'

'I was hoping you'd be able to make a quick stop at Fenside Prison.'

Tanner's broad square brow creased into a curious frown. 'May I ask why, sir?'

'Vincent O'Riley is due to be released at six o'clock this evening.'

'Am I supposed to know who that is?'

'The man behind the infamous Montgrave Robbery, back in 1994?'

'Wasn't he the guy who killed one of his accomplices with a sawn-off shotgun?' Tanner asked, trying to remember the details.

'Shortly before his other accomplice shot and killed PC Deborah Clarke,' Forrester added. 'I think I'd better email the file over, to help remind you.'

'You don't have to,' Tanner replied, hoping he wouldn't.

'It's already done.'

'Oh, great. But you still haven't told me why you want me there?'

'You'll understand when you read the report.'

'I don't suppose you could give me the gist?'

Tanner heard him huff indignantly down the line at him.

'In a nutshell,' the superintendent eventually began, 'O'Riley's been on the receiving end of a string of death threats, ever since the British press inaccurately reported him as being responsible for PC Clarke's murder. HQ is simply keen to make sure that nobody acts on them, the moment he's released.'

'And what do you expect me to do about it, if someone does decide to have a go?'

'Good point,' Forrester mused. 'Tell you what, why don't you take a couple of uniform with you? Maybe you could ask someone from CID to tag along as well? Hopefully that should be enough to deter anyone from doing anything silly.'

- CHAPTER TWO -

WITH DETECTIVE CONSTABLE Townsend in the passenger seat of his somewhat dated jet-black Jaguar XJS, and with a squad car following closely behind, Tanner steered into the road leading down to Fenside Prison to find three film camera crews and no less than two-dozen reporters, all jostling for position around a pair of ten-foot high steel mesh prison gates.

'For Christ's sake,' Tanner moaned, looking on as two lanky cameramen began pushing and shoving each other near the front of the unruly pack. 'Looks like we're going to need more men.'

'Who is this guy, anyway?' Townsend queried, as Tanner brought his car to a graceful halt alongside a large, nondescript white van. 'The one who's about to be released?'

'Vincent O'Riley. He was charged with theft and murder, back in 1994.'

'But that was over thirty years ago! Why all the media attention?'

'According to the police report, the one Forrester kindly emailed over to me, a young policewoman was murdered with a shotgun, when O'Riley and his accomplices were caught making a run for it. Despite not having actually pulled the trigger, the papers blamed him, awarding him with the auspicious title of being the most hated man in Britain. Since then, he's been on the receiving end of numerous death threats, which, apparently, have continued to this day. Forrester thinks the press are here for the same reason he sent me. Just in case someone attempts to turn their threat into a reality.'

'But if he didn't kill her, why was he convicted of murder?'

'Because of what happened after he and his partners in crime tried to walk off with a Turner.'

'Sorry,' interrupted Townsend, 'but what's a Turner?'

'William Turner?' Tanner lamented. 'The famous British artist?'

'Oh, *that* Turner!'

'Anyway,' Tanner continued, shaking his head, 'they had some sort of an argument at some point, which was when he killed one of them.'

'Who, Turner?'

'No, O'Riley, you idiot!'

'Oh, right.' Townsend replied. 'I must admit, I don't remember learning all that much about William Turner at school.'

'That's probably because you weren't paying attention.'

'When?' the young detective constable asked, his eyes being caught by an attractive female journalist.

'Ever,' Tanner remarked, rolling his eyes.

'That's hardly fair!' Townsend protested, glancing around at Tanner, before his eyes drifted back to the journalist. 'Although, saying that,' he added, trying to catch the woman's eye, 'Sally would probably agree with you. She says that the only time I ever pay her any attention is when she's bouncing up and down on top of me.'

Tanner closed his eyes in reticent despair.

'Don't tell her this,' he heard Townsend continue,

'but to be completely honest, I rarely give her my full and undivided attention even then. I'm normally doing my best to imagine she's Gina.'

'Are there really no depths to your sexual depravity, Townsend?'

'Not that I'm aware of,' his detective constable shrugged.

'Anyway, bringing us back to the here and now,' Tanner continued, desperate to change the subject, 'personally, I'm not convinced that the press are here to film someone trying to assassinate him, but more because of the painting.'

'What about it?'

'Apparently, it's never been found,' Tanner replied. 'Ever since he was caught, O'Riley has always insisted that he never had it; that it was either in one of the bags left at the scene, or was taken by his accomplice, Coby Morgan.'

'And what happened to him?'

'He fled to Malta, with his son. Attempts were made to repatriate him, to face charges for the murder of the policewoman, but with the country having recently declared itself as being politically neutral, their government didn't feel we had enough evidence to oblige.'

'Couldn't he have taken the painting with him?'

'He could have done, but it wasn't considered likely.'

'Why not?'

'Because he set himself up in business, shortly after he arrived.'

'Sorry, but why does that mean he didn't have the painting?'

'Because it was to clean people's swimming pools, and he declared bankruptcy a year later.'

'Fair enough.'

Seeing another scuffle break out within the jostling press pack, Tanner glanced anxiously around at Townsend. 'I think we'd better try to do something about that lot, preferably before our prisoner is released. If you could put a call into the office, requesting a couple more squad cars, I'll see if I can get something sorted out with our uniformed chums parked behind us.'

- CHAPTER THREE -

W ITH THE ARRIVAL of an additional four uniformed constables, Tanner was able to have the press herded back behind a line of flickering blue and white tape, just in time for a gleaming black C Class Mercedes to come sweeping down the road towards them.

Seeing Townsend flag it down to have a brief word with its driver, Tanner stepped cautiously back as it drove sedately past, before coming to an eventual halt on the other side of the road from the high wire mesh prison gates.

Making his way over to Townsend, Tanner asked, 'I assume they said who they were?'

'The prisoner's wife and daughter,' Townsend replied, as a large, square-jawed chauffeur could be seen climbing slowly out.

'They seem to have done alright for themselves,' Tanner commented, as the man made his way around to the boot to lift out a folded black and chrome wheelchair, as if it weighed no more than a bag of flour, 'all things considered, that is.'

'Apparently, the family owns a boatyard.'

'I'd have thought they'd have needed to own a lot more than that to afford to be driven around in a chauffeur driven Mercedes,' mused Tanner, offering Townsend a curious frown.

Hearing some of the press pack's cameras begin

clattering into life, Tanner glanced back to see a beautiful dark haired woman, step gracefully out from one of the car's rear passenger doors.

Offering the on-looking journalists a disdainful glare, she set about helping the chauffeur assemble the wheelchair, before wheeling it around to the other side of the car.

'I assume that's the daughter?' said Tanner, finding himself transfixed by her enigmatic beauty.

'Maybe it's the wife?' Townsend proposed, raising an eyebrow beside him.

Falling silent again, they watched her position the wheelchair to the side of the car before helping a sombrely dressed elderly woman to swing her stick-thin legs carefully out.

After a brief discussion between them, the younger woman helped the older one to shuffle herself off the car's plush leather seat, to eventually rest herself down in the wheelchair.

The moment she had, the entire press pack burst into life, as the figure of a tottering old man dressed in a crumpled, ill-fitting black suit, came into view on the other side of the intimidating prison gates.

Flanked by two sour-faced prison guards, the man inched his way forward, his gaze flickering nervously at first the uniformed police officers, then at the squirming press, before resting more gently on the women waiting for him.

'OK, here we go,' Tanner muttered, glancing nervously about as the gates began to inch slowly open.

'Surely nobody's stupid enough to try anything here?' whispered Townsend, shifting his stance.

'I don't know,' Tanner murmured, his eyes resting on the nondescript white van he'd left his car beside, part-hidden by the branches of a large, overhanging tree. 'It's the first time O'Riley has stepped foot outside those prison gates since 1994, which is a very long time for someone to have an itch they've been unable to scratch.'

Bringing Townsend's attention to the van, he eventually asked, 'I assume someone's checked that out?'

'As best we could,' the young detective constable replied. 'It looked like it had been there a while.'

'There's no one inside?'

'Not that we could see.'

As Tanner turned back to watch the old man leave his prison guards to shuffle his way through the still opening gates, the journalists began calling out numerous questions, some asking what prison was like, others if he knew where the missing painting was.

As one particularly insensitive reporter demanded to know what it was like to have spent the last thirty years touted as being the most hated man in Britain, Tanner thought he heard the sound of an engine, barely noticeable above the cacophony of noise.

A flash of white from the corner of his eye had him spinning around, just in time to see the van he'd been examining a few moments before come flying out from under the tree.

Realising it was heading straight for them, Tanner was barely able to pull Townsend out of its way before it charged past, its wing-mirror missing Tanner's shoulder by a matter of inches.

Falling hard to the ground, Tanner was left to look on in dismay as the van came skidding to a halt, directly outside the now fully open gates.

As two masked men leapt suddenly out, each wielding a particularly lethal-looking sawn-off shotgun, Tanner was about to charge headfirst at the nearest, when the blast from one of the guns brought him stumbling to an ungainly halt.

When another blast split the air, turning the press pack into a screaming mob, the old man was shoved violently inside.

With one of the men following behind, the other leapt into the driver's seat to wheelspin away, leaving Tanner gasping for breath amidst an impenetrable cloud of thick, grey, swirling dust.

- CHAPTER FOUR -

'PLEASE, GOD,' TANNER pleaded, glaring dementedly about at the stunned faces of his surrounding officers, 'tell me that one of you, at least, got a look at the numberplate?'

'I did,' said one, raising his hand. 'I made a note of it when we were checking it over.'

'That's something, I suppose. Do we know who it belongs to?'

'Not yet, boss,' he replied, shaking his head.

'And why was that again?'

'Because I – er – haven't called it in.'

'May I ask if there's some reason in particular as to *why* you haven't called it in?'

The fresh-faced officer continued to stare gormlessly at Tanner for a moment longer, before appearing to realise that he'd just been given an order. 'No reason, boss. I'll – er – do it now.'

Waiting for him to spin fretfully away, Tanner resumed his chastising glare at those officers remaining. 'Being that we have no less than three squad cars here, didn't any of you think to chase after them?'

'Sorry, boss,' apologised the nearest, glancing earnestly around at his colleagues. 'It all just happened so quickly.'

'These things generally do,' Tanner responded, casting his eyes over at the reassembling press pack.

Accidentally catching the wheelchair bound elderly woman's tear strained eyes, glaring at him with demonic intent, he looked shamefully away. 'I assume everyone's OK?' he eventually asked, taking a more compassionate tone.

'Only cuts and bruises,' the same officer replied, 'but I've requested an ambulance, just in case.'

'OK, good,' commented Tanner, feeling a stinging sensation on one of his knees.

Looking down to see a small tear in his trousers, he cursed quietly to himself. It was a brand new suit, bought with some of the additional money he'd been paid when he'd officially taken over Norfolk Constabulary's Western Division.

Wondering if Christine would be able to repair it, he glanced around again to see the frail old lady manoeuvre her wheelchair around before wheeling it towards him.

'Right,' he continued, in a more urgent tone, 'if none of you have anything better to do, I want you out looking for that van. The moment it's found, I want an armed unit in place before anyone's to go within a hundred yards of it.'

'What about the abducted prisoner?' the same officer enquired.

'With any luck, he'll still be inside.'

'And if he isn't?'

'Then we'll have to find him, obviously!'

'Yes, of course, boss, it's just...'

'It's just... what?'

'I'm sorry, boss, but... nobody's told us who he is.'

Tanner raised his eyes to the sky above. 'His name's Vincent O'Riley. If you need to know any more, DC Townsend, here, should be able to help. Now, if there's nothing else, it looks like the abducted man's wife is looking to have a not so quiet word with me, which is hardly surprising, given the fact that we've managed to allow her husband to be abducted, right in front of our eyes, and only about three-and-a-half feet from the prison he'd only just been released from.'

- CHAPTER FIVE -

' A RE YOU THE person who's supposed to be in charge here?' demanded the approaching silver-haired old lady, her dark hooded eyes glaring up into his.

Holding out his formal ID, Tanner held his ground to introduce himself. 'I'm Detective Chief Inspector Tanner, Norfolk Police.'

As she wheeled herself to a halt, Tanner continued by asking, 'Am I safe to assume that you're Mrs O'Riley, the abducted victim's wife?'

'Who the hell else would I be?' she snapped, as the press behind them began taking an interest. 'Do you have any idea how long I've been waiting for my husband to be released?'

'I'm...er...'

'Over thirty years!' she stated. 'That's how long!'

'I'm – er – most dreadfully sorry,' he uttered, unsure what else to say.

'Are you really?'

'Had we known something like this was going to happen, we would have been more prepared.'

Mrs O'Riley took a moment to stare about at all the uniformed policemen, levering themselves into their various squad cars. 'If you didn't suspect that my husband was going to be shoved into the back of a van at gunpoint, then why were you all here?'

It was a good question, one which, unfortunately,

he didn't have an answer to. 'As I said, I really am most dreadfully sorry.'

'I don't want your apology, Detective Chief Inspector whatever-your-name-was, I want my husband!'

'And we are doing all that we can to find him.'

'If that's true, then what are you all still doing here?'

It was another good question.

'More to the point,' she continued, 'why the hell didn't any of you try to stop them?'

'The men who took him were armed, which again, wasn't something we were expecting.'

'Then perhaps you should have been, don't you think?'

'In hindsight, yes, of course, but we only deploy armed police units to situations where there is a clear and present danger to the general public.'

'You do know who my husband is, don't you?'

'I was briefed before my arrival.'

'So you know that the British press have spent the last thirty-odd years referring to him as the most hated man in the entire country?'

Tanner nodded in response.

'Then didn't it occur to you that someone *might* try something like this, so presenting a clear and present danger to one particular member of the general public, i.e. my husband? Or let me guess, he doesn't count, as he's a convicted criminal?'

Hoping to change the focus of the conversation, Tanner pulled in a breath to ask, 'I don't suppose you have any idea as to who may have taken him?'

Mrs O'Riley's eyes flickered momentarily between Tanner's, before regaining their laser sharp focus. 'Didn't I just tell you what the press has spent the last thirty years calling him?'

'You did, however, thankfully, there aren't all that many people in the UK in possession of sawn-off shotguns.'

'And you think I have a list of them, do you?'

'No, of course, but I thought you might have your suspicions?'

'Even if I do, Chief Inspector, I'm not about to start pointing my finger at random people. I believe that's your job, something I'd appreciate if you could start actually doing!'

'If you'd prefer not to say, then perhaps you could provide us with a possible motive?'

'And what use would that be?'

'Knowing why someone may have wanted to would go a long way towards helping us to find them.'

'How about revenge, being that the entire population were led to believe that my husband was responsible for murdering that poor policewoman.'

Seeing her clench at her chest in pain, Tanner stepped forward with earnest concern.

'I don't need your assistance,' she spat. 'I need you to find my husband. Can you at least *try* to do that for me?'

'I promise to do the very best that I can.'

Then I suppose I'm going to have to trust you,' she replied, fixing his eyes for a moment longer before glancing around to see the woman Tanner presumed to be her daughter, stepping up behind her.

As Mrs O'Riley steered herself around to begin pushing herself back to her car, Tanner was left staring into the mesmerising, sapphire blue eyes of the woman left standing in front of him.

Unwilling to be on the receiving end of yet another tirade of abuse, Tanner turned to head off, only to hear her call out, 'I really must apologise for my mother.'

Glancing around to find her smiling apologetically at him, he turned back to say, 'Unfortunately, she has every reason to be upset.'

'Maybe so, but that's no excuse.'

'Detective Chief Inspector Tanner,' he announced, presenting his ID. 'May I ask who you are?'

'Rebecca O'Riley,' she replied, reaching for her narrow, cream leather clutch bag. 'I'm sorry, but I'm not sure I have any identification on me.'

'There's no need to see your ID,' Tanner replied, his face flecking with colour as he caught the scent of her warm, seductive perfume. 'There's also no need to apologise for your mother. After all, it was our fault, at least in part.'

'Were you one of the men who abducted my father?'

'Well, no, but it was our job to protect him. That *was* why we were here, after all.'

'I can assure you, Chief Inspector Tanner, we're as much to blame as you are.'

'Forgive me,' Tanner replied, 'but how could it have possibly been *your* fault?'

'For a start, we should have made more of an effort to keep quiet about the date of his release.'

'You told the press?'

'Well, no, but we did tell all our friends. My brothers also mentioned it to our staff.'

'At your boatyard?'

'Oh, no. That was our father's business. We sold that a while back to move into construction.'

'May I ask what your father had to say about that?'

'Nothing good!' she laughed, her captivating eyes sparkling gently in the evening sun. 'But he did eventually agree. Sadly, none of us had the same passion for boats that he did, and with him being away for such a long time, and everything...'

'You mentioned your brothers.'

'You're about to ask why they're not here.'

'I was thinking about it.'

'Me too,' she replied, glancing back to see her mother being helped into the back of their car. 'They had planned to, but the date clashed with a deal closing on our latest building project, which is another reason why what happened today was our fault. Had they been, whoever took our father would have thought twice before doing so.'

'Your brothers walk around with sawn-off shotguns, do they?'

'Well, no,' she laughed again, 'but if they had, I doubt they'd have let him be taken quite so easily. They're both quite large, you see, and when not in the office, they spend their time studying martial arts. I'm fairly sure they're going to be gutted to have missed the opportunity to have finally had a chance to put their training to good use.'

'If that's the case, then I'm pleased they weren't here. It doesn't matter how good someone may be at hand-to-hand combat, there's little defence against a shotgun, especially in the hands of people who clearly don't have a problem using them. Speaking of which, I don't suppose you have any idea who they could have been?'

Rebecca presented Tanner with a look of cautious uncertainty. 'I think that's something you're going to have to ask my mother.'

'Actually, I already did.'

'And... what did she say?'

'Almost nothing.'

'If she didn't think it appropriate to tell you, then I'm afraid I'm going to have to respect her decision.'

'Even if doing so would help us to find your father?'

The woman glanced briefly back at the Mercedes. 'The problem is,' she replied, leaning towards him, 'as nice as you would appear to be, you're still a policemen.'

'You noticed.'

'Which, unfortunately,' she continued, 'means that I probably shouldn't be talking to you at all, certainly not with quite so many cameras around. I shudder to think what my brothers would say if they found out.'

'We're not *that* bad.'

'I dare say, but as I'm sure you can appreciate, with my father's history, and everything, the British Police aren't exactly a family favourite.'

'I can assure you that we're very much on your side.'

'Maybe now,' she muttered.

'Then why can't you tell me who you think took your father?'

She hesitated for another moment, before holding his eyes to say, 'I think the most likely suspects would have to be the Priestlys. Jake Priestly was the man my father shot, just before he was caught. He left behind a wife and two sons, who are a similar age to my brothers. It's probably no great surprise to learn that they've held a grudge against us ever since. Of all the people who'd want to hurt my father, I think his sons would have to be top of the list.'

Hearing the sound of someone clearing their throat, Tanner glanced around to find one of his police officers, lurking behind him.

'Sorry to bother you, boss, but we've managed to find the van's registered owner.'

'Yes, and...?'

'It's someone by the name of Andrew Priestly.'

Tanner turned to offer Rebecca a conspiratorial frown.

'Anyway,' she said, backing away. 'It was nice to meet you, Detective Chief Inspector Tanner, but my mother's waiting for me.'

'OK, well, thanks for your help.'

'I wasn't aware I had been,' she smiled, spinning gracefully away.

Turning back to find the young police constable grinning at him, Tanner locked his jaw to ask, 'Is something funny?'

'Er... no, boss,' he replied, instantly straightening his face.

'I assume you have an address for this Andrew Priestly character?'

'Yes, boss. He lives in Lingwood, not too far from here.'

'Then on the off chance that they were stupid enough to use it, I suppose we'd better head down there to take a look.'

- CHAPTER SIX -

W ITH TOWNSEND SITTING beside him, Tanner was soon turning his XJS into the road of the address he'd been given to see a squad car, parked discreetly on the kerb ahead.

Pulling up alongside it, Tanner wound his window down to ask, 'What've we got?'

'Not sure,' came the constable's measured response. 'We've only just arrived. We drove past the house before circling back.'

'Did you see anything?'

'Just a white van, parked in the drive. The vehicle registration matches the one given over the radio.'

'OK, stay there,' Tanner instructed, pulling away.

'Can they really have been stupid enough to abduct someone with their own van,' mused Townsend, 'knowing they'd be photographed by half the nation's press whilst doing so?'

Tanner inched his XJS up to what was a normal looking detached house on the other side of the busy suburban road, to see the van the police constable had described.

'I must admit,' Tanner replied, continuing slowly past before pulling over, 'it is difficult to believe.'

Silence followed, as both Tanner and Towsend stared over their shoulders at the house, searching the outside for even the remotest signs of life.

'What are we going to do?' Townsend was soon

asking, having neither of them seen so much as a net curtain twitch.

'Go and take a look,' shrugged Tanner, turning off the engine to begin stepping out.

'Don't you think we should call for an armed response unit first?'

'I'm not proposing that we break down the door, or anything.'

'Sorry, boss, but what do you mean, "we"?'

Tanner turned to offer him an encouraging smile. 'I thought you'd like to come with me?'

'If it's all the same to you, I think I'd rather stay here.'

'But that means I won't have anyone to hide behind when they start shooting.'

'I think that's why I'd rather remain where I am, unless, of course, you don't mind if I stand behind you?'

'Don't worry, I was only joking,' Tanner replied, stepping quickly out.

'You're still going?'

'As I said, I'm only taking a look.'

Standing up to close the door, he heard Townsend climb out to join him.

'I thought you'd chickened out?' Tanner asked, taking him in over the Jag's low sloping roof.

'I was just thinking that they'd be less likely to shoot if there were two of us. Besides, I don't like being on my own.'

Offering him a paternal smile, Tanner led him across the road, just out of sight from the house in question.

Raising a reassuring hand to the officers inside the squad car, they walked back up the road before stopping on the pavement, directly outside the house.

With Townsend standing uncomfortably beside

him, Tanner perched himself on a low brick wall to pull out his phone. 'Can you see anyone?' he asked, pretending to look at the screen.

'The place looks deserted,' Townsend replied, casting his eyes over Tanner's shoulder.

'OK, I'm going to take a quick look around the van. Let me know if anyone comes out.'

Leaving Townsend where he was, Tanner shoved his hands down into his pockets to nonchalantly amble his way towards the van.

On reaching it, he stopped to listen at the back before trying the handle.

Looking over to see Townsend, watching the house as he'd been instructed, Tanner made his way to the driver's side door, resting a hand on the tyres as he did.

Stopping briefly to peek inside the cabin, he touched the bonnet as he continued around, before heading slowly back.

'What do you think?' Townsend asked, as Tanner glanced casually about.

'It's difficult to tell. The tyres and bonnet feel warm to the touch, but it's the middle of August.'

'You think someone may have used another van, making it look like this one?'

'It would've been easy enough. It's an unmarked white Ford Transit, like about twelve million others. All they'd had to do was to buy a matching set of numberplates. As you said yourself, they'd have to have been incredibly stupid to have used their own van.'

'Or perhaps that's what they were hoping we'd think, which is why they did?'

'It's possible, I suppose. But if that was the case, they'd need to be either criminal masterminds, or to have balls of steel. Either way, at some stage we're going to have to ask them, so it may as well be now.'

Seeing Tanner turn to begin marching his way up to the front door, Townsend called after him in a low, demanding voice, 'What about that armed police unit?'

'Don't worry. I doubt they'll come out shooting. But maybe you should stay there, just in case they do.'

- CHAPTER SEVEN -

A S TANNER WAS about to ring the doorbell, the sound of an approaching car had him turning around to see a dark red Audi TT rumble slowly into the drive.

Gesturing for Townsend to remain where he was, Tanner fished out his formal ID to watch two tall, well-built men step warily out, each wearing similar blue jeans and pastel coloured office shirts.

'May I help you?' queried the car's driver, staring first at Tanner, then Townsend.

'DCI Tanner, and my colleague, DC Townsend,' Tanner announced.

'Shit,' the driver cursed, staring over the car's roof at the man on the other side. 'I told you we shouldn't have been doing seventy-one down the A47, not when the designated speed limit was seventy. Now what am I going to do? I can't go to prison. I've got nothing to wear!'

'Don't worry,' the other man replied, 'I'm fairly sure they'll provide something suitable. Isn't that right, Inspector... sorry, what was your name again?'

'Tanner,' he repeated, with an affable smile. 'We were actually looking to speak to the owner of the van.'

'Let me guess,' the driver continued, 'the MOT's run out.'

'Not that I'm aware of.'

'Then it must be the road tax. God damn it! I was about to pay, I promise!'

'May I ask who I'm talking to?'

'Yes, of course,' he smiled, only to fall stoically silent.

Tanner shook his head before repeating the question, this time with a little less ambiguity. 'Can you please tell me your name?'

'Andrew Priestly. And this, here, is my brother, Richard.'

'Hello!' Richard waved, like an over-enthusiastic children's TV presenter.

'You both live here, do you?'

'Er, no,' Andrew replied. 'My brother lives down the road.'

'May I ask where the two of you were, about half-an-hour ago?'

'Sorry, I thought I'd already said. We were driving down the A47, at just a fraction over the speed limit.'

'I assume nobody would be able to vouch for you, apart from your brother, of course?'

'I suppose that would probably depend on if we *did* get caught speeding.'

'And before that?'

'Er...' Andrew began, gazing thoughtfully up at the sky, 'I think it was the A1042.'

'I think Mr Tanner is trying to find out *what* we were doing on the A1042,' his brother interjected.

'I'd have thought that was obvious. Trying to get onto the A47.'

Hearing Townsend laugh down his sleeve, Tanner glared at him, before returning his attention to the brothers. 'I don't suppose there's any chance we could skip the comedy routine?'

'We were driving back from work,' Andrew answered, straightening his face. 'We own an estate

DAVID BLAKE

agency in Norwich.'

'Thank you!' Tanner replied.

'No problem.'

'May I ask when you last used your van?'

'I think it was a couple of weeks ago.'

'You haven't used it today?'

'Is there any particular reason why we should have?'

'It's just that a Ford Transit van, remarkably similar to this one, was involved in an armed abduction about half-an-hour ago.'

'OK, well, I'm fairly sure it isn't the only Ford Transit van in Norfolk.'

Tanner paused for a moment, before asking, 'I don't suppose either of you have heard of a man by the name of Vincent O'Riley?'

'Who?'

'He was convicted of murdering your father, back in 1994.'

'Oh *that* Vincent O'Riley!'

'Did you know that he was released from prison today?'

'Good for him.'

'You didn't take a day off to say hello?'

'Unfortunately, neither of us were able to make it. We didn't even have time to send him a card.'

'It's just that two men matching your description were seen helping him into the back of the van I described earlier, less than a minute after his release.'

'OK, well, as I said, about half-an-hour ago, we were on our way back from work. You can ask our secretary, if you like. I'm sure she'd be able to vouch for us.'

'Yes, I'm sure she would.'

'You know, I'm not normally a suspicious person,' Andrew continued, 'but it almost sounds like you

44

don't believe me.'

'Had it not been for the fact that the abducted man was the same person who'd just finished a life sentence for murdering your father,' Tanner began, 'that the men seen taking him matched you and your brother's description, and that the van they used was remarkably similar to yours, I wouldn't have any reason to. However, what does make it somewhat difficult is that, not only was the van the same colour, make, and model, but it had the same numberplate as well.'

'Then someone must have used it when we were away,' Andrew retorted.

'I must admit, we have considered that, but if a vehicle is stolen to help carry out some unlawful activity, the culprits don't normally bring it straight back afterwards.'

'Do you really think we'd be stupid enough to use our own van to abduct someone?'

'Not before meeting you, I didn't. But now that I have, I'm not so sure. Do you mind if I take a look inside?'

The two brothers glanced around at each other, before Andrew looked up at the house. 'I'd have to get the keys.'

'Be my guest,' Tanner replied, standing to one side.

Allowing Andrew to make his way in, Tanner watched his brother lean back against the car, before wandering over to have a quiet word with Townsend.

'What do you think?' he eventually asked, making sure neither of them could hear.

'They're definitely not stupid enough to have used their own van.'

'That's what I was thinking.'

'I assume that means you think they did?'

Tanner glanced furtively back at the house. 'It

wouldn't have been difficult for them to have dropped it off here, jumped into their car, do a quick loop around the block, before driving back with a previously rehearsed comedy routine.'

'What about Vincent O'Riley?'

'Either thrown into a ditch, or left inside a lock-up, somewhere.'

'And their alibi?'

'It's unlikely their secretary will be of much use. I think we'd have more luck checking CCTV cameras in Norwich, but not before I've had a quick look inside their van,' he continued, seeing Andrew emerge from the house.

Leaving Townsend again, Tanner made his way back up the drive, just in time for Andrew to heave open the van's double back doors.

'As you can see,' he said, standing to one side, 'it's empty.'

'It's also remarkably clean,' Tanner commented.

'That's because we don't use it much.'

'What *do* you use it for, if you don't mind me asking?'

'Oh, you know, this and that.'

'May I see the cabin?'

'By all means,' Andrew replied, leaving his brother closing the rear doors to lead him to the front.

'Also spotless,' Tanner remarked, stepping up. 'There's also no sign that it had been stolen.'

'Have you considered the possibility that whoever you're looking for used fake numberplates, to make theirs look like ours?'

'It's something else we're considering,' Tanner replied, stepping down.

'OK, well, I've shown you inside the van. Now, if there's nothing else?'

'Would you mind if we took a quick look inside

your house, as well?'

'Actually, yes, I would!'

'I can come back with a warrant.'

'Then I look forward to seeing you then,' Andrew replied, fixing Tanner's eyes with a resolute glare.

- CHAPTER EIGHT -

JOINING TOWNSEND ON the pavement, they took a reflective moment to watch the two brothers discuss something quietly together, before seeing them make their way up to the front door.

'I assume there was nothing inside the van?' Townsend quietly asked.

'Not so much as an empty crisp packet. To be honest, it looked like the whole thing had been wiped clean.'

'So, you *do* think it was them?'

'At this stage, I'd be surprised if it wasn't. They certainly had the motive. The question is, what to do about it?'

'Can't we just arrest them?'

'We could, I suppose, but I'm not sure it would help. Not when our priority is to find O'Riley, preferably alive. At this stage, I think it would be more sensible for us to get hold of their prints and DNA. Can I leave that with you?'

'Of course!'

'Then I think we should apply for a search warrant. I'll get Sally to do that. At least then we'd be able to get forensics to take a look at that van of theirs. Inside their homes, as well. Meanwhile, I think it may be an idea to have them followed. With any luck, they'll lead us straight to him.'

Presenting Townsend with a questioning frown, Tanner turned to ask, 'I don't suppose you'd be up for the job?'

'Well, I'd love to, of course,' the young DC replied, 'but, unfortunately, I don't have my car with me.'

'What if I sent someone over to pick you up?'

'I also said that I'd see my mum tonight, but I know Gina's free. Vicky, as well.'

'May I ask *how* you know?' Tanner queried.

'Because Gina's fiancé has gone on a golfing holiday with his mates, and she was going out for drinks with Vicky, although, if you do ask them, I can already see a problem.'

'What's that?'

'There are two suspects, so you'd need two cars, unless you'd want to separate them.'

'I suppose I could pair them up with uniform,' mused Tanner, his eyes drifting towards the squad car down the road, and the officers who looked as if they'd fallen asleep inside it. 'I think I'll give the office a call, to see if they wouldn't mind driving down. Then I'll have a word with those two. With any luck, the prospect of spending a few hours working undercover with a couple of our female CID members will be enough to incentivise them.'

'If you want them incentivised, you should ask Sally!'

'I'd have thought you'd have wanted to keep her as far away from other men as possible – unless – don't tell me – you've broken up again.'

'We're actually getting on rather well at the moment,' Townsend replied, looking sagaciously away. 'Sally bought me a self-help book a few weeks ago, which has certainly helped.'

'Oh, right!' said Tanner, somewhat surprised. 'Which one was that?

'Men are from Mars, Women don't have a Penis.'

'Er... don't you mean, "Men are from Mars, Women are from Venus"?' Tanner suggested.

'Mine's the adult version,' he smirked. 'Actually, whilst we're on the subject, I don't suppose you've read it, by any chance?'

'About thirty years ago. My wife at the time gave it to me when it first came out.'

'I don't suppose you can remember what it was about?'

Tanner turned to stare at him. 'I thought you said you'd read it?'

'Fat chance!' he laughed. 'I haven't even read the cover!'

'I'm sorry, I'm confused. If you haven't read it, then how's it helping your relationship with Sally?'

'Simple. Whenever she's around, I pretend to, so making her think that I'm the caring, thoughtful individual she wants me to be, when instead I'm watching the rugby on my phone.'

- CHAPTER NINE -

LATER THAT EVENING, Tanner crept inside his unusually quiet house to whisper, 'Honey, I'm home,' whilst gently closing the door behind him.

Laying his keys on the sideboard, he made his way inside to find Christine asleep on the sofa, with baby Samantha snoring gently on her chest.

Smiling down at them, he continued to the breakfast bar, and the bottle of rum he could see nestled at the end.

As he poured himself a glass, he heard Christine stir behind him.

'You're back,' she murmured, taking him in through a pair of bleary, half-closed eyes.

'Sorry, I didn't mean to wake you.'

'That's fine,' she replied, levering herself up to cradle Samantha in her arms. 'I wasn't supposed to fall asleep.'

'How was your day?'

'Not bad. Samantha spent most of it watching Peppa Pig.'

'And you?'

'Watching it with her,' she laughed. 'How about you?'

'No Peppa Pig for me today.'

'I meant your work, you idiot, particularly the part when I saw you chatting up a rather attractive, wealthy-looking woman.'

'Which attractive, wealthy-looking woman was that?'

'I don't know. How many were there?'

'I suppose that depends on the time of day.'

Shaking her head with a distinct lack of amusement, she stood up to add, 'It was on the news.'

'What, that I was chatting someone up?'

'When they were reporting from outside Fenside Prison, just after that man was taken.'

'Oh, *that* rather attractive, wealthy-looking woman! You should have said.'

'Are you going to tell me who she was?'

'The daughter of Vincent O'Riley, the person who was abducted.'

'And may I ask what you were talking to her about?'

'You're not jealous, I hope?'

'Just curious,' she replied, with an unreadable smile.

Tanner downed his drink to pour himself another. 'She wanted to know why we'd allowed her father to be abducted, right from under our noses.'

'And why did you?'

'Not you as well!'

'Sorry, but that *is* what it looked like. I mean, you were all standing around doing nothing much in particular, when two masked men pulled up in a van, grabbed him, and drove off.'

'Well, for a start, I wasn't *just* standing there. I was trying to avoid being run over. And secondly, they were both heavily armed.'

'You're not afraid of masked men wielding shotguns, are you?'

'Are you deliberately trying to wind me up?'

'Only a little,' she laughed. 'I don't suppose you'd

like to take Samantha, while I get you something to eat?'

'That will probably depend on if she needs her nappy changed.'

Christine hoisted her up to smell the nappy under discussion. 'I think she's alright.'

'Go on then,' he replied, swapping his tumbler for the half-comatose baby.

As Christine made her way to the sink, she glanced back to ask, 'So anyway, did you find him?'

'Not yet,' Tanner replied, resting Samantha against his chest to begin pacing up and down.

'Any idea who took him?'

'We're currently following two lines of enquiry, literally!'

'In what way?'

'Vicky's following one suspect around in her car, alongside a handsome young police constable, whilst Gina's following another, albeit with a slightly less attractive one.'

'Dare I ask what Forrester had to say about it?'

'That Vicky and Gina are doing nothing more productive than following a couple of suspects around?'

'I was thinking more about the armed abduction.'

'Oh, that. Not much.'

'Have you told him?'

'Uh-huh.'

'And?'

'I think he was happy enough that nobody got hurt.'

Hearing his phone ring, Tanner laid Samantha carefully between a couple of cushions on the sofa.

'Hello, Vicky,' he answered, having made sure to check the caller ID. 'I don't suppose you're calling to tell me that the man you were following has led you straight to O'Riley?'

'Not yet, boss, and to be honest, I think he's unlikely to.'

'And why's that, may I ask?'

'Because he's just given us the slip.'

'That's not good.'

'Sorry, boss. He must have cottoned-on to the fact that we were following him.'

'Have you tried his house?'

'That's where we are now.'

'And he's not there?'

'Well, his car isn't.'

'Then you'd better give the station a call to ask everyone to keep their eyes open for him. Maybe someone could plug his car's numberplate into the ANPR. Speaking of which, has anyone had any luck with their alibi?'

'Unfortunately, we've been unable to find any CCTV cameras outside their office.'

'Then I suppose we'll have to have a word with their secretary in the morning. Any idea how Gina's getting on?'

'They're still outside the other brother's house.'

'The suspect hasn't moved?'

'She doesn't think so.'

'OK. Before you go, can you do me a favour? Can you arrange for another two squad cars to position themselves outside each of their houses. Then I suppose you'd all better call it a day.'

Thanking Vicky for her help, Tanner ended the call to find Samantha had fallen asleep.

'Any news?' asked Christine.

'Yes. Samantha's snoring.'

'Oh, crap! Can you wake her up? She's not supposed to sleep again until ten.'

'And just how am I supposed to do that?'

'Try picking her up. That should do it.'

Reaching down to do what he was told, he heard Christine ask, 'What did Vicky say?'

'The guy she was supposed to be following gave her the slip, leaving me even more convinced that he and his brother are responsible.'

'Who are we talking about?'

'Jake Priestly's grown-up children.'

'And who's Jake Priestly?'

'The man O'Riley was convicted of murdering.'

'Oh, right. Then I can see why you think it was them.'

'The problem is, it was their van that was seen outside the prison gates.'

'And that's a problem because...?'

'Because, when I spoke to them, it was obvious they weren't stupid enough to have used it, leaving me to think that it's probably more likely that someone was trying to make it look like it was them. Unfortunately, with O'Riley touted as being the most hated man in the UK, to be honest, that means it could have been just about anyone.'

- CHAPTER TEN -

Tuesday, 15th August

ARRIVING AT WORK the next day, Tanner made a beeline for Vicky's desk, only to find she wasn't there.

'Morning boss,' he heard Gina say, staring at her monitor with her phone pressed to her ear. 'Vicky's in the ladies.'

'Oh, right,' Tanner responded, glancing awkwardly around. 'How'd you get on last night?'

'Apart from that police officer you lumped me with staring at me for three hours, before eventually asking for my phone number, nothing much happened.'

'Sorry about that. I should have put you with someone who was married.'

'He was!' she laughed. 'Three children, as well!'

'OK, then next time, I'll try to have you working alongside another woman.'

'That would be nice, thank you.'

'If I can find one,' he muttered to himself. 'I don't suppose you know if O'Riley turned up anywhere?'

'Not that I've heard,' she replied, as the office phones burbled into life around them. 'But I did hear that the guy Vicky had been following eventually turned up outside his house, and guess who was with him?'

'Not O'Riley, presumably?'

'His brother, Richard!'

'I thought Vicky said you didn't see him leave?'

'He must have slipped out the back,' she shrugged.

'And nobody knows where they went?'

'I don't think so, at least nobody's registered it on the system.'

'How about that search warrant I asked for?'

'I'm on hold for them now,' she replied, sitting suddenly up to take hold of the receiver. 'Yes, I'm still here!' she announced, only to roll her eyes up to the ceiling. 'Can you at least tell me how long it will take?'

Tanner remained where he was until Gina ended the call.

'I take it the search warrant hasn't come through?' he eventually asked.

She shook her head in response. 'They don't know how long it will be, either.'

'Did they say why it was taking so long?'

'I'm sorry, they didn't.'

Hearing someone clear their throat behind him, Tanner glanced around to find DC Henderson's pale, goat-like face, staring at him.

'Yes, Henderson, what is it?'

'Sorry to bother you, boss, but a call's come in.'

'That doesn't sound good,' Tanner commented, seeing Vicky heading over.

'A body's been found along Fritton Road, just outside Ludham.'

'Is it O'Riley?' Tanner demanded.

'Sorry boss, I don't know.'

'OK, call Doctor Johnstone. Have him meet me there. Forensics, as well.'

'What's going on?' questioned Vicky, as Henderson nodded to spin away.

'Grab your coat, I'll tell you in the car.'

'But I haven't even had a coffee yet!'
'Me neither. We'll just have to pick something up on the way.'

- CHAPTER ELEVEN -

NEARING THE END of the meandering country lane he'd been directed to, Tanner was beginning to wonder if he'd taken a wrong turn, when he finally saw two squad cars, each one parked on a narrow grass verge to his right.

Leaving his on the opposite side, about ten feet from a gated entrance to someone's grand country home, he climbed wearily out, grabbing the coffee Vicky was holding out for him.

When he saw two uniformed police constables, waiting for him on the opposite side, he spent a frustrating moment trying to remember their names, before giving up to call out, 'What've we got?'

'It's a dead body, boss,' replied the larger of the two.

'So I've heard,' Tanner responded, unable to tell if the man was being deliberately facetious. 'A man, or a woman?'

'Looks like an old man. Judging by the state of him, he was probably just some homeless drunk.'

'Any ID?'

'None that we've seen.'

With the disquieting sense that he didn't need the victim's ID to know who he was, Tanner drew in a reticent breath. 'And he's definitely dead?'

'Well, he certainly looks like he is, but as neither of us are paramedics, I wouldn't want to put money on it.'

'Speaking of paramedics,' Tanner lamented, glancing earnestly about, 'where's the bloody ambulance?'

'I'm – er – not sure, boss.'

'And what about the person who found him?'

The two police constables stared gormlessly around at each other, before the larger one looked back to say, 'Sorry, boss, but there was nobody here when we arrived. We had to find the body ourselves.'

'Which is where?'

'Behind us,' he gestured. 'Just past the treeline.'

'OK, you two had better get busy. We need the lane closed from both ends. Then this whole area needs to be sealed off. And let me know the minute the medical examiner shows up. The ambulance, as well!'

Making their way through the trees, it didn't take them long to find the reported body. It took Tanner even less time to recognise the crumpled, three-piece suit.

'Looks like he's been beaten to death,' Tanner remarked, crouching down to examine what was left of O'Riley's blackened, blood-spattered face.

'That must have been why the Priestly brothers took him,' whispered Vicky, in a low, reverent tone. 'To exact their revenge for what happened to their father.'

Climbing slowly to his feet, Tanner let out a world-weary sigh. 'Maybe, maybe not. Unfortunately, it's too early to say, not without some evidence.'

'You mean, apart from the fact that the van they used was found parked outside their house, and that one of the suspects deliberately gave us the slip?'

'Aren't you normally the one telling *me* not to

jump to conclusions?' Tanner queried, presenting her with an accusatory frown.

Before she had a chance to reply, the sound of someone crashing through the undergrowth had them turning around to see Dr Johnstone, fighting his way through a tangle of uncooperative branches.

'Ah, Tanner!' he eventually exclaimed, coming to a breathless halt in front of them. 'I thought I recognised that car of yours.'

'I don't suppose you happened to see an ambulance there as well?'

Shaking his head, Johnstone stared down at the crumpled, sprawled out body. 'They must have taken a wrong turn. Anyway, whilst we wait, I suppose I may as well take a look. Do we have any idea what happened to him?'

'I was hoping you'd be able to tell us.'

'Fair enough,' Johnstone replied, stepping between them to take a closer look.

The sound of raised voices, drifting over the air towards them, brought Tanner's attention back to the lane.

Leaving Vicky with Dr Johnstone, he made his way back through the trees to eventually see a police constable on the other side, attempting to prevent a gleaming black Range Rover from driving out from the gated property opposite.

Realising the officer was taking his orders far too literally, he cursed quietly to himself before stomping quickly over.

'What's going on here?' he demanded, staring first at the police officer, then up at two large, square-jawed men he could see sitting in the front, each with the same coloured hair, and similar sun-bronzed faces.

'This idiot won't let me out of my own bloody house!' the one perched behind the wheel declared, undoing his tie as if it was strangling him.

'Sorry, boss,' began the fresh-faced constable, 'but I've been trying to explain to them that we've had to close the lane due to a major incident.'

'I understand,' Tanner replied, fixing the young man's eye, 'but that doesn't mean we need to prevent the local residents from leaving their homes, now does it?'

'Yeah, you moronic fuckwit!' cursed the driver, grinning around at the man sitting next to him.

'Er... excuse me, sir,' interjected Tanner, catching the driver's eye, 'but there's no need to speak to one of my officers like that.'

'I'm sorry, but if you don't mind me asking, who the fuck are you to be telling *me* what to do?'

'Detective Chief Inspector Tanner, Norfolk Police,' Tanner smiled, presenting him with his formal ID.

'What's this so-called major incident, anyway?' the driver huffed, giving the ID the most cursory of glances. 'I suppose some idiot's driven into the drainage ditch, again.'

'The body of a man has been found in the trees opposite, which unfortunately means we're having to restrict access to the lane. However, if you tell the officers at either end that you live here, I'm sure they'll let you through.'

'What do you mean, "a man's body"?' the driver continued, staring out at Tanner with a look of questioning uncertainty.

'Forgive me, sir, but as I'm sure you can appreciate, I'm unable to go into detail.'

'I assume you know who we are, or more importantly, who our father is?'

'I'm sorry, but why should I know who either you or your father is?' Tanner responded, flabbergasted by the man's extraordinary assumption that he, and everyone else on the planet, should have known who they were.

'Vincent O'Riley?' the driver declared, glaring at Tanner as if he was a complete imbecile. 'You know, the man your lot released from prison yesterday, only for him to be abducted about five seconds later?'

'Vincent O'Riley is your father?' Tanner repeated, struggling to think of anything else to say.

'Is it him?' the man continued, casting an anxious eye at his passenger. 'The person you found. Is it our father?'

Seeing Johnstone stumble out from the trees to urgently beckon him over, Tanner glanced back to say, 'Perhaps you'd be kind enough to provide my colleague, here, with your contact details?'

'That doesn't answer my question!'

'I'm aware of that, but until we've been able to identify the victim, I won't be able to. Now, if you'll excuse me.'

Without waiting for a response, Tanner turned to make his way over to where Johnstone was standing with seeming fretful impatience.

'Where's that bloody ambulance?' the medical examiner muttered, the moment Tanner was in earshot.

Glancing behind him to see both men climb out of the Range Rover, Tanner turned back to ask, 'Why? What's up?'

'Because that body of yours,' Johnstone began, his voice a low, conspiratorial whisper, 'he's still alive!'

'Shit!' Tanner exclaimed, diving instantly back

through the trees to find Vicky, kneeling quietly beside the victim, watching his mouth open and close like a drowning fish.

'Dad?' came the earnest voice of the car's driver, from over Tanner's shoulder.

'You can't be here!' Tanner stated, spinning on his heel to block the man's way.

With the apparent realisation that the victim lying on the ground was indeed his father, the man charged forward, shoving Tanner to one side to fall hard to his knees.

Taking hold of the old man's pale, withered hand, he stared in abject horror along the length of his twisted, broken body.

'Who did this to you?' he demanded, his own body shaking with rage. 'Tell me who did this to you?'

As if gasping for one final breath, the victim pursed his lips together to whisper, 'Burton. Leonard Burton.'

'Is that who did this? Leonard Burton?'

The victim opened his mouth again to try and say something else, but instead of words came the ghostly sound of rasping air, hissing listlessly out from his steadily parting mouth.

'Dad!' the victim's son exclaimed, his body shaking as he began to openly sob. 'Please, don't leave me! Not now!'

As Tanner watched the light from the victim's eyes ebb slowly away, he knew with absolute certainty that he was now most definitely dead. There was also a chance that he knew the name of the person responsible. If that was true, all he had to do was to identify him to have discovered the old man's killer.

- CHAPTER TWELVE -

W ITH THE SOUND of an ambulance, fast making its approach, Tanner prised the victim's son away from the body to guide him back through the trees.

Seeing him safely back to his car, Tanner left him to explain to his brother what had happened, before slowly returning.

'I really am truly sorry about your father,' Tanner eventually said, keeping his voice respectfully low. 'Do you think you'll be able to talk?'

Wiping tears from their eyes, both men nodded quietly in response.

'I assume you're able to confirm that the victim *was* your father, Mr Vincent O'Riley?'

'Of course it was!' spat the one who'd seen the body.

'And may I ask your names, just so I know who I'm talking to?'

The man hesitated for a moment, before eventually saying, 'I'm Michael. This, here, is my brother, Jonathan.'

'And is this where you live?' he continued, glancing up at the gates.

'It is.'

Tanner searched his pockets for his notebook, before glancing up to say, 'I spoke to your sister yesterday, shortly after your father was abducted.'

'This is my fault,' Michael interrupted, fresh tears appearing in his eyes. 'None of this would have happened if we'd been there.'

'Considering the fact that the men who took him were heavily armed, I sincerely doubt that. Had you been, then I suspect the situation would have been considerably worse.'

With both men glaring at the ground, Tanner attempted to catch their eyes. 'May I ask why you weren't?'

Still staring down, Michael drew in a juddering breath. 'The date coincided with the sign off on a new building development project. We asked our father if we should reschedule, but he insisted that we continue. He said we'd have plenty of time to catch up at home afterwards. Turns out he was wrong, as were we for listening to him.'

'The name your father mentioned, before he passed away. Leonard Burton. Do you have any idea who that is?'

'Not a clue,' he shrugged back in response.

'He hadn't mention him to you before?'

'Not that we can remember,' Michael replied, glancing around at his brother.

'Could he be one of his old friends, or perhaps someone he met in prison?'

Michael looked back to fix Tanner's eye. 'If you're thinking he was responsible for murdering my father, then you're most definitely barking up the wrong tree.'

'He certainly seemed determined enough to tell you his name before he passed away.'

'We know it wasn't someone called Leonard Burton, because we already know who murdered him!' Michael stated, his eyes burning with furious rage. 'It was Jake Priestly's family, his two sons in particular. They've wanted him dead ever since their father tried double-crossing ours. That's why our father ended up having to spend half his life in prison.'

'I'm sorry, but I thought that was because your father was found guilty of murdering him with a shotgun?'

'Not before Jake Priestly tried shooting him first, no doubt to take all the money for himself. He would have done, as well, had our father not had the good sense to load his gun with empty cartridges. Then there's the painting, of course. For some unknown reason, they've always been under the impression that it belongs to them. Personally, I think that's why they took him, to force him to tell them where he'd hidden it.'

'I thought your father said he never had it?'

'He didn't!'

'Then why would the Priestly brothers think he did?'

'Because that's the story the newspapers have been pedalling, ever since he was arrested.'

'If your father never had the painting, then where do you think it ended up?'

'We've no idea,' Michael replied, shrugging his shoulders at his brother. 'All we know is that our dad didn't have it. Nor did he hide it. He'd have told us if he did. If you really want to know where it is, your best bet would be to ask their other accomplice, Coby Morgan.'

- CHAPTER THIRTEEN -

HAVING ARRANGED A time to have samples of their fingerprints and DNA taken, Tanner left Michael and Jonathan to start contacting their family and friends with the tragic news.

Seeing Vicky on the other side of the lane, directing a unit of tardy police forensic officers to where the body could be found, he caught her eye to make his way over.

'Why's everyone so late?' he moaned, watching the forensic unit disappear beyond the tree line.

'A lorry went over on the A1062. There's a two mile tailback in both directions.'

Gesturing over at the O'Riley brothers, she continued by asking, 'Did you manage to speak to them?'

'Only briefly.'

'Did they have anything to say?'

'Perhaps unsurprisingly, they were of the impression that the Priestly family were responsible, the two brothers in particular. What surprised me more was what they considered their motive to have been.'

'Not to avenge their father's death?'

'To find the missing Turner,' Tanner replied, shaking his head.

'I thought O'Riley didn't have it?'

'That's what he always said. I'm just not sure

anyone believed him.'

'I assume you asked his sons what they thought?'

'They simply repeated their father's claim; that he'd never had it, suggesting instead that it was taken by their father's other accomplice,' Tanner continued, checking his notes. 'Coby Morgan.'

'And where is he?'

'Malta, apparently,' Tanner replied. 'Assuming he is, we'll need to see if he's been back recently, possibly to say hello to his old partner in crime, with the help of a man and a van, and a couple of shotguns.'

'Are we considering the possibility that O'Riley managed to give the painting to either his wife or children, before he was arrested? They could have then sold it in secret on the black market. If they had,' she continued, staring over at their fancy car, and the enormous, black wrought iron gates it was parked between, 'it would go a long way to explain their apparent wealth.'

'That may also explain why they seemed to have no interest in finding it,' Tanner replied, tapping a pensive finger against his dark, stubble covered chin.

'Unless it's hanging up in their living room?' mused Vicky.

'Either way,' Tanner continued, watching the brothers end their various calls to begin climbing back into their car, 'the missing painting is only of interest to us in that it provides a possible motive for what happened to their father. At this stage, I'm far more interested to know who Leonard Burton is, the person O'Riley used his last dying breath to tell them about.'

'I assume you asked?'

'They said they'd never heard of him.'

'Did you believe them?'

'I'm not sure. Considering it was the last thing

their father said, they seemed remarkably dismissive of it.'

'How about the location of the body?'

'I assume you're referring to the fact that it was left less than twenty metres from the gates to their home?'

Nodding her head, Vicky pulled out her notebook. 'I've been doing a little digging of my own. Apparently, they all live there; O'Riley's wife, sons, and daughter, all on the same estate.'

'Making it likely that his body was left there to send them some sort of a message.'

'Which, again, points back to the Priestly brothers, don't you think?'

'Possibly,' Tanner replied, looking wistfully away, 'but it could just as easily be someone else, like Vincent O'Riley's other accomplice, Coby Morgan, or even Leonard Burton – whoever he is – which reminds me,' Tanner continued, seeing Johnstone fight his way out from the trees. 'Could you ask someone to find out? Then maybe get someone else to try and locate this Morgan character. Meanwhile, I'm going to have a quick chat with our medical examiner.'

Raising a hand to help garner Dr Johnstone's attention, Tanner left Vicky to start making some calls.

'Did you find anything of interest?' he queried, coming to a standstill in front of him.

'I'd say he most likely died from either blunt trauma to the head, or internal haemorrhaging. I won't be able to say for certain until I open him up.'

'I don't suppose you'd be able to hazard a guess at what caused the blunt trauma to the head, or the internal haemorrhaging?'

'It could have been any number of things; from a baseball bat to a golf club, but it's what didn't kill him that may be more of an interest.'

'Go on.'

'For a start, one of his fingers had been removed. There are also clear signs that he'd been electrocuted.'

'You're saying he was tortured?'

'Well, he didn't do it to himself, not when his hands and feet had been tied to something.'

'OK, thank you,' said Tanner, glancing around to see Vicky, beckoning for his attention. 'Let me know if you find anything else.'

'I suppose you'd like my post mortem report on the normal expedited timescale?'

'Of course!' he smiled back, before leaving him to return to his colleague.

'Yes, Vicky, what've you got?'

'Nothing on the suspects, but the search warrant has come through for the van. The Priestly brothers' properties, as well.'

'Finally!' he exclaimed, clasping his hands together. 'Right, tell them to start with the van, then the houses. Actually, don't bother. We'll tell them ourselves when we get there.'

- CHAPTER FOURTEEN -

A S TANNER SPED them towards Andrew Priestly's house, and the van that was hopefully still parked outside, a thin plume of dirty grey smoke could be seen in the distance, growing larger with every passing mile. It was only when they entered the next village for a fire engine to blast its way past, did it occur to him that the thickening pillar of smoke could be marking their very destination.

'Do you get the feeling that they're going to the same place we are?' Vicky queried, leaning forward in her seat to stare through the windscreen.

'I sincerely hope not,' Tanner replied, speeding after it as a knot tightened in his stomach.

With the fire engine making the exact same turns that they were, it wasn't long before Tanner's fears became a reality, when he saw it come to an ungainly halt next to a white Ford Transit van, the same one he'd been so keen for forensics to examine, burning like a Pagan effigy on the drive outside Andrew Priestly's house.

'This must prove it was them, surely?' Vicky urged, her eyes transfixed by the vicious orange flames, dancing in the sky before them.

'Maybe so, but it's just made it ten times harder to prove.'

Taking a moment to stare at her with a questioning

frown, he opened his mouth to ask, 'I assume there was a reason why I didn't arrest them yesterday?'

'Something to do with a lack of evidence, wasn't it?'

'Even less, now,' he responded, returning to stare at the flames.

'But we didn't have a body then. With any luck, it will help shed light on who's behind all this. We also still have their homes to search.'

'Unless they're about to set fire to them as well,' came Tanner's disgruntled response. 'Speaking of whom, there's one of them now!' he exclaimed, seeing Andrew Priestly, deep in conversation with a large burly fireman, at the furthest edge of his drive.

Stepping quickly out, Tanner crossed the road to call, 'Mr Priestly! May we have a word?'

'Christ! Not you again,' Andrew moaned, rolling his eyes. 'I didn't know I'd called the police.'

'But you did call the fire brigade?'

'I'm sorry, but what else was I supposed to do? Walk down to the corner shop to buy some marsh mallows?'

'I was just wondering why you bothered, when you were the one who set fire to it.'

'Why the hell would I set fire to my own van?'

'Because you used it to abduct your least favourite person in the whole wide world, Vincent O'Riley.'

'Jesus Christ! You're not still going on about that?'

'Before taking him somewhere to torture,' Tanner continued.

'What are you talking about?'

'I think you know exactly what I'm talking about, which is why we're standing here, watching your van burn.'

'I know who set fire to my van. I saw them throw a petrol bomb at it from inside my house.'

'May I ask what you were doing inside your house, being that it's Tuesday?'

'Shouldn't you be asking who I saw from inside my house, instead of wondering what I was doing inside it?'

'Only if I thought that you *had* seen someone set fire to it.'

'Well, I think the evidence is pretty clear, being that my van is right there, on actual fire.'

Instead of replying, Tanner simply stared at him with an accusatory glare.

'You're seriously suggesting that I set fire to my own van?'

'Didn't you?'

'Of course I didn't! I was on the phone to a client, staring at my bloody computer, when the whole thing went up.'

'If you were on the phone to a client, staring at your computer, how could you have seen someone drive past your house to throw a petrol bomb at it?'

'Because I – I got up to make myself a drink,' Andrew eventually replied.

'Tea, or coffee?'

'What?'

'This drink you made for yourself, at the exact same time someone drove past your house to throw a petrol bomb at your van, was it a tea or a coffee?'

Shaking his head as if trying to clear it, Andrew pulled back his shoulders to fix Tanner's eyes. 'I'm sorry that you don't believe me, Chief Inspector, but it's not my job to convince you that I'm telling the truth. It is, however, your job to prove that I'm not.'

'OK, then what did this person look like?'

Andrew held Tanner's eyes for a moment longer, before glancing away. 'I don't know. I didn't see his face.'

'Then maybe you can tell me what sort of a car they were driving?'

'Alright, I admit, I didn't see them, but I heard a glass smash, and when I looked outside, my van was on fire.'

'Maybe it was your brother?' Tanner queried.

'My brother?'

'That's right.'

'Why on Earth would it have been him?'

'Because that would allow you to honestly say that someone else did it.'

'But – for what possible reason?'

Sidestepping the question, Tanner changed the subject. 'May I enquire as to your whereabouts last night, between the hours of ten o'clock, and two o'clock the following morning?'

'What's it to you?'

'If you could just answer the question.'

'I was here.'

'Are you sure?'

'Of course I'm sure. I wouldn't have said so otherwise.'

'Then why did one of my officers see you return home, shortly after the time previously mentioned?'

Andrew glared at Tanner with incredulous dismay. 'May I ask what one of your officers was doing outside my house at two o'clock in the morning?'

'Keeping an eye on you,' he smiled.

'Don't I have some sort of legal right to privacy?'

'Not when you're the suspect in a murder investigation.'

'A murder investigation?'

'That's right.'

'But – who's been murdered?'

'My apologies. I thought I said. We found Vincent O'Riley's body about half-an-hour ago. It would appear that someone spent the night torturing him, before dumping what was left of him opposite where the O'Rileys live.'

The briefest of smiles flickered over Andrew's mouth. 'Well, whoever it was,' he eventually replied, 'it wasn't me.'

'I never said it was.'

Andrew looked momentarily confused. 'You just said I was a suspect.'

'Sorry, I meant it wasn't *only* you. I'm fairly sure your brother is equally responsible, which is why you told him to set fire to your van.'

'This is ridiculous!'

'It's certainly easy enough for you to clear up. All you have to do is to tell us where you were last night, between the hours previously mentioned.'

Andrew glowered at him for a moment longer, before eventually saying, 'I think the time has come for you to either arrest me for the crime of *not* setting fire to my own van, or to get the fuck off my property. The choice is yours.'

Tanner glanced around to nod briefly at Vicky, before turning slowly back. 'Mr Andrew Priestly, we're placing you under arrest.'

'You must be fucking joking!' he exclaimed, staring with open-mouthed disbelief at first Vicky, then Tanner.

'You do not have to say anything, but it may harm your defence if you do not mention when questioned something that you later rely on in court. Anything you do say may be given in evidence.'

'Aren't you supposed to say what your arresting me for?'

'To be honest,' Tanner began, taking the handcuffs Vicky was holding out for him, 'I haven't decided yet. But don't worry, I've got the journey from here to the police station to make up my mind.'

- CHAPTER FIFTEEN -

ARRIVING AT WROXHAM Police Station a few minutes later, Tanner prised Andrew Priestly unceremoniously out from his Jag's cramped back seats to frogmarch him inside, straight into the hands of the awaiting DS Taylor.

'As soon as he's been processed,' Tanner instructed, removing the man's handcuffs, 'I want him placed inside Interview Room One.'

'What about my phone call?' he heard his disgruntled suspect demand.

'Yes, sorry, of course,' Tanner replied, looking again at DS Taylor. 'The suspect will need access to a phone, at some point at least. But if it's to call his brother, tell him not to bother. We've already got someone heading over to pick him up.'

'Right you are, boss,' Taylor replied, manhandling Andrew towards the back of the building. 'Oh, sorry, boss,' the duty sergeant added, glancing over at two smartly dressed men in the corner, 'I forgot to mention. There are a couple of gentlemen waiting to see you. *They're from the National Gallery,*' he whispered, in a low, conspiratorial tone.

Raising an eyebrow, Tanner took a moment to look at the two men, the older, grey-haired one in particular, who was wearing the most ridiculous bright yellow bow tie.

Heading over to see them, Tanner offered them an

affable smile. 'I understand you're looking to speak to me?'

'Detective Chief Inspector Tanner?' the older one enquired, in a distinctly clipped British accent.

'That's correct.'

'My name's Edward Phillips,' he continued, handing Tanner an elegantly designed business card. 'This is my assistant, Thomas Ward. We're curators for the National Gallery.'

'You mean *the* National Gallery, the one in Trafalgar Square?'

'So, you've heard of it, then.'

'Not only have I heard of it, I've actually been there!'

'Excellent!' Phillips exclaimed, looking at Tanner in a new light. 'I take it you're something of an art connoisseur?'

'Not exactly,' Tanner grimaced. 'I was forced to go, when I was at school. I assume you're here to make enquiries about the missing Turner?'

'How very insightful of you.'

'Then you'd better come through to my office, although I'm not sure how I'll be able to help.'

Having guided them inside, he offered them first a seat, then a coffee, before settling down behind his desk.

'So,' he eventually continued, 'as I said before, I'm not sure I'm going to be of much use.'

'We were simply wondering if you had any idea as to where it might be? I don't know if you're aware, but it was only on loan to Lord Montgrave, when it was taken.'

'And now, presumably, you'd like it back?'

'Well, to be honest, we've wanted it back since it

went missing!' Phillips chuckled. 'But yes, you're right, of course, especially in light of recent events.'

'You mean, because the man found guilty of having taken it was released from prison?'

'Actually, more because of the painting's value. You see, at the time it was taken, it was considered to be one of Turner's lesser works, which is why we were willing to loan it out. However, since then, interest in its whereabouts has grown with each passing year. With interest comes demand, and with demand comes value. We've subsequently just had rather a generous offer from an American buyer, one we'd be rather foolish to turn down.'

Tanner leaned back in his chair to take a sip from his coffee. 'So, what you're trying to tell me is that it's worth rather a lot of money.'

'You could say that,' Phillips replied, returning to Tanner a conniving smile.

'That's certainly very interesting, but I still don't see how I can help.'

'We thought that now the man found guilty of taking it has been released, you'd be able to ask him where it is.'

'OK, well, first of all, he's always denied it, and secondly, I think you should watch the news a little more often.'

'I'm sorry, Chief Inspector, but may I ask what the news has to do with it?'

'Because the man who was found guilty of having taken the painting, Mr Vincent O'Riley, was abducted at gunpoint, the moment he was released.'

'Oh, right,' Phillips responded, his entire face sagging with despondent despair. 'I suppose that means you don't know where he is?'

'Not at all. As of this morning, we know exactly where he is!'

The curator's face immediately brightened. 'Then do you think it would be possible to ask him where it is, perhaps under cross-examination, or whatever it is that you call it?'

'Cross-examination is the term given to the interrogation of a witness by one's legal opponent, normally during a trial,' Tanner replied. 'Mr O'Riley would need to be first arrested, then charged before that could happen.'

'But you could at least ask him, though, couldn't you?'

'In theory, we could, but he'd be under no legal obligation to tell us. As I said before, we'd need to arrest him first.'

'Then why can't you do that?'

'Because he's already served his sentence. It would be both immoral, and illegal, for us to arrest him for the same crime again. However, there is another more pertinent reason as to why it would be impractical for us to do so.'

'Which is...?' Phillips demanded.

'Because he's dead.'

The old man's head jolted back in surprise. 'What do you mean, he's dead?'

'His body was found just over an hour ago,' Tanner replied, glancing nonchalantly at his watch. 'We've yet to establish the cause, but from what we can make out, it would appear that he was tortured, probably for the same reason that you're sitting in front of me today.'

Having been staring at Tanner with incredulous incomprehension, Phillips eventually opened his mouth to ask, 'Do you have any idea who was responsible?'

Tanner raised a curious eyebrow at the question. 'May I ask why you'd like to know?'

'Because, if it's true that he was tortured, then isn't it likely that the victim would have told them where the painting was?'

'Perhaps,' Tanner replied, with a nonchalant shrug, 'although, if he did, that might not be a good thing, at least not for you.'

'May I ask why?'

'Because it would mean that his abductors may have already found it. For all we know, at this precise moment in time, it could be on an EasyJet flight, winging its way to a collector's vault in Zurich.'

'Forgive me for saying this, Chief Inspector, but you don't seem to be taking this very seriously.'

'That's probably because I'm not.'

Phillips sat back in his chair to offer Tanner a perturbed scowl. 'Then I think it's probably best if we speak to your commanding officer.'

'You're more than welcome to,' Tanner replied, rummaging around his desk. 'I'll even give you his business card, if I can find one. But you do need to understand that our priority is to identify Vincent O'Riley's murderer, not to locate some painting that went missing over three decades ago.'

A short knock at the door was followed by Vicky's head, poking around from the other side.

'Sorry to bother you, boss,' she began, casting a curious eye over at Tanner's academic-looking guests, 'but I just thought I'd let you know that Mr Priestly is waiting for you in Interview Room One.'

'Any sign of a solicitor?'

'Not yet.'

'OK, good,' Tanner replied, eagerly pushing himself up from his chair.

'His brother is on his way in, as well.'

'Even better!'

'There's also news on the other.'

'The other... what?'

'The other potential suspect,' came her more guarded response, glancing again at the two men. 'The one whose name the – er – victim mentioned?'

'Right, yes, of course. Give me a minute, will you?'

With Vicky ducking out, Tanner turned back to his guests. 'If you'll excuse me, gentlemen, but there are matters that need my attention.'

As they reluctantly prised themselves out from their chairs, the older one caught Tanner's eye. 'Are all these suspects in relation to the murdered victim, Mr Vincent O'Riley?'

'I'm sorry, but I'm unable to comment on an ongoing investigation.'

'If they are, then don't you think we have the right to know?'

Tanner stopped where he was to glare at him. 'And why is that, may I ask?'

'Because one of them might know where the missing Turner is.'

'Maybe, maybe not, but as I've already said, locating the missing painting is very low on my list of priorities.'

'You're talking about a work by one of England's most celebrated artists, possibly the best this country has ever produced!'

'As I just said...'

'Something that could be worth over a million pounds!'

'...it isn't a priority!' Tanner stated, raising his voice with irritated annoyance. 'How much someone who's clearly got more money than sense is willing to pay for it doesn't change that. Now, you're more than welcome to take this up with my superior, but in the meantime, you really must excuse me.'

- CHAPTER SIXTEEN -

'A LL SET?' TANNER enquired, hovering outside the door to Interview Room One.

'Just about,' came Vicky's breathless response, as she hurried down the corridor towards him, 'although his solicitor hasn't arrived yet.'

'Which is why I want to get started.'

As Vicky gave him a disapproving scowl, the screeching sound of the corridor's door had them turning around to see a tall, fresh-faced young man dressed in a scruffy grey suit, squinting down the dimly lit passageway towards them.

'Detective Chief Inspector Tanner?'

'Yes, may I help?'

'I'm looking for a... er...' the young man continued, lifting his glasses to glance down at a tablet, '...Mr Andrew Priestly?'

'May I ask what it's in connection with?'

'Sorry, yes, of course. I've been appointed to be his solicitor for the day.'

'He might need you for a little longer than that,' Tanner whispered to Vicky. 'We're actually heading in to speak to him now, if you'd care to join us?'

'Oh, yes, great!' the young solicitor replied, tucking his tablet into a blue, child-sized rucksack.

'Do you have a name?' Tanner enquired, wondering if the young man he could see lolloping down the hallway towards them was still at school.

'Lucas, George Lucas,' he replied, presenting Tanner with a cheerful smile.

'Oh, right! Any relation?'

The solicitor stopped in front of them to offer Tanner a quizzical frown. 'Sorry, any relation to who?'

'Er... the creator of Star Wars?'

'Oh, right, of course. Sorry. It was a little before my time.'

'*No kidding*', Tanner muttered, under his breath. 'May we get you something to drink? Tea? Coffee? A glass of milk, perhaps?'

'I've actually brought a carton of orange juice with me,' he replied, diving into his rucksack to retrieve the carton in question.

'Is there a lunchbox in there as well?'

'Actually, yes, there is!'

As the solicitor reached back inside, Vicky jabbed Tanner in the arm.

Glancing around to offer her an innocent shrug, Tanner turned back to find the solicitor holding out a small plastic box covered in Lego Ninjago characters.

Doing his best to keep a straight face, he glanced down at the solicitor's feet. 'And I see that you're wearing a pair of sensible shoes, so you must be ready!'

With Lucas staring at him with a particular gormless expression, Tanner grinned at him to say, 'Shall we go in?'

Opening the door to find Andrew Priestly, slumped miserably on the other side of a small wooden table, Tanner cleared his throat. 'Mr Priestly, I'm delighted to announce that your solicitor has arrived!'

Priestly lifted his gaze from the table's empty surface to rest his eyes on his appointed solicitor, staring at him from the doorway like an over-excited puppy. 'Just my bloody luck,' he eventually muttered, shaking his head to stare back down at the table.

'My name's Mr Lucas, George Lucas,' the solicitor announced, taking his backpack off. 'I've been sent from BHJC Solicitors to represent you.'

'Any relation?' Priestly enquired, with seemingly little interest in hearing the answer.

'That's funny, but that's what Detective Chief Inspector Tanner asked.'

'Shall we push on?' proposed Tanner, pulling out a seat for first Vicky, then himself.

'Yes, of course. If I may, I'd like to start by enquiring as to what my client's been arrested for?'

'Good question!' Priestly exclaimed, sending Tanner a resentful glare.

'Hasn't he told you?' the solicitor enquired.

'Not yet.'

'I'm sorry, Chief Inspector, but you really must tell my client why he's been arrested.'

'Fair enough, I suppose,' Tanner replied, casting his eyes pensively up to the ceiling. 'I think we're going to start with arson, and see how we go from there.'

'And may I ask what he's supposed to have set fire to?'

'His van.'

'You mean, his own van?'

'That's correct.'

'Oh, right,' Lucas replied, taking the seat next to his client to remove a notebook from his backpack. 'And what evidence do you have to support such a claim?'

'We found his van on fire, parked outside his house.'

'And that means he set fire to it, does it?'

'It is our belief that he, and his brother, used the van to abduct someone the day before.'

'But you haven't arrested him for that?'

'Not yet.'

'May I ask why not?'

'Because, at this precise moment in time, we're unable to prove it, more so since he set fire to the van we believe he used.'

'So, your evidence that my client set fire to his own van is because he'd used it to abduct someone, something you've not yet been able to prove?' the young solicitor queried, glancing up from his notes.

'Something like that,' Tanner replied.

'But isn't that following the erroneous assumption that two wrongs make a right, or in this particular instance, two unproven criminal acts make one proven one?'

With the unfortunate realisation that the solicitor wasn't as stupid as he looked, Tanner returned to him a thin smile. 'The abduction provides a motive, which is enough for us to have him arrested under suspicion of setting fire to it. He's also suspected of murdering the person he abducted.'

'May I ask who the murdered victim was?'

'A man who'd just been released from prison for having shot and killed your client's father, a Mr Vincent O'Riley.'

'And again, may I ask if you have any evidence to support the theory that my client was responsible?'

'Only that the victim's body was found this morning, lying opposite the gates to the O'Riley family's residence.'

'But that doesn't prove my client was responsible, though, does it?'

'No, it doesn't, which is why we haven't arrested him for it.'

'OK, so, just to clarify; the only thing my client is under arrest for is because you suspect him of having set fire to his own van?'

'That's correct.'

'OK, great!' the solicitor replied, placing his pen down to offer Tanner a placating smile. 'You may begin.'

Forcing a smile back in return, Tanner switched on the interview room's recording device to speed his way through the various formalities. Taking a breath, he then fixed the suspect's eyes. 'Andrew Priestly, in your own time, can you please tell us where you were between the hours of ten o'clock last night, and two o'clock this morning?'

'Is that when the fire started?' interrupted the solicitor.

'No, that was later.'

'How much later, exactly?'

Tanner turned to Vicky for help.

'We arrived at the suspect's house at just after ten o'clock this morning,' Vicky began, flipping through her notebook, 'at which time the van was already on fire, so it must have been sometime shortly before that.'

'I see,' the solicitor continued, returning to his notes. 'But if that is the case, why do you need to know where he was last night?'

Tanner let out an exasperated sigh. 'Because it relates back to the previously mentioned crimes of abduction and murder.'

'Neither of which my client's been arrested for.'

'Correct again,' Tanner replied, beginning to doubt his previous deduction that the young man was more intelligent than he looked.

'OK, good. Sorry, please carry on.'

'Mr Priestly,' Tanner sighed, 'where were you last

night, between the...'

'Forgive me,' the solicitor interrupted once again, 'but when I said please carry on, I actually meant with another line of questioning.'

Tanner shook his head in confused consternation. 'I'm sorry, Mr Lucas, but why are you asking me to move on to another line of questioning?'

'Because, asking my client about his whereabouts last night wouldn't appear to have anything to do with what you've arrested him for.'

'I beg to differ.'

'For what reason?'

'Because I'm looking to establish motive.'

'And how, may I ask, are you attempting to do that?'

'By connecting the abduction and the murder of Vincent O'Riley to the suspect's attempt at concealing evidence of his involvement, by deliberately setting fire to his own van.'

'I'm more than happy for you to attempt to establish a motive for what my client's been arrested for, Chief Inspector, but not by exploring other suspected crimes for which he hasn't. If you'd like to do that, then I'm going to have to insist that you arrest him for those crimes as well.'

- CHAPTER SEVENTEEN -

L EFT WITH LITTLE choice but to take a premature break in the proceedings, Tanner paused the interview with a disgruntled huff to lead Vicky back out into the corridor.

'Sounds like that solicitor isn't quite as naive as you expected him to be,' Vicky postulated, the moment the door was closed.

'Maybe not,' Tanner replied, leading the way to the end, 'but you can't blame me for thinking he was. I mean, the guy looks like he's still at school.'

'The problem is,' Vicky continued, 'if he's not going to let us question Priestly about either the abduction, or the murder, then what are we going to do?'

'What we always do. Keep searching for evidence. Besides, we still have his brother to interview, their houses to search, as well. We've also yet to hear from Dr Johnston, or to see the forensics report for the scene where O'Riley's body was found.'

'And if none of that unearths anything?'

Tanner stopped in front of the door at the end to stare at her with an agitated frown. 'I assume you have a better idea?'

'Actually,' she continued, 'I was thinking that it may be a better option to let them go.'

'Why on Earth would we want to do that?'

'Because of the painting.'

Tanner shook his head in dismay. 'I'm sorry, but

what's the painting got to do with it?'

'Because, if they did torture O'Riley with a view to finding it, I'd have thought the chances are fairly high that he'd have told them. Assuming he did, and we let them go, then I reckon there's an above average chance that they'd lead us straight to it.'

'But finding the painting won't prove anything, certainly not that they tortured and killed him.'

'Maybe not directly, but how else would they have known where it was if he hadn't told them? Then there are the other suspects to consider.'

'You mean Leonard Burton and Coby Morgan?'

'For all we know,' she nodded, 'one of them could have abducted him, and are at this precise moment in time recovering the painting in preparation to sell it to the highest bidder. Meanwhile, we're doing nothing more productive than being unable to interview two people who possibly didn't have anything to do with any of it.'

'If they're so innocent,' Tanner responded, 'then why are they so reluctant to tell us where they were last night?'

'I've no idea, but at this stage, I think it's a mistake for us to focus solely on them, not when there are other suspects to consider, and not when letting them go may help us to recover the painting.'

'There you go about the bloody painting again,' Tanner muttered. 'Finding it clasped in someone's hot sweaty hands may help identify who murdered O'Riley, but it won't prove they did. They could simply say that they found it whilst walking their dog.'

'So, the plan is to keep the Priestly brothers locked up for the next twenty-four hours, whilst being unable to ask them a single question about what happened to O'Riley?'

'Only until we find some more evidence.'

Giving her shoulders a petulant shrug, Vicky glanced away to mumble, 'You're the boss,' under her breath, leaving Tanner staring at the back of her head with a look of tired exasperation.

'Please don't let us fall out over this, Vicky. We are allowed to disagree, occasionally.'

'Yes, of course,' she replied, turning back. 'I just thought it might help speed things up a little if we let them go.'

'With you're inability to follow anyone without losing them three seconds later, probably nowhere!' Tanner laughed.

Seeing her face fleck with colour, Tanner quickly added, 'That was a joke, Vicky.'

'And it was an exceptionally good one.'

'Anyway, I like the idea, in theory, at least, I'd just be happier if we could keep hold of them for a little longer. I'm sure something in the form of evidence will turn up at some point. Speaking of which, perhaps you could chase forensics for me? Maybe give Dr Johnstone a call, as well?'

Vicky glanced down at her watch. 'It's a little soon, isn't it?'

'Perhaps,' Tanner replied, peering absently through the door's circular window to see none other than Superintendent Forrester, standing in the middle of reception, deep in conversation with someone just out of view, 'but it's possible that something's turned up. Then maybe you could see if anyone's had any luck working out who Leonard Burton might be, or if Coby Morgan's been back in the country?'

With his mind consumed by Forrester's unannounced appearance, he glanced back to add, 'Whilst you're doing that, I'm going to see what our superintendent is doing here. I could have sworn he promised to call ahead before doing so.'

- CHAPTER EIGHTEEN -

TANNER HAD BARELY stepped through the door when he heard Forrester's booming voice calling over to him.

'Ah, Tanner! I was wondering if you were around.'

Turning to face him, Tanner's heart leapt inside his chest when he saw the smirking face of the person his superintendent had been talking to.

'Have you met Mr Elliston?' he heard Forrester ask. 'Norfolk's latest Member of Parliament?'

With memories of his previous investigation flooding through his mind, beginning with a body found at the bottom of an open grave, to watching in anguished horror as the man who had been the prime suspect plummeted to his death off the back of a cross-channel ferry, Tanner felt an acrid mixture of guilt and rage crash over his head. Standing directly in front of him, talking to his superior officer in the middle of Wroxham Police Station, was the very man who'd confessed to the crimes, on the actual day of the election.

'Are you alright, Tanner?' Forrester enquired, as if speaking to him from some distant shore. 'You look like you've seen a ghost.'

'Sorry, sir,' he eventually responded, 'it's just that I've – I've got a lot on my mind at the moment. *Even more now,*' he mumbled, under his breath.

'I've actually met the Chief Inspector before,' Elliston chirped, his gaze casually shifting from Tanner to Forrester. 'If you remember, he was the one who arrested me on suspicion of murder, shortly before the election.'

'Oh – right – yes – of course,' came Forrester's embarrassed response. 'I must admit, I'd completely forgotten about that.'

'*I hadn't,*' Tanner muttered, his eyes latching onto Elliston's like two military-grade lasers.

'Yes, well, water under a bridge, and all that,' Forrester laughed, somewhat nervously.

'May I be so bold as to ask what the right honourable gentlemen is doing here?' Tanner queried, his eyes never leaving Elliston's.

'I offered him a guided tour,' came Forrester's magnanimous reply, 'to explain why we're in such desperate need of investment.'

'And now that I've had a chance to see Wroxham Police Station, this time from the more comfortable side of a holding cell,' Elliston smirked, 'I'm confident that such an investment will be possible. After all, I won the election on a pledge to improve our local police service, and I fully intend to keep that promise.'

'That's funny,' mused Tanner, 'I thought there was another reason for your landslide victory. Something about your political opponent falling off the back of a ferry, in the middle of the North Sea.'

Elliston presented Tanner with a malevolent grin. 'From what I read in the papers, Chief Inspector, I thought *you* were responsible for the loss of our dearly departed colleague, Sir George Fletcher?'

'In part, perhaps,' Tanner snarled back, 'but only because I had my sights set on the wrong person.'

Elliston opened his mouth in mock consternation. 'I sincerely hope you're not about to accuse me, again?'

'Of course he isn't!' Forrester interrupted, turning his head to send daggers into Tanner's eyes.

With Tanner still glaring at Elliston in brooding silence, the MP looked back at Forrester with an apathetic shrug. 'Anyway, thank you for your time, superintendent. You and your wife must come over to dinner some time. Maybe you could bring Chief Superintendent Thornton and Assistant Chief Constable Walker with you as well? I know my wife would simply love to have you all over.'

'That sounds absolutely delightful!' Forrester exclaimed, shaking the man's extended hand with gleeful enthusiasm.

'Excellent! I look forward to seeing you then.'

Tanner continued to glower at Elliston as he watched Forrester escort him to the door. The moment he'd left, Forrester pivoted around to charge back towards him.

'What the hell was all that about?' he demanded, his voice a portentous growl.

'What was all what about?' Tanner replied, presenting Forrester with an innocent frown.

'You may as well have accused the man of being a psychotic serial-killer! Do you have any idea who he is?'

'I know exactly who he is, thank you very much.'

'Then why were you talking to him as if he was a prime suspect in a murder investigation?'

'If you remember, sir, he was.'

'And if *you* remember, Tanner, he was fully exonerated, shortly before the predatory paedophile who did kill all those people drowned in the North Sea.'

'But we never proved he did. Not beyond a reasonable doubt.'

'No, we didn't, but only because you let him slip through your fingers, quite literally, I may add.'

'Thank you for reminding me, sir,' Tanner replied, glaring back at him with resentful rage. 'Very much appreciated.'

With a look of instant regret, Forrester pulled himself back. 'I apologise, Tanner. I didn't mean to insinuate that you had anything to do with what happened to Sir Charles. But what I don't understand is why you've suddenly got it into your head that Elliston was responsible?'

Replaying the conversation the two of them had had on the day of the election, Tanner remembered why he hadn't told a single solitary soul. Because that would have meant admitting to the fact that his actions, and his actions alone, had allowed an innocent man to plummet to his death, leaving the person who was actually responsible for murdering all those people to not only walk away, scot-free, but to go on to become one of the most powerful people in the whole of Norfolk. His only chance of redemption had been to somehow prove Elliston's guilt. But with the investigation officially closed, and without a single shred of evidence to support it being opened again, he hadn't known where to start. And up until a few minutes before, when he'd discovered his own boss giving the man a tour of the station, he'd largely managed to forget about him.

'No reason in particular,' he eventually replied.

'Then can you please show the man a little more respect?'

'I'm sorry sir, but that's going to be difficult. The only reason he won the election was because of what happened to his opponent. Besides, who's to say he *wasn't* behind the whole thing?'

'The law says he wasn't, Tanner, which is why the investigation was closed. And now Mr Elliston is promising to give us an additional two-and-a half million pounds, which I can assure you we most desperately need. Bearing all that in mind, I'd rather you didn't deliberately go out of your way to upset the man.'

'I see. So what you're basically saying is that he's paying us off to make sure he's never investigated, ever again.'

'For God's sake, Tanner, it's not a bribe, it's a re-allocation of government funding.'

'Sounds like a bribe to me,' Tanner muttered.

'And what's he supposed to be bribing us for?' Forrester continued. 'He's not under investigation!'

'But if he was, though,' Tanner countered, 'wouldn't the fact that he was promising to pay you two-and-a-half million, whilst inviting Norfolk's highest ranked police officials around to his house for dinner, give you reason to look the other way if something untoward did come up?'

'Of course it wouldn't!'

'Uh-huh,' Tanner replied, his eyes drifting slowly away.

'This is ridiculous! It's not as if the money would be going anywhere near me. Not personally, at least.'

'Then I suppose we'll just have to wait and see.'

'Wait and see for what? If the Right Honourable Mr George Elliston is about to come under the spotlight for some major crime he's yet to commit, or if I'm about to announce to the world that I'm open to accepting bribes?'

'I'm not saying you are, sir.'

'Then what are you saying, Tanner?'

'That I don't trust Elliston.'

'Unless you have actual evidence that he's committed some sort of a crime, I suggest you keep your mouth shut, is that understood!'

Realising he was fighting an uphill battle, one that he'd be unable to win any time soon, Tanner let out a capitulating sigh.

'Sorry, was that a yes?'

'Yes, sir,' Tanner reluctantly replied, his head dropping despondently to the floor.

'Anyway, how about filling me in on what's been going on with regards to your current investigation? The last thing I heard was that Vincent O'Riley's body had turned up outside someone's house, something I only found out about during a conversation with Vicky, I may add.'

'I can't update you all the time, sir,' Tanner replied, pulling himself up straight.

'And I don't expect you to, but when a body turns up, it would be nice if someone did.'

'Then I apologise again, sir.'

'What do you mean, again, Tanner? I wasn't aware you'd apologised a first time?'

'I must have done, at some point,' Tanner mumbled.

'And what about those men from the National Gallery?'

'What about them?'

'You gave one of them my number, telling him to call me.'

'That's right.'

'Having told him that you couldn't give a shit about his missing painting, despite the fact that it's a long lost Turner, one that's estimated to be worth over a million pounds.'

'I simply told him that our current priority is to find Vincent O'Riley's killer, sir.'

'Did it not occur to you that the painting may lead us straight to those responsible?'

'Or finding those responsible may lead us to the painting,' Tanner rebutted.

Forrester glowered at him for a moment longer, before re-opening his mouth. 'I assume you're considering the men who abducted O'Riley to be the same men responsible for his murder?'

'Naturally,' Tanner replied. 'At least, that is our current assumption.'

'So that means the Priestly brothers are the prime suspects, correct?'

'For now.'

'OK, so, where are we with them?'

'One's inside Interview Room One, the other's on his way over.'

'Oh, right!' exclaimed Forrester, in a clear note of surprise. 'And how are we doing for evidence?'

'Well, we did have their van, the one we believe they used for the abduction.'

'Don't we still?'

'Unfortunately, someone set fire to it.'

Forrester let out a frustrated sigh. 'I don't suppose we have any idea who it was?'

'Not yet,' Tanner replied, glancing around at the door leading through to the interview rooms.

'Do you have anything else in the form of evidence?'

'We're hoping something will turn up from either O'Riley's body, or the location where it was found.'

'But you said you've arrested them?'

'Only under suspicion of arson.'

'You think they set fire to their own van?'

'If they used it to kidnap O'Riley, then it's certainly a possibility. The only problem is, their solicitor won't allow us to question them about anything relating to either O'Riley's abduction, or his murder, as we didn't pull them in for that. So I'm now hoping to hear back from either Dr Johnstone, or forensics, before the clock runs out, and I'm forced to let them go.'

'Are they likely to come back to you by then?'

'Probably not,' Tanner replied, glancing down at his watch with an air of despondency.

'Then you may as well let them go.'

'I'm sorry?'

'If you only arrested them on a charge of arson, then you may as well let them go,' Forrester repeated. 'You could then get someone to follow them, to see if they lead us to the painting.'

Tanner shook his head in consternated despair. 'Why's everyone constantly obsessed with that bloody painting?'

'Apart from the fact that it's a long lost Turner, one that's worth a considerable amount of money, imagine the publicity we'd get if we were the ones to actually find it!'

'The publicity?'

'It may surprise you to learn, Tanner, that we spend a considerable amount of time, effort, and money to maintain a positive working relationship with the general public. What do you think all these bloody posters are for?' he continued, gesturing around at the surrounding walls. 'Like most constabularies, we tread a very thin line between everyone demanding to have us patrolling the pavement outside their homes, to wishing we didn't exist. Finding the missing Turner would generate a bout of PR that money simply couldn't buy.'

'You're saying that you want me to let them go to have them immediately followed?'

'Why not? After all, it's not just the painting they could lead us to, but where they tortured O'Riley, as well. If they did, then I'd be very surprised if forensics weren't able to find enough evidence to have them put away for a very long time.'

'And what if we were to let them go, only for them to torture and kill someone else?'

'As long as they're being followed, then I don't think that's very likely, do you?'

- CHAPTER NINETEEN -

T ANNER CREPT INSIDE his house at just after half-past five that evening to hear the sound of Christine, singing softly in the living room. Placing his keys ever-so gently down on the sideboard, he took a reflective moment to listen.

Row, row, row your boat,
Gently down the stream,
Merrily, merrily, merrily, merrily,
Life is but a dream.

Peering inside their main living area to see her pacing up and down like a comatosed zombie, whilst patting baby Samantha gently on the back, he stepped inside to remark, 'You know, I'm really not convinced that it is.'

'Oh, hello,' she whispered, offering him a tired, but caring smile. 'I didn't hear you come in.'

'I was in full stealth mode,' he replied, heading over to the breakfast bar to pour himself a much needed glass of rum. 'Furthermore,' he continued, 'you'd be far more likely to find yourself rowing a boat down a river, than a stream. Certainly around here. I'm not even sure *how* you could row a boat down a stream, but I suppose the word "river" doesn't rhyme with "dream", hence the rather peculiar choice.'

'Huh?'

'The nursery rhyme you were singing. It definitely has some factual errors.'

'Ah,' she replied, with a sagacious frown, 'but does it?'

'You don't seriously think that you could row a boat down a stream, do you?'

'Maybe not, but I'm fairly sure life is but a dream, at least, it feels like it is, especially at the moment, but that's probably because I've barely slept since yesterday.'

'I assume that means Samantha has been struggling?'

'She only seems to want to sleep if I either carry her around the house, or take her for a walk in the pram. Either way, it's hardly ideal.'

'Do you want me to take her for a while?' he asked, half hoping she'd say yes, the other half desperate for her not to.

'It's OK. She's asleep now. I'm going to try and put her down.'

Two drinks later, Tanner turned to see Christine come weaving her way back into the room.

'Can I get you something to eat?' she asked, her hands held out in front of her as if unable to see.

'Only if you don't mind.'

'No problem at all,' came her cheerful response, stopping in the middle of the room to begin turning blindly around. 'I don't suppose you know where the kitchen is?'

'I can guide you, if you like?'

'Don't worry,' she continued, peeling thick strands of hair away from her face, 'I can see it now. What do you fancy, a very ready meal, or a not quite so ready one?'

'Either / or would be fine, thank you.'

'I'll do the first. It's quicker.'

Debating whether or not to have a third glass of rum, Tanner said, "sod it" to himself, and poured himself another.

'So anyway,' he said, swirling the drink around the bottom of the glass in anticipation of drinking it, 'apart from not getting any sleep, how was your day?'

'Oh, you know. Same old, same old. How about you?'

'It had its ups and downs, but we at least managed to find O'Riley.'

'That's something, I suppose. Was he alright?'

'Not really. Someone had tortured him to death.'

Sliding a ready meal out from the fridge, Christine offered him a peculiar look. 'Not seriously?'

'Pretty much, although, when we first found him, he'd only *nearly* been tortured to death. But the only reason I knew that was because he started talking.'

'You mean, he's not dead?'

'No, sorry. He is. He passed away about ten seconds later.'

'I'm sorry to hear that.'

'Me too!'

'Does that mean you heard him utter his very last words?'

'Something like that.'

'Out of morbid curiosity, may I ask what they were?'

'He said a name. Leonard Burton.'

'Do you think that's who killed him?'

'Possibly, but at the moment, our prime suspects are a couple of comedians known as the Priestly brothers. I even managed to arrest them.'

'That was quick!'

'Only to let them go about two hours later.'

'But I thought you could hold suspects for twenty-four hours?'

'We can.'

'So why did you let them go?'

'Because Forrester told me to. Vicky, as well.'

Placing the ready meal inside the microwave to close the door, Christine turned to ask, 'Any particular reason why?'

'They're both under the impression that O'Riley must have told them where the missing painting is, and that if I were to let them go, they'd be stupid enough to lead us straight to it.'

'And have they?'

'Not yet. Vicky's following one as we speak, at least I hope she is.'

Tanner was about to down his third glass, when he heard the demanding tone of his mobile phone ring.

Placing his tumbler down, he dug it out to see Vicky was calling.

'Hello Vicky,' he began. 'Christine and I were only just this second talking about you. How've you been getting on?'

'Not great, I'm afraid.'

'Let me guess. You've lost them again?'

'Only the one I was following,' she replied, 'but that's not why I'm calling. I've just had a call from the station. I'm afraid Mrs O'Riley has been taken into hospital.'

'Oh, right. I'm sorry to hear that, although, I'm not sure why you had to tell me.'

'It's the reason *why* she was taken to hospital that's important,' Vicky continued. 'Someone broke into her house a few hours ago. They've beaten her up pretty badly. When the paramedics arrived, they said she was barely breathing.'

- CHAPTER TWENTY -

PLEASED, AT LEAST, that he hadn't drunk his third glass of rum, Tanner made his way wearily back to his car to make the relatively short journey over to Wroxham Medical Centre, where Mrs O'Riley had been taken, and where Vicky said she'd meet him.

Seeing her waiting for him on the steps outside reception, he left his car in the nearest space to climb slowly out.

'Any news?' he asked, making his way over.

'I just spoke to one of the nurses. She's alive, but apparently, it's touch and go if she'll make it through the night.'

'Is she conscious?'

'Just about.'

'Have you asked if we'd be able to talk to her?'

'I thought I'd wait for you.'

Reaching the top of the steps, Tanner peered in through the glass doors. 'I don't suppose there were any witnesses?'

'It doesn't look like it. Her children were out at the time.'

'Do we know where they are now?'

'Waiting inside,' she replied, gesturing behind. 'They're a little upset, the brothers in particular.'

'That's hardly surprising.'

'They want to know what we're doing to find who's responsible.'

'No doubt,' Tanner sighed. 'I don't suppose there's been any sign of Andrew Priestly, the suspect you managed to lose, again?'

'Nothing yet.'

'How about his brother?'

'Townsend's still keeping an eye on him. He says he's at home, and has been since he was released.'

'Wasn't that what we thought last time?'

'You think it was them?'

'Don't you?' Tanner questioned.

'If it was, that must mean they're still looking for the painting, which means O'Riley didn't tell them where it was after all.'

'Or maybe he did, but it wasn't where he said it was?'

'So they thought they'd try asking his wife instead,' mused Vicky.

Tanner glanced thoughtfully back through the glass doors. 'If this *is* all about the painting, and whoever's looking for it is prepared to torture and kill to find it, then the children could well be next on the list.'

'If that's the case,' Vicky began, 'then anyone they think might know its location could be as well, like the third accomplice, Coby Morgan, for example?'

'Or maybe Coby Morgan is the one looking for it, together with the person O'Riley told us about, just before he died. What was his name again?'

'Leonard Burton,' Vicky replied.

'I don't suppose there's been any news on either?'

'As far as we know, Morgan is still in Malta. At least, he hasn't used his passport to leave the country. Neither has he done to enter ours.'

'And Leonard Burton?'

'The jury's still out on him. There are at least a dozen in the UK.'

Tanner took a moment to think, before drawing in a fortifying breath. 'OK, I suggest we start by asking if it's possible for us to speak to Mrs O'Riley. If we can, then there's a good chance that she'll be able to identify whoever it was who attacked her. She may be able to tell us why they did, as well.'

'And if she can't do either?'

'Then we'll at least be able to talk to her children, if for no other reason than to warn them that they could be next.'

- CHAPTER TWENTY ONE -

TANNER HAD BARELY made it through the hospital's doors before the man he recognised as being the victim's son, Michael O'Riley, came charging towards him like a rampaging rhino.

'Have you caught the people who did this to my mother?' he demanded, blocking Tanner's way as his brother, Jonathan, came storming up behind him.

'I'm sorry, Michael, but we've only just found out what happened.'

'Then what are you doing here?'

'To be honest,' Tanner replied, glancing around to see Vicky come to a jittery halt beside him, 'we came to see if she's OK.'

'What do you mean, to see if she's OK?' Michael responded, his body shaking with rage. 'She's been beaten half-to-death, just like our father had. Of course she's not OK!'

'We also came to see if it would be possible to speak to her. If she's able to tell us who her attackers were, then we'd be able to take the appropriate action.'

'What do you need to ask her for? Everyone knows who did it. The only people who don't seem to know are the police, i.e., you!'

'We've already spoken to the Priestly brothers about what happened to your father.'

'Then why the hell didn't you arrest them?'

'Actually, we did.'

Michael's head baulked back in surprise. 'You mean, they're currently locked behind bars?'

'They *were*,' Tanner replied, casting an admonishing eye at Vicky, 'but, unfortunately, due to a lack of evidence, we had no choice but to let them go.'

'You must be fucking joking!' Michael spat. 'You're honestly telling us that you couldn't find any evidence, despite the fact that they abducted my father, right from under your nose, before dumping his half-dead body outside the gates to our family home?'

'As I'm sure you can appreciate, we can only prove it was them when we're in possession of some actual evidence.'

'What about the van they used to abduct him? Did you at least make the effort to trace the numberplate?'

'We did.'

'And...?'

'On the surface, it did appear to be registered to them, however...' Tanner immediately added, as Michael's face looked like it was about to explode, '...that doesn't mean it was their van. Someone could have easily used fake numberplates to make it look like it was.'

'But they do own a white van. I know they do!'

'That still doesn't mean it was theirs.'

'Have you at least taken a look at it?'

'We have, or at least we were about to, when...'

'When... what?'

'Someone set fire to it, just before we arrived.'

Michael threw his head back to laugh at Tanner in a vicious, condescending manner. 'I wonder who that could have been?'

'Anyway, we need to warn you, both of you,' Tanner continued, looking at each of them, 'your sister as well, I'm afraid, that whoever *did* do this to your parents, may well have something similar in mind for yourselves, especially if this is all in an effort to find the missing painting.'

'If I were you, I'd be more worried about the Priestly brothers than us,' Michael sneered.

'Whatever retaliatory action you're considering, I beg you to reconsider. You'll only end up in the same place your father did. Besides, as much as you may want to believe it, we still don't know it was them.'

'I'm sorry, Chief Inspector, but we can't promise anything, especially if they do make the mistake of attempting to come after us.'

'Self-defence is one thing, but a pre-meditated attack is something completely different.'

'We'll see,' Michael muttered, glancing away.

'OK, look, for now, at least, I suggest you focus your attention on looking after your sister,' Tanner continued, turning to see her slumped in one of the reception chairs, her beautiful face staring despondently down at the carpet, 'and leave finding whoever did this to us.'

As both Michael and Jonathan followed his compassionate gaze, Tanner continued by asking, 'I don't suppose either of you would be able to help us in that regard?'

'In what way?' Michael queried, turning back.

'We were wondering if anyone has been in contact with you about the missing Turner?'

'Not in a threatening manner.'

'But someone has been in touch?'

Michael glanced briefly around at his brother. 'We had a call from someone from the National Gallery, asking if we'd be prepared to meet them to discuss its possible whereabouts.'

'Presumably someone by the name of Edward Phillips?'

'It was something like that,' Michael nodded.

'May I ask what you said?'

'The same thing we told you; that we don't have any interest in its whereabouts, and that as far as we know, my father never had it.'

'You didn't agree to meet them?'

'To be honest, we didn't see the point.'

'Do you think they might have been in contact with your sister?'

'I – I don't know,' he replied, glancing around at her again.

'Then perhaps you could ask her for me, maybe when she's a little more... herself?'

'Yes, of course.'

'We'd also like to ask about your mother, in particular, if you know if there were any witnesses?'

'She was on her own.'

'May I ask where you were?'

'At the gym.'

'And Rebecca?'

'I've no idea.'

'But, you do all live in the same house?'

'We're on the same estate. Only our sister lives with our mother, in the main house.'

'So, where do you live?'

'I'm in a flat above the garage. My brother's in an annex, just off to the side of the main building. We find living on the same estate helps keep us together. We've always been close, especially since our father was dragged away when we were children.'

'How about security?'

'The property is surrounded by a ten-foot high brick wall, which I suppose would be easy enough to climb over. You've seen the gate at the front.'

'Do you have CCTV?'

'There are seven motion sensitive cameras. Two at the front, one at each side, and three around the back. They send a notification to our phones if they're triggered.'

'And were they?'

'Nothing came through,' Michael replied, digging out his phone. 'Unfortunately, it's relatively easy to avoid setting them off. All someone would need to do would be to move slowly, and keep close to the walls.'

'What about inside?'

'It has an alarm, again motion sensitive, but it's turned off when someone's inside, for obvious reasons.'

'May I ask who found her?'

'Rebecca, which probably explains why she's so upset.'

'How long was it before the two of you arrived?'

'Just before the ambulance.'

'I assume that means you saw inside the house?'

'Someone had completely trashed the place. It was an absolute mess!'

'And your mother? Did it look like she'd been... she'd been tortured?'

Tanner watched each of their jaws tighten.

'She'd been tied to a chair. Rebecca said that a plastic bag had been placed over her head. She'd also been beaten to the point that we can barely recognise her. So, yes, I'd say she'd been tortured!'

'OK, thank you for your time. I can assure you that we'll be doing everything we possibly can to find out who did this, to both your mother and father, which will include speaking again with the Priestly brothers.'

'Are you going to arrest them, again?'

'If the evidence is there.'

'And if it isn't?'

'Then we'll keep looking until we find some. But the fact that whoever was responsible spent a considerable amount of time inside your house, should give us a better than average chance. Meanwhile, I'd recommend keeping a watchful eye over your sister. And although I'm sure you're both more than capable of looking after yourselves, I'd advise you to be careful. It would be easy enough for you to be caught off guard, especially when whoever did this, be it the Priestly brothers, or whoever else,' Tanner made sure to add, 'have at least two shotguns between them, and don't seem to have an issue with murdering people in order to get what they want.'

- CHAPTER TWENTY TWO -

H ANDING EACH OF the brothers his business card, Tanner left them and led Vicky over to the reception desk.

'Excuse me,' he whispered to the sour-faced nurse they found sitting there. 'DCI Tanner, and DS Gilbert, Norfolk Police. We understand you had a patient brought in here about an hour ago, someone by the name of Mrs Sarah O'Riley?'

The nurse glanced down at her computer screen before returning to him a perfunctory nod. 'She's currently being examined by Dr Ashcombe.'

'We were actually wondering if it would be possible to have a very quick word with her?'

The nurse looked up with a disapproving eye.

'We wouldn't need long. Only a minute, or two.'

'You can ask the doctor, if you like. You'll just need to wait for him to come out. Although, to be honest,' she added, as Tanner stared impatiently at his watch, 'I think you'd be better off coming back in the morning.'

Tanner glanced behind him to see the O'Riley brothers comforting their sister. 'Sorry,' he continued, leaning over the desk, 'this may sound a little insensitive, but... do you have any idea if the patient is likely to last that long?'

The nurse returned to Tanner a contemptuous glare. 'As I said, you'll have to speak to the doctor.'

'Then I don't suppose you know how long he'll be?'

'I've no idea.'

'It's just that we're investigating the murder of her husband,' Tanner continued, 'and there's a very strong possibility that whoever attacked her, killed him as well.'

The nurse presented Tanner with a look of mortified horror. 'That poor woman's husband was *murdered?*'

'I'm afraid so,' Tanner replied, in a low, clandestine tone. 'We're now very concerned that the same people might target their daughter,' he added, gesturing behind him. 'The woman who's sitting just over there.'

'If that's the case,' the nurse announced, pushing herself up from her chair, 'I suggest the two of you had better come with me!'

- CHAPTER TWENTY THREE -

W ITH TANNER AND Vicky following her along a series of windowless corridors, the nurse eventually stopped outside a door to turn suddenly around.

'If you wait here, I'll have a quick word with the doctor. It will be up to him whether you'll be able to speak to her or not.'

Answering with a nod, they waited obediently as the nurse knocked on the door to slip quietly inside.

Leaning forward to try and hear what was being said, Tanner jumped back with a start when the door was flung suddenly open, leaving him staring into the exhausted hollow eyes of a stick-thin elderly man.

'I understand you're looking to speak to my patient?' the doctor asked, nudging a pair of wired-framed glasses up the ridge of his nose.

'If that would be possible?'

'In theory, I suppose, but I'm not sure she'll be of much use, especially after the medication she's just been given.'

'We *could* come back tomorrow, I suppose,' began Tanner, watching the nurse slink her way out. 'I'm just worried that she might not make it through the night, and it's vitally important that we speak to her.'

'Well, she's sustained numerous injuries to her head. There are also third degree burns on her forearms. Perhaps unsurprisingly, her heart is very weak. So, if you *really* need to talk to her, then it's probably best if you try now, but please, make it quick.'

With the doctor standing to one side, Tanner gave him an understanding nod to lead Vicky in.

Entering a small, dimly lit private room to see Mrs O'Riley, lying peacefully on the bed ahead, Tanner glanced over at a heartrate monitoring device, then up at a saline drip, hanging above.

Following the clear plastic line down, his eyes rested on her heavily bandaged face, the only parts visible being the dark red lips of a half-open mouth, and a single swollen eyelid.

'Mrs O'Riley?' Tanner whispered, crouching beside her. 'It's DCI Tanner, Norfolk Police.'

'I think she's asleep,' commented Vicky, from the other side of the bed.

'Mrs O'Riley,' Tanner repeated, gently shaking her shoulder. 'Can you hear me?'

Seeing her unbandaged eye flicker open to focus on his, he pulled in a breath to ask, 'Do you remember me? We met briefly, yesterday, when your husband was taken by those two men.'

Seeing her blink in response, he smiled around at Vicky, before turning back. 'Are you able to talk?'

'A little,' came her thin, rasping voice.

'We need to ask about what happened.'

She blinked once more.

'Did you see the people who attacked you?'

Moving her head from side to side, she mumbled something unintelligible.

'I think she said they were wearing masks,' commented Vicky, to which she blinked again.

'How about their voices? Did you recognise them?'

As a single tear pooled at the corner of her eye, she seemed to hesitate for a moment, before shaking her head.

'Are you sure?' Tanner demanded.

Another blink followed, forcing the tear to spill out over the side.

'OK,' Tanner continued, taking a breath. 'We're going to leave you now. The doctor says you'll be back on your feet in no time,' he lied, 'so we'll be able to have more of a chat then.'

About to leave, he felt one of her hands rest gently down onto his arm.

Turning back, he watched her lift her head to try and say something else.

'I – I can't understand,' he eventually responded, leaning forward to listen more closely.

'The – p – painting,' he heard her say. 'They wanted the painting.'

Tanner took hold of her hand. 'Did they find it?'

With her head falling back, she blinked twice before shaking her head.

'Do you know where it is?'

She opened her mouth again, only for the unbandaged eye to close as her head drifted slowly to the side.

Fearing the worst, Tanner stared frantically up at the heartrate monitor.

'Don't worry,' came Vicky's reassuring voice. 'She's still breathing. I think she's just fallen asleep.'

- CHAPTER TWENTY FOUR -

'A T LEAST WE know what they were after,' commented Tanner, heading back to reception.

'It's just a shame she didn't recognise her attackers,' added Vicky, following after him.

'To be honest, I'm not entirely convinced that she didn't.'

'How do you mean?'

'When I asked if she had, she seemed to hesitate before answering. It may be that she was too afraid to say, and for good reason. Whoever did that to her is clearly prepared to stop at nothing to find that bloody painting. If that involves abducting, torturing, maybe even killing her children, then I wouldn't be surprised if she is keeping her mouth shut, more so if they told her to.

'Anyway, let's just hope she makes it through the night. If she did recognise them, and we're able to allay any fears she may have that her children could be in harm's way, her testimony could prove vital. With that in mind, maybe we should have someone posted outside her door, just in case someone tries to finish the job.'

'What about her children? Is it worth having a squad car parked outside the family's estate?'

'At this stage, I'm more concerned about what her sons might do to those they're assuming to be responsible, than the other way around.'

'But what if something does happen to the them, and HQ decides that we didn't do everything we could to protect them?'

'If it does turn out to be the Priestly brothers, then I'd be able to lay the blame squarely at Forrester's feet. After all, it was his idea to let them go.'

'I told you to as well,' Vicky replied, in a subdued tone of guilty reticence.

'Er... no, Vicky. You only offered your opinion. Forrester was the one who ordered me to.'

'Either way, I was wrong to have done so.'

Coming a gradual halt, Tanner turned to face her. 'Tell you what, you can make it up to me by doing what you suggested.'

'Remind me what that was again?'

'Arrange to have a squad car parked outside the gates to their family's estate.'

Seeing her pull out her phone, he added, 'Can you also ask someone to head over to do the same thing here? Whilst you're there, maybe you can find out if we know where the Priestly brothers are?'

Seeing her nod, he was about to continue their journey to reception, when he heard his own phone ring from the depths of his sailing jacket.

'Tanner speaking!' he answered, failing to check who it was.

'Tanner, it's Johnstone. I hope it's not too late?'

'Not at all!' Tanner replied, glancing down at his watch to see just how late it actually was.

'I just thought you'd like to know that I've finished Vincent O'Riley's post mortem.'

'I don't suppose anything interesting turned up?'

'Nothing I hadn't already suspected. He died from internal haemorrhaging, caused by repeated blunt force trauma to the upper and lower torso. Basically, he'd been beaten to death.'

'What about the other injuries?' Tanner enquired, thinking back to what the doctor had said about the injuries Mrs O'Riley had suffered.

'Just the missing finger, and the fact that he'd been electrocuted, but neither would have been fatal.'

Tanner raised a curious eyebrow at Vicky, only to find her still on the phone.

'Anyway,' Johnstone continued, 'I'm happy for the body to be released. Would you like me to give someone a call, to let them know?'

'That would be useful, thank you, but perhaps not his wife. Unfortunately, she's just been admitted to hospital, apparently having suffered a similar fate to her husband.'

'I'm sorry to hear that. Is she going to be alright?'

'We'll have to see. Do you know when I'll be able to see a copy of your report?'

'I just emailed it to you. Give me a shout if you have any questions.'

'Will do, thank you.'

Before ending the call, Tanner remembered to ask, 'I don't suppose you've heard anything from forensics?'

'Only that they finished at the scene where O'Riley's body was found, so their report should be with you soon.'

Checking his inbox to find emails from both Dr Johnstone and forensics, he ended the call to open them up.

Speedreading his way through the forensics report, his attention was caught by one particular paragraph, just as he saw Vicky, making her way over.

'Townsend radioed in to the station,' she announced, stopping in front of him. 'He's seen Andrew Priestly, arriving at his brother's house.'

'Is his brother in?'

'He thinks so.'

'Then at least they're both at the same place. I don't suppose he's managed to catch sight of the painting?'

'He didn't say, but that doesn't mean they haven't found it.'

'OK, whether they have, or haven't, I definitely want to have another word with them, preferably sooner rather than later.'

'Does that mean something's turned up?'

'Yes, their DNA, at the scene where Vincent O'Riley's body was found,' Tanner replied, glancing up from his phone to present her with a victorious grin.

- CHAPTER TWENTY FIVE -

STEERING HIS XJS into the narrow congested residential road where Andrew Priestly lived, Tanner looked ahead to see Townsend's car, parked discreetly to the side, as he'd been expecting. What he hadn't expected was to see its doors swing open for Townsend to climb out, closely followed by an over-weight uniformed police constable.

'You didn't tell them we were coming, did you?' Tanner queried, glancing around at Vicky.

'Don't look at me!' she replied, staring ahead. 'They must have seen your car in the mirror. After all, it is rather conspicuous.'

But as they watched them slam their respective doors closed, neither turned to look at Tanner's approaching XJS. Instead, they bolted over the road, heading towards where he could see four men, having some sort of an altercation outside Andrew Priestly's house, where what remained of his burnt out van still smouldered.

As Tanner drove closer, it didn't take him long to recognise who two of them were; the Priestly brothers, pushing and shoving the other two as they forced their way down the drive.

'For fuck's sake,' Tanner moaned, assuming the two trying to stop them to be reporters. 'How the hell did the press find out?'

It was only when he saw one of them fall to the ground did he realise that they weren't reporters after all, but were the curators from the National Gallery.

Unsure which was worse, nosey journalists, or interfering museum curators, Tanner double-parked alongside Townsend's car to climb quickly out, only to be nearly run over by a giant-sized van, charging up the road behind him.

Jumping back with a start, he watched the van come skidding to a halt, blocking both his path, and more annoyingly, his view.

Unable to see what was happening, Tanner shook his head as he clawed his way around the back to find himself being rudely beeped at by another car, screeching to a stop behind the now stationary van.

Raising an apologetic hand up to the young woman behind the wheel, he continued around to be met by the van's driver, an enormous man who was about as wide as he was tall, clambering down from his cabin.

'You need to watch where you're goin', mate!' he exclaimed, coming to a breathless standstill in front of him. 'I nearly ran you over!'

'I noticed,' Tanner remarked, with a disgruntled grimace.

'Anyways, I fought I better stop, to make sure you was alright.'

'Quite alright, thank you,' Tanner replied, attempting to step around him.

'Are you sure, mate?' the driver continued, deliberately blocking his way. 'You look a little red in the face.'

The van driver's words brought Tanner grinding to a halt. 'Don't worry,' he replied, glaring up at him. 'It's probably got more to do with the fact that I was nearly run over by a van who's driver failed to look where he was going, than because I'm in the throes of having a cardiac arrest.'

'Excuse me, mate, but you're the one who wasn't looking where he was going, not me!'

'Right, yes, of course,' Tanner responded, shaking his head. 'It was entirely my fault. What was I thinking? Now, if you wouldn't mind getting out of my way?'

'Sorry, mate, but you're gonna have to apologise first.'

'What the hell would I want to do that for?' Tanner demanded.

'For stepping out in front of me, then having the balls to say it was my fault!'

'Tell you what. Either you get out of my way, or I'm going to arrest you for dangerous driving.'

'What?' the driver replied, his head jolting back in surprise.

'DCI Tanner, Norfolk Police,' Tanner replied, pulling out his formal ID to present to the man's fat, sweaty, unshaven face. 'Now, are you going to move, or am I go to have to read you your rights?'

'Alright, alright,' the driver replied, stepping back. 'Keep your 'air on.'

Finally able to see around the driver, Tanner stared over at the other side of the road, just in time to see the Priestly brothers jump into their car.

'OI!' he yelled, sprinting over, as the Audi TT came wheel-spinning towards him.

Forced to leap out of its way, he watched it speed off down the road before running back to his car, only to realise that the van was still there, and was blocking him in.

'Are you alright, boss?' came Townsend's voice behind him.

With his eyes tracking the Priestly's car as it disappeared into the distance, he was about to order Townsend to drive after them, when it dawned on him that his subordinate's car was blocked in beside his.

'I really wanted to have a word with them,' he muttered, glaring ahead in frustrated consternation.

'About anything in particular?'

'Forensics discovered traces of their DNA where Vincent O'Riley's body was found.'

'So, it was them, after all!'

'We'll probably never know now,' he huffed, looking past Townsend to see the elderly museum curator and his younger associate, sitting in a somewhat dishevelled state on the drive.

'Are they OK?' Tanner enquired, nodding over at them.

'They should be, but we've called an ambulance, just in case.'

'What the hell was going on, anyway?'

'We're not exactly sure. We were watching the front of the house, as instructed, when those two appeared as if from nowhere to start banging on the front door. When one of the Priestly's came out to answer it, they started having a discussion that quickly escalated, which was when we went over to break it up.'

'Did you hear what it was about?' Tanner continued, glancing around to see Vicky approach.

'The missing painting. The Priestly brothers kept saying that they didn't have it, whilst the other two kept insisting that they did.'

'OK,' said Tanner, letting out an exasperated sigh, 'I suppose I'd better have a word with them. Whilst I do, if you could get an All Ports Warning out for the

Priestly brothers, just in case they try to leave the country, that would be useful.'

- CHAPTER TWENTY SIX -

'**MR PHILLIPS AND** Mr Ward!' exclaimed Tanner, surprised to have remembered their names. 'To what do we owe the pleasure?'

'We came here to ask the Priestlys if they had any idea where the painting was,' Philips replied, prodding a finger at his bloodied nose, as if it was a mysterious ancient artifact.

'And you thought they'd tell you, did you?'

'I wasn't expecting them to punch me in the face, I know that much!'

'Then you must have said something to provoke them.'

'I suppose I may have been a little overly persistent in my questioning.'

'From what I could tell, you appeared to be trying to stop them from leaving their house.'

'I just had the feeling they weren't telling us something, that's all.'

'About the painting?'

'Of course about the painting? What else would it be about?'

'Then may I ask why you've suddenly come to the conclusion that they must be in possession of it?'

'Isn't it obvious?' Phillips continued, pushing himself off the tarmacked drive to adjust his ridiculous-looking bow tie.

'Strangely no, it isn't.'

'Because of what happened to Vincent O'Riley!'

'Oh, I see. So you think they abducted him, hoping to make him tell them where the painting was?'

'Yes, of course! And please don't tell me you don't. That *was* why you came here, wasn't it? To arrest them for O'Riley's murder?'

'I must admit, we *were* looking to have a word with them about it. But that doesn't mean they know where the painting is. To be honest, at this precise moment in time, I'm not convinced anyone does. What I do know is having the two of you going around trying to find it, as if you're starring in some sort of Indiana Jones movie, isn't helping. And given the fact that I did come to arrest them, only to have them disappear in a cloud of dust, because of your efforts to interrogate them I may add, is proof of that. If you really want to find the painting, the very best thing you can do is to go back to London and await a call. Anything else is only going to undermine our efforts, as it has done today.'

'Unfortunately, we're unable to do that.'

'And why, pray tell, is that?'

'Because the National Gallery's Board of Directors tasked us with the job of finding it.'

'Then I suggest you go back and tell them that you've sadly been unable to. If you don't, and you end up continuing to hinder our efforts to solve a murder investigation, then you may well find yourself having to stay here far longer than you'd planned, locked behind bars under a charge of obstruction.'

Taking a breath, Tanner turned to find Vicky standing behind him, staring up at him with an anxious look.

'Sorry to bother you, boss,' she said, keeping her voice low as she glanced awkwardly down at her phone, 'but another body's been found.'

'For fuck's sake!' he moaned, leading her away from the curators. 'Please don't tell me it's the same M.O.?'

'From what I've been told,' she continued, 'unfortunately, it does sound like it is.'

'Is there a name attached to the body?'

'Not yet.'

'But it's not one of the O'Riley children?'

'I'm sorry, boss, I don't know.'

'Do we at least have an address?'

'We do.'

'How far?'

'About twenty minutes.'

Casting his eyes down at his watch to see it was nearly seven o'clock, Tanner let out an exhausted sigh. 'Very well! Make sure someone lets Dr Johnstone know, then I suppose you'd better tell whoever's at the scene that we're on our way.'

- CHAPTER TWENTY SEVEN -

TURNING INTO A deserted country lane on the outskirts of Martham, Tanner rounded a corner to see an ambulance and two squad cars, parked outside the entrance to a quaint, rustic cottage.

Seeing Johnstone's boxy old Volvo Estate, left behind a delivery van, Tanner brought his car to a stop alongside to climb wearily out.

As he led Vicky along an overgrown gravel path, heading towards the cottage at the end, he saw a rather pale-looking PC about halfway up.

'The body's in the kitchen at the back, boss,' the young officer announced, holding out a pair of latex gloves and pale blue shoe coverings.

'Jenkins, isn't it?' he queried, taking the proffered items.

'It's actually Jennings, boss,' the officer responded, with a dutiful nod.

'Well, at least I got the first part right,' Tanner laughed, returning to him an affable smile. 'Do we know who the victim is?'

'Sorry, boss, I haven't been told.'

'How about the person who found it?'

'That would be the delivery van's driver. You'll find him getting some air around the back.'

'Right, thank you, Jennings.'

'Oh, and you may wish to consider wearing a mask,' the young PC added, 'if you have one.'

'Why's that, may I ask?' Tanner enquired, looking over his shoulder to see a dilapidated Citroen 2CV, left to rot under the branches of a sprawling sycamore tree.

'Because of the smell, boss,' he heard Jennings continue, 'although it probably won't help much, even if you do have one.'

Tanner's gaze drifted over to the cottage to find it in a similar state to the car. 'Dare I ask what's causing it?' he asked, already feeling his stomach churn.

'Sorry, boss. I didn't stick around long enough to find out, but I suspect it has something to do with the cats.'

'The cats?' Tanner repeated, with a questioning glance.

'Yes, boss. The house is full of them!'

Casting a curious eye around at Vicky, Tanner thanked the young PC before continuing on.

As he reached the open front door to see one of the previously mentioned cats, slinking its way out with an air of aloof indifference as to what Tanner was doing there, he stopped on the doorstep to peer cautiously in.

Unable to see anything but a shadow-filled hallway, he took a single step inside, only for his head to jolt instantly back.

'Jesus Christ!' he exclaimed, gasping at the untainted outside air. 'The man was right. The place absolutely stinks!'

'Do you mind if I stay here, boss?' Vicky requested, backing away. 'I'm really not much of a cat person. To be honest, I'm fairly sure I'm allergic.'

'Tell you what, why don't you find the delivery van's driver, and I'll meet you back here.'

Watching her disappear around the corner, he donned the gloves and shoe coverings to stare back inside. 'Right then,' he said to himself, drawing in a fortifying breath. 'I suppose I'd better get on with it.'

Doing his level best to ignore the repugnant smell, he inched his way slowly inside. As his eyes adjusted to the low level of light, he began to see an increasing number of cats, some watching him in curious silence from the stairs above, others darting erratically between his legs.

When he eventually reached a door at the end, he nudged it open with his foot to see Dr Johnstone, gazing studiously down at a man's half-naked body, staring unblinkingly up at the ceiling on a large wooden kitchen table. It was only then that he noticed the dozens-upon-dozens of cats, of every shape, colour, and size, all glaring at him, as if daring him to come any closer.

Seeing a particularly large ginger one suddenly bolt between his legs, he stared down to realise where the appalling smell had been coming from. Just about every square inch of the tiled kitchen floor was covered in curling clumps of faeces, circling each were pools of stinking yellow urine.

Realising he'd already trodden in one particularly disgusting lump, he involuntarily threw-up into his mouth.

'Ah, Tanner!' Johnstone exclaimed, glancing around. 'I was wondering when you were going to make an appearance.'

Unable to speak, Tanner lifted a hand to say hello, before swallowing the acidic bile to take a very deliberate backwards step.

'Are you alright?' the medical examiner enquired, gazing over at him with a concerned frown. 'If you don't mind me saying so, you look a little peaky.'

'Haven't you seen what you're standing in?' Tanner queried.

'Oh, that!' Johnstone replied, glancing down at his shoes, and the coverings protecting them. 'When you spend half your life wallowing around inside a human's large intestine, a little cat poo is like water off a duck's back.'

'If you say so,' Tanner muttered, using the sleeve of his suit in a failing attempt to mitigate the smell. 'I don't suppose you have any idea what they're all doing here?'

'The cats, or their excrement?'

'How about both, being that the presence of one would have to be the result of the other.'

'I've no idea,' Johnstone replied, turning his attention back to the body. 'I can only assume that the person we see lying before us had a soft spot for them.'

'A soft spot is one thing. Keeping them by what must be the hundreds is something completely different. There's probably even a law against it, I just don't happen to know what it is.'

'Well, if you can think of one, I'm not sure there's much point in arresting their owner for it, being that he's dead, and everything.'

Tanner took a moment to take in the body. 'I heard the M.O. was the same as for Vincent O'Riley?'

'It certainly appears to be similar. A little more extreme, perhaps.'

'In what way?'

'If you were to come inside, I could show you?'

'Er... thanks for the offer, but if it's all the same to you, I think I'd rather stay here.'

'Suit yourself,' the medical examiner shrugged, turning back to the body. 'There are severe burn marks to his forearms. I think it's possible that a blowtorch was used. There's no sign of a struggle, so I'd say he was overpowered fairly rapidly before having his wrists and ankles cable-tied to the table legs. The main difference is the cause of death. Vincent O'Riley died from internal haemorrhaging. The most likely cause in this instance was from a massive release of adrenalin, elevating both his heart rate and blood pressure to the point where he had either a stroke, or a heart attack.'

'Time of death?' asked Tanner, digging out his notebook.

'Between six and nine hours ago.'

'I don't suppose we have an ID, by any chance?'

'I found a wallet, inside one of his pockets. It's on the counter, in the corner, if you'd care to take a look.'

'If that means having to go back inside the kitchen, then I think I'd rather wait until your report comes out.'

'For goodness sake, Tanner!' Johnstone huffed, spinning around to retrieve the wallet. 'It's only animal excrement,' he continued, holding it out. 'Before Joseph Bazalgette invented the sewer back in 1859, we virtually had to live in the stuff!'

'I didn't know you were a historian,' Tanner remarked, taking the wallet being presented.

'It's common knowledge, Tanner!'

'I really don't think it is,' Tanner replied, under his breath. 'Anyway, thanks for this. If it's all the same to you, I'll take a look at it outside.'

Heading out to the front of the cottage, he prised it open to find some cash, credit cards, and, eventually, a driver's licence.

Seeing Vicky return, he glanced up to ask, 'How'd you get on?'

'The van's driver said he had a parcel to deliver that needed a signature. He saw the body when he looked through the letterbox.'

'I don't suppose he knows anything about all the cats?'

'Only that the owner had a soft spot for them. He used to take them in whenever the local animal shelter had one they couldn't find a home for.'

'Fair enough, but why on Earth would he then keep them all locked up inside his house?'

'Not a clue. Perhaps you could ask him?'

'That might be difficult,' Tanner grimaced, glancing back at the cottage.

'What did Johnstone say?'

'That he'd been tortured, possibly with a blowtorch.'

'I assume we know his identity?' Vicky continued, gesturing down at the driver's licence.

'Arthur Shaw.'

'Arther *who?*'

'Not a clue,' Tanner shrugged, 'but he must have something to do with what's been going on. I can't imagine he'd have been tortured to death just for the hell of it.'

'Maybe they were using him for practice?'

Wondering if she was being serious, Tanner opened his mouth to ask, when he heard some sort of a commotion, drifting up from the lane beyond.

About to head down to take a look, he saw a tall elderly man come charging up the driveway towards them, leaving a red-faced uniformed police constable trailing in his wake.

'May I help you?' Tanner enquired, stepping forward to block the man's way.

'I'm sorry, boss,' came the constable's breathless voice, running up behind him. 'He just barged straight past.'

'And why shouldn't I have?' the elderly man questioned, coming to a halt in front of Tanner. 'This is my house, after all!'

'This is *your* house?' Tanner queried, in an incredulous tone.

'Of course it's my house! Who else did you think it belonged to?'

'Sorry, sir, it's just that – well, we seem to have found someone else inside.'

'Oh, right!' the man exclaimed, in a relieved tone. 'I suppose that's OK then. For a minute there, I thought he'd gone out and left the front door open.'

'I take it that means you know who it is?

'Of course I know who it is! I'm not in the habit of letting complete strangers inside my home. What I want to know is what you're all doing here? He hasn't done anything stupid, I hope? He was supposed to be looking after my babies, whilst I went away for a few days.'

'Your *babies?*' Tanner enquired, even more confused.

'Sorry, I meant my cats. They're alright, I hope?'

'*They're* alright,' Tanner confirmed, 'Unfortunately, I can't say the same for your cat-sitting friend.'

'Why? What's happened?' the man demanded, lifting his gaze to the cottage.

'Someone would appear to have gained entry into your property in order to ask him a few questions.'

'Why on Earth would they want to do that?'

'To be honest, I was hoping you might be able to tell me.'

'How should I know?'

'I don't suppose you know a man by the name of Vincent O'Riley, by any chance?'

'Not that I'm aware of.'

'How about Coby Morgan, or Jake Priestly?'

'I've never heard of any of them?'

'Then what about Leonard Burton?'

The man tilted his head to stare at Tanner with a supercilious frown. 'Are you trying to wind me up?'

'I'm sorry, sir, but why would I be trying to wind you up?'

'Because you're asking if I've heard of someone by the name of Leonard Burton.'

'Yes, and...?'

'That's *my* name! *I'm* Leonard Burton!'

- CHAPTER TWENTY EIGHT -

E XPLAINING TO THE cottage's owner at least *some* of what had taken place inside his home, warning him that he could well have been the intended target, Tanner left instructions for him to be checked into a local hotel under a different name before leading Vicky back to his car.

'Do we know how many other Leonard Burtons have been found living in and around the Norfolk area?' he asked, searching for his keys.

'Two more,' she replied, referring to her notebook, 'one of whom is only ten.'

'And the other?'

'A retired school teacher.'

'And where abouts is he?'

'In Acle, not too far from here.'

'Then I suggest we head straight over there,' Tanner announced, opening the car door to begin climbing inside. 'Let's just hope that whoever did that to our cat-sitting friend doesn't know about him as well.'

'How about the boy?' questioned Vicky, opening the passenger door to climb in beside him.

'Surely they wouldn't think that a young boy could know anything about a missing painting?'

'Can we really take that chance?'

Knowing she was right, Tanner shook his head in reticent acknowledgment. 'Then I suppose you'd better arrange a squad car to be parked outside their house. Maybe they need to advise whoever they find living there to stay indoors for a while, but perhaps not to tell them why, at least, not exactly. I don't particularly want a rumour flying around that someone is on the lookout for ten year old boys to torture with a blowtorch.

'When you've done that,' he continued, watching Vicky exchange her notebook for her phone, 'we need to discuss who else knew about Leonard Burton. As far as I can remember, the only people who were there when Vincent O'Riley brought his name up were you, me, Dr Johnstone, and the person he told, his eldest son, Michael. We haven't mentioned Leonard Burton's name to the press, so I'm not sure how anyone else could have found out, certainly not the people we've been considering to be our prime suspects, the increasingly elusive Priestly brothers.'

'You're thinking that it may not have been them after all?' Vicky queried, dialling the office.

'I'm thinking about it,' Tanner muttered, starting the engine as he heard someone answer.

Ending the call a few minutes later, Vicky put her phone away to ask, 'What were you saying again?'

'I was responding to your question,' Tanner began, his eyes fixed on the road ahead, 'whether or not the Priestly brother's should remain our prime suspects, when we've just left a house belonging to some random person by the name of Leonard Burton, whose cat-sitting friend was tortured and murdered instead of him, and the only people who knew we were looking to speak to someone sharing his name were you, me, Dr Johnstone, and the dead guy's son, Michael O'Riley.'

'You're not seriously suggesting that it could have been the O'Riley brothers?' Vicky questioned, gazing over at him with astonished incredulity.

'I wasn't about to, but now you've brought them up, perhaps we should?'

'You do realise that if it was them, they'd needed to have tortured not only their own father, but their mother as well, all to locate a painting that they haven't shown the slightest interest in finding.'

'Unless the exact opposite is true,' Tanner proposed, 'and they're desperate to get their hands on it.'

'Desperate enough to take a blowtorch to their parents?'

'I'm fairly sure that there are other children who've done worse. If you take the fact that they are the victim's children out of the equation, it begins to make a lot more sense. If you remember, they just happened to have a vitally important business meeting the day their father was released, giving them the excuse not to attend. They also just happened to be out when their mother was attacked.'

'So was their sister.'

'But not with them, meaning that she'd be unable to vouch for their whereabouts. Then there's the location where their father's body was found,' Tanner continued. 'I always thought it was odd that someone would choose to leave him outside the gates to his own family estate.'

'Didn't we think that was to send them some sort of a message?'

'Maybe, but if that was the case, it would have been far easier just to have sent them a postcard.'

'You're suggesting that the O'Riley brothers did so to allay suspicion that it was them?'

'Why not? It would certainly have been the smart move. There's also the fact that their father wasn't dead when we found him, in much the same way that their mother wasn't. If it had been someone else, like the Priestly brothers, for example, I'd have thought they would have made sure he was, to prevent them from being identified. Thinking about it now, it may have been them who called the ambulance, hoping they'd arrive in time to save him.'

'I suppose,' Vicky replied, not sounding particularly convinced, 'however, if it had been them, then surely their parents would have recognised them? Even if they'd worn masks, their voices would have been a bit of a giveaway. Then there's the painting, of course. If their father did hide it somewhere, just before he was arrested, why on Earth wouldn't he have told his family? I can understand why he might not have wanted to let his wife know, just in case she did a runner with it, straight into the arms of another man, but his children as well?'

'Perhaps he didn't want them to end up where he was,' Tanner responded, 'which they would have done, had they been caught trying to sell it.'

'Maybe,' mused Vicky, 'but I still find it hard to believe that they'd have resorted to torturing their parents to get their hands on it. And it still doesn't explain how neither parent seemed to know it was them.'

'Maybe they did, but they didn't want to tell us?' Tanner replied, his mind thinking back to the way their mother appeared to have hesitated, before denying any knowledge of who her attackers were.

'It also doesn't explain why their father would have used his last dying breath to tell them the name of someone who doesn't appear to have a single thing to do with any of this.'

'Well, somebody seems pretty convinced that they do. Anyway, let's just hope we're in time to warn them,' Tanner added, his mind re-focussing on the road ahead, 'before the same thing happens all over again.'

- CHAPTER TWENTY NINE -

SCREECHING TO A halt outside a red bricked terraced house in the middle of Acle, Tanner climbed quickly out to make his way up to a faded painted wooden door.

Unable to find a bell, he hammered on it with the knocker, before standing back to examine the front, searching the windows for signs of life.

'Is anyone in?' he heard Vicky ask, joining him on the doorstep.

'Hopefully,' Tanner murmured, staring expectantly about.

When he saw a net curtain twitch from one of the ground floor windows, he turned to add, 'Sorry, make that definitely!'

Knocking hard again, he stood back to the sound of footsteps whilst clawing inside his jacket to pull out his formal ID.

'Who is it?' came a thin, wispy voice, from behind the still firmly closed door.

'Leonard Burton?' Tanner demanded, as loudly as he felt was necessary.

'Yes, I'm Leonard Burton.'

'DCI Tanner and DI Gilbert, Norfolk Police. We'd like to have a quick word, if that's OK?'

'May I ask what it's about?'

Tanner drew in an impatient breath. 'This would be a lot easier if you could open the door, Mr Burton.'

'I'm sure it would, but just because you say you're from the police, doesn't mean you are.'

'Would it help to see our identifications?'

'Do you have them on you?'

'Of course,' Tanner replied, wondering why they wouldn't. 'We're currently holding them in our hands.'

A long drawn out pause followed, leaving Tanner wondering if whoever had been behind the door had done a runner.

'Could you put them through the letterbox?' the voice eventually requested.

Tanner rolled his eyes at Vicky.

'At least he's being careful,' she whispered.

'There's being careful, and there's being bloody annoying,' Tanner replied, before lifting his voice again. 'Tell you what. How about if we hold them up to the letterbox? Would that suffice?'

'They could still be fake, and it would be difficult for me to know, just looking at them through the letterbox.'

'It would be difficult for you to know whatever we did, but more to the point, why would we go to the trouble of faking a couple of police IDs to do nothing more nefarious than to ask you a couple of questions?'

'I've no idea, but people come around here all the time saying they just want to ask me a couple of questions, whether it's about a new roof, double glazing, gardening services, or to find out who my current energy supplier is. If it's not that, then it's to offer me a guaranteed place in Heaven, in exchange for my life long dedication to some dodgy-sounding religion.'

'I do understand,' came Tanner's sympathetic reply, 'but has anyone come around before, saying they're from Norfolk Police?'

'Well, no, but I had a couple of people around earlier who said they were from the National Gallery, and I hadn't had that before, either!'

Tanner sent Vicky an anxious frown. 'May I ask what they wanted?'

'They had some cock and bull story about a missing painting, saying that if I helped them find it, there'd be a reward.'

'What sort of a reward?'

'They said I had to let them in before they'd tell me, at which point I told them to F-off.'

'Does that mean you don't know anything about a missing painting?'

'Christ, not you as well!'

'It's a Turner, taken from Lord Montgrave's house, back in 1994. You may have heard about it on the news?'

'I don't watch the news.'

'Does that mean you have, or you haven't?'

'OK, yes, I have heard about it. Is that what you want to talk to me about?'

'We've actually come to warn you.'

'About what?'

'That someone might come around, asking about it.'

'You mean, like you?'

'Like the two men who were here before.'

'Does that mean they *weren't* from the National Gallery?'

'All we know at this stage is that someone by the name of Arthur Shaw has just been found lying dead on his kitchen table.'

'And what's that got to do with me?'

'Because we believe it was a case of mistaken identity, and that the person they were really looking for was someone with the same name as yours.'

There followed a momentary silence, before hearing the man ask, 'Am I in danger?'

'It's a possibility, which is why we came to see you. We're also trying to find out why someone would appear to be so keen to talk to you about the missing painting.'

Hearing the door's security chain being slotted into its latch, the door opened slightly for Tanner to see the thin, pale face of an elderly man, his narrow, elongated jaw covered by a thick layer of stubble.

'I'm not opening it any more than that,' he eventually said, glaring out at first Tanner, then Vicky, 'but if you show me your identifications, I'll be happy to help if I can.'

Allowing him to see them, Tanner put his away to ask, 'Do you have any idea why someone might think you would know something about the missing painting?'

'Not a clue! I only remember hearing something about it at the time it went missing.'

'So you don't know the person accused of stealing it, a man by the name of Vincent O'Riley?'

'Nope!'

'What about Coby Morgan, or Jake Priestly?'

'Again, I've never heard of them.'

'You don't have any idea why Vincent O'Riley would have mentioned your name to his son, a few moments before he died?'

The old man's body shivered, as if someone had stepped on his grave. 'Is that what happened?'

Tanner replied with a solemn nod. 'And now two people are dead, and another is in hospital, all having been tortured in an attempt to find it.'

'Was it those people who came round to see me; the ones from the National Gallery?'

'It's possible, but it could equally have been someone else. With that in mind, we strongly recommend that you either remain indoors, or, preferably, check yourself into a hotel under a different name.'

'Until when?'

'Until we find those responsible.'

'And how long will that take?'

'I'm sorry, I don't know.'

Burton thought for a moment, before eventually saying, 'OK, thank you, but I think I'd rather stay here. I'm pretty good with security, as you can probably tell.'

'Right, well, thank you for your time, Mr Burton,' Tanner concluded, offering him a benevolent smile. 'Actually,' he added, digging out his wallet, 'before we go, I may as well give you my card. If those men from the National Gallery decide to make a reappearance, or anyone else comes around asking about the painting, then perhaps you could give me a call?'

'Yes, of course,' Burton replied, taking the card through the gap in the door.

'But whatever you do,' Tanner added, fixing the man's eye, 'do not let them in!'

'Don't worry, I won't!'

As Tanner turned to lead Vicky back to his car, he heard the man call out, 'Mr Tanner! Sorry, but – I don't know if it's relevant?'

Tanner turned back with a curious frown.

'You asked me earlier if I knew Vincent O'Riley?'

'Yes, that's right. Go on.'

'Well, it was a while back now, before the painting was stolen, but I'm fairly sure I taught his children at school. Michael, Jonathan, and Rebecca? Is that them?'

- CHAPTER THIRTY -

'THERE ARE THOSE names again,' muttered Tanner, leading Vicky back to his car to the sound of the door being locked and bolted behind them.

'Do you think it's relevant; that he used to teach the O'Riley children?'

'It's difficult to see how, especially when he said it was before the painting was stolen. However, at this stage, I'm not prepared to rule anything out, which includes taking a closer look at our curator friends.'

'Edward Phillips and Thomas Ward,' interjected Vicky, retrieving her notebook from her handbag.

'That's assuming those are their real names. For all we know, they just pulled them out of a hat.'

'Do you want me to check with the National Gallery?'

'Someone needs to, but maybe ask Sally. We also need to find them, if for no other reason than to take samples of their fingerprints and DNA. If we discover that they'd been anywhere near Vincent O'Riley's body, the room where his wife was tortured, or where the other Leonard Burton's cat-sitting friend was found, then I think we most definitely need to treat them as suspects, especially if we find out that the National Gallery has never heard of them.'

'One more question,' Vicky asked, taking notes. 'Where does all this leave us with the Priestly brothers?'

'To be honest, I don't know,' Tanner replied, hearing Vicky's phone ring, 'but I'm still keen to talk to them, if for no other reason than to ask what Phillips and Ward said to them outside their house. It couldn't just have been to ask them if they'd seen the painting,' he continued, as Vicky lifted her phone to her ear, 'not when one of them ended up being punched in the face.'

Leaving Vicky to her call, Tanner continued back to his car.

By the time he'd opened the door, he heard her come running up behind him.

'I think we'd better head back to the station.'

'For any particular reason?' Tanner enquired, in a dubious tone.

'The Priestly brothers have just been arrested!'

Tanner raised an intrigued eyebrow. 'Not for murder, I assume?'

'Someone drove into the back of them on the A47, after which a fight ensued. The attending officers found the driver to be over the legal alcohol limit, charging him with drunk driving, and the other assault.'

- CHAPTER THIRTY ONE -

W ITH THE WARM summer sun drifting lazily beneath Norfolk's endless horizon, Tanner arrived back at the station to find its reception to be far busier than normal.

Asking Vicky to grab him a coffee, he had to fight his way to the front of a disorderly queue to try and catch the eye of a flustered-looking duty sergeant.

'What's going on?' he was eventually able to ask. 'Why's it so busy?'

'Buses,' came DS Taylor's distracted response.

'You're not seriously going to tell me that one's crashed into another?'

'I mean they're like buses,' he grimaced. 'You can go for hours without seeing a single person, then two-dozen show up at the same time. I assume you're looking for the Priestly brothers?'

'Uh-huh,' Tanner replied, edging himself away from a drunken youth, looking as if he was about to throw up all over his shoes.

'Interview Rooms One and Two. I thought you'd appreciate them being kept separate.'

'Have they been processed?'

'They have.'

'And have they called for a solicitor?'

'They each made a phone call. I don't know who it was for.'

Nodding his thanks, Tanner headed back past the queue in search of Vicky, and a much needed coffee, when he saw none other than George Elliston, Norfolk's brand new Member of Parliament, stepping gracefully out from his gleaming black Bentley Continental to make his way towards the entrance.

'What the hell's *he* doing here?' he muttered to himself, debating if he should head outside to ask him in person.

Seeing Elliston run his eyes over his XJS with aloof disdain, Tanner made up his mind.

Pulling open the entrance door for him, the moment Elliston's hand reached for the handle, Tanner smiled to himself as he watched him leap back to avoid walking straight into him.

'May we help you?' Tanner enquired, offering the man a disingenuous smile.

'Detective Chief Inspector Tanner! Just the man I came to see!'

'As I said,' Tanner continued, blocking Elliston's way, 'may we help you?'

'Isn't that your car, that rather sad looking XJS?'

'I know it isn't as fancy as your Bentley Continental,' Tanner responded, 'but at least I didn't have to go around murdering people in order to get it.'

'Surprisingly, neither did I.'

'Do you mind telling me what you're doing here, or would you like me to arrest you for loitering with intent.'

'With the intent of doing what?' Elliston enquired, returning to Tanner an innocent grin.

'That's what I'm endeavouring to find out,' said Tanner, smiling back.

'I was actually looking to speak to you about a couple of people who I believe you currently have in custody,' he eventually replied, casting his eyes along the length of the building.

Tanner stared at him with apprehensive suspicion. 'I don't suppose you could be a little more specific, it's just that there are currently quite a few people inside?'

'Andrew and Richard Priestly?'

On hearing the suspect's names, Tanner's head baulked back in surprise.

'I understand they were arrested for some minor misdemeanour,' Elliston continued.

'I would hardly describe drunk driving and assault as minor misdemeanours, but when you compare them to stabbing people to death, maybe they are.'

'Off the record, Chief Inspector, I only stabbed one person to death,' Elliston replied, in a frank, cheerful manner, 'someone who most definitely had it coming, I may add. It was my wife who dealt with the others; not forgetting the last one, of course, the one you were kind enough to lend a hand with. Although, someone did tell me that if you'd had the sense to use two hands, the outcome may have been dramatically different.'

'You're treading on very thin ice, Mr Elliston,' Tanner growled. 'Actually, that's not true. You've fallen through the ice and are in the process of sinking to the bottom, or at least you will be, just as soon as I'm able to prove what you've already confessed to.'

'And there was me thinking that I was standing on a concrete step, at the entrance to Wroxham Police Station.'

Fighting the temptation to frogmarch him inside under a murder charge, Tanner held his ground. 'May I enquire as to your interest in the Priestly brothers?'

'I was actually hoping you'd be able to let them go?'

'I beg your pardon?'

'I was hoping you could let them go?' Elliston repeated, offering Tanner a disarming smile.

'I heard you the first time, thank you.'

'So, you wouldn't mind, then?'

'I assume you're joking?'

'Was that a no?'

'What do you think?'

'Oh dear. That's a shame.'

'What I fail to understand is why you thought I would?'

'Because I asked; rather nicely, I may add.'

'Was that it?'

'Also, that we're doing some business together, and it's proving rather inconvenient to have them locked inside a holding cell.'

'Are they helping you to eliminate some more of your troublesome political opponents?'

'Actually, they're helping me to sell a large commercial development project, which should prove to be rather lucrative.'

'For them, or for you?'

'It wouldn't be much of a business deal if both parties didn't come out with something to show for it.'

'Tell you what, I just need to ask them a few questions, mainly about their whereabouts at the time of a recently released prisoner's abduction, torture, and murder. After I'm done, I'll be happy to oblige. Unless, of course, I've been able to unearth the evidence needed to convict them by then.'

'When you say a released prisoner, I assume you're referring to the recently deceased Vincent O'Riley?'

'You knew him, did you? Now, why doesn't that surprise me?'

'And you think the Priestly brothers may have had something to do with it?' Elliston continued, ignoring Tanner's comment.

'They're amongst a growing list of suspects.'

'Then I think I can help you to narrow that list down a little.'

'And how, may I ask, do you think you'd be able to do that?'

'Because I was in a meeting with both Andrew and Richard Priestly at the time Mr O'Riley was abducted.'

'That's extraordinarily convenient,' Tanner remarked, studying Elliston's smirking face.

'Not with them locked up it isn't!' he laughed back in return.

'Not that I don't trust you, or anything, but I assume you'd be able to provide some sort of proof?'

'What sort of proof do you need?'

'Anything that isn't just you, standing there telling me.'

'OK, well, the meeting took place in the Council's main office building. I'm fairly sure it has CCTV cameras, both inside and out, which should provide proof beyond a reasonable doubt. Tell you what, if you give me your email address, I'll ask someone to confirm that for you.'

'Then I suppose I'd better give you my card,' Tanner huffed, levering one out from his wallet with grudging reluctance.

'And then you'd be able to let them go?'

'If you can provide confirmation in the form of video evidence, then I'd be forced to consider it.'

'Then I'd better get on the phone to my secretary!' he exclaimed, with an enthusiastic nod. 'Before I do, I don't suppose I could have a quick word with them now? It's just that something fairly urgent has come up that needs to be discussed.'

'If I were you, Mr Elliston, I wouldn't push your luck. The next time you find yourself stepping through those doors,' Tanner continued, gesturing behind him, 'you may just find yourself unable to leave.'

- CHAPTER THIRTY TWO -

R EMAINING WHERE HE was to watch Elliston climb back into his car, Tanner headed inside to find Vicky, waiting for him with two mugs of steaming coffee.

'Wasn't that George Elliston?' she enquired, gazing out through the reception doors, as his Bentley Continental drove sedately away.

'Annoyingly, yes, it was,' Tanner remarked, taking one of the mugs.

'Then why didn't you invite him in?'

'I'm sorry, but why would I have wanted to do that?'

'Er... to say hello? I mean, it's not every day we have a Member of Parliament gracing our doorstep.'

'You seem to be forgetting, Vicky, that it was only a couple of months ago when he was a prime suspect in a murder investigation.'

'Oh, right,' she replied, 'although, I could have sworn the man responsible was a predatory paedophile, someone who fell off the back of a ferry in the middle of the North Sea, whilst attempting to make a run for the Swiss border.'

Tanner cursed Elliston once again. If the man hadn't openly confessed to the murders, he would have been in the same position as Vicky, and everyone else for that matter; blissfully unaware that Norfolk's latest MP was in fact a cold blooded killer.

'Anyway, shall we head in to have a chat with the Priestly brothers?'

'You still haven't told me what Mr Elliston was doing here?'

'Not much,' Tanner shrugged.

'Not much, as in...?'

'Apparently, our suspects are helping him sell some sort of commercial development project, and having them locked up is proving to be somewhat troublesome.'

'Oh, right!'

'He's also decided to provide them with an alibi.'

Vicky presented Tanner with a dubious frown. 'Did you ask him for one?'

'Nope!'

'You mean, he just came forward, of his own accord?'

'Looks like it. Unless, of course, the Priestly brothers phoned him up to request one.'

'Are you thinking Elliston may have something to do with the missing painting?'

'I think it's a possibility. I'm also not ruling out the idea that he had a hand in what happened to Vincent O'Riley, his wife, and our recently deceased cat-sitting friend, as well.'

'Surely you don't think he's capable of murder?'

Opening his mouth to tell her what Elliston had confessed to, directly outside his house on the day of the election, Tanner thought better of it. Regretfully, there was little point. For a start, he sincerely doubted that she'd believe him, and if she did, she'd be on the phone to Forrester, demanding to have the investigation re-opened. But without the necessary evidence, and with the alleged suspect already using his elevated position in society to cosy-up to as many high-ranking police officials as possible, Tanner knew it would be a waste of time. It could also end up with them losing their jobs – or worse!

'I wouldn't go *that* far,' he eventually replied, in a disingenuous tone.

'You think he is, don't you?'

Tanner let out an apathetic sigh. 'Only in so much that I think anyone with the right motive would be, and that he's a politician, of course.'

'Does he have evidence to support his alleged alibi?'

'He said he'd be emailing me some CCTV footage. Meanwhile, I believe we have a couple of suspects to interview?'

Remaining where she was, Vicky glanced earnestly about. 'Are we not going to wait for their solicitor?'

Tanner gave her a sideways glance.

'Sorry, of course not,' she responded, shaking her head. 'What was I thinking? So, which one do you want to start with first?'

'How about the youngest, for a change?'

With Vicky nodding to lead the way, Tanner followed after when he heard his phone ring from the depths of his sailing jacket.

Digging it out to see it was Forrester, he called over to Vicky, 'Hold on, I've got the boss on the line.'

Watching her come to a halt to roll her eyes, he turned away to take the call.

'Yes, Forrester, sir. How can I help?'

'Ah, Tanner! Thanks for picking up. It certainly makes a change. I was about to leave you a message!' he exclaimed, in a tone of wry amusement.

'I assume you're calling about the body discovered at Martham.'

'I wasn't,' Forrester continued, 'but whilst you're on the phone, you may as well update me.'

'No problem at all, sir. We found a body, over at Martham.'

'Thanks for that. Now I know what to tell Chief Superintendent Thornton, the next time he calls.'

'Then I assume it's OK for me to get back to work?'

'I was joking, Tanner!'

'*I wasn't,*' Tanner muttered, under his breath.

'So.... are you going to update me, or not?'

Tanner drew in an impatient breath. 'The body was someone by the name of Arthur Shaw. He'd been tortured to death, in much the same way Vincent O'Riley had.'

'What about O'Riley's wife? Sally told me she's in hospital. Is she going to be alright?'

'We're not sure. She was badly hurt.'

'What about her attackers? Do you think they're the same people?'

'The injuries are similar, so we're assuming them to be.'

'And the latest victim? What do we know about him?'

'At the moment, we're proceeding on the basis that it was a case of mistaken identity. The victim was only there to look after the pets found inside. We believe the intended victim was the home owner himself, a man by the name of Leonard Burton.'

A momentary pause followed, before Forrester asked, 'Haven't I heard that name somewhere before?'

'It was the name Vincent O'Riley uttered with his last dying breath.'

'And who was there at the time?'

'Only myself, Vicky, Dr Johnstone, and the victim's eldest son, Michael O'Riley.'

'Then it must be him!' stated Forrester, with categorical certainty. 'His brother, as well!'

'Thank you, sir,' Tanner replied, shaking his head.

'I assume you've spoken to them about it?'

'Not yet.'

'Is there any particular reason why not?'

'Well, first, I haven't had the chance to, second,' he continued, using his fingers to count, 'we don't have any evidence, and third, it seems unlikely that they'd have tortured their parents with a blowtorch to locate a painting that they haven't shown the slightest interest in finding. But the main reason is because I was just this second about to start interviewing the Priestly brothers, who, by chance, have been picked up for drunk driving and assault.'

'Which reminds me of the reason for my call.'

'Let me guess,' Tanner pondered, 'you've just been contacted by the Right Honourable George Elliston, requesting their immediate release?'

'That's – er – correct, Tanner. May I ask how you knew?'

'Because the man was around here about five minutes ago, asking me the exact same thing.'

'Oh, right. Anyway, he was wondering if we'd be able to bend the rules a little, just this once.'

'For drunk driving and assault?'

'I understand it's their first offence.'

'I don't care if they'd previously only been found guilty of parking on a double yellow line. We don't let people off for either!'

'Not normally, I know, but apparently, they're doing some business together.'

'That's what worries me.'

'I'm sorry, but what's that supposed to mean?'

'That I wouldn't trust Elliston as far as I could throw him, sir. Same for those so-called business associates of his.'

'Listen, Tanner, I'm sorry that you've taken a dislike to Mr Elliston, but at some point you're going to have to accept the fact that he's our local MP, which means it's important that we all get on. Failure to do so could lead to budget cuts, which, in turn, could mean redundancies. So, unless you want to start telling your staff that they're all out of a job, this time because you couldn't be arsed to make the slightest effort to get on with him, then I suggest you bite your tongue and get on board!'

'On board the gravy train, you mean?'

'Do you want a job, Tanner, or would you prefer to spend the rest of your life stacking shelves down the local supermarket?'

About to tell Forrester that the job he was promoting actually sounded rather appealing, he did what he'd been told, bit his tongue to change the subject. 'Whether I have a job at the end of the day is frankly irrelevant, sir. I'm not letting the Priestly brothers go, not until I've had a chance to speak to them about what happened to Vincent O'Riley.'

'And why, may I ask, is it so important for you to ask them about that?'

'Because they're prime suspects in a murder investigation!' Tanner replied, talking to Forrester as if he was a complete imbecile.

'But Mr Elliston said he's provided them with an alibi.'

'I'll believe it when I see it.'

'He told me that he's already sent you CCTV footage of them both arriving, and leaving the Council's offices at the time O'Riley was abducted.'

'Then I suppose I'd better check my email,' Tanner grudgingly replied.

'OK, good, and call me back when you have. If it has come through, and it does show them doing so, then I want them to be released immediately. Is that understood?'

'Yes, *sir*,' Tanner replied, with as much disdain as he thought was possible. 'Anything you say.'

Ending the call with a silent curse, Tanner navigated to his phone's email account.

'What was all that about?' he heard Vicky ask, her dark red hair looming into view beside him.

'Forrester wants me to let the Priestly brothers go.'

'For any particular reason?'

'He's reached the conclusion that they couldn't have had anything to do with the abduction, torture, or murders.'

'On what basis?'

'Because George Elliston told him so,' Tanner sneered, finding an email from the man under discussion at the top of his inbox. 'And it looks like the promised CCTV footage has arrived.'

'What, already?'

'You're right. That *was* too quick. He must have had it ready to go before even speaking to me.'

Opening up one of two attachments, he held out his phone for them to watch some low resolution colour footage of what did appear to be the Priestly brothers, ambling their way inside an office building, with Norfolk County Council's signage hanging above the doors.

'The date and time looks good,' commented Vicky, bringing Tanner's attention to the screen's bottom right hand corner.

'I'm still not convinced,' he replied. 'It could easily have been manipulated.'

Opening the next attachment to see them leaving, he closed it down to begin tapping out an email. 'I'm going to send it to our digital forensics department. It shouldn't be too difficult for them to tell if it's been doctored. Meanwhile,' he continued, putting his phone away, 'I suggest we push on with our suspects, preferably before their solicitor arrives.'

'Detective Chief Inspector Tanner?' came the shrill, demanding tone of a woman's voice behind him, one he couldn't help but think he'd heard somewhere before.

Turning around, he mouthed an unspoken curse when he found himself staring into the large round face of a woman he instantly recognised, the belligerent solicitor George Elliston had used when he'd been in custody. Annoyingly, he could even remember her name.

'Ms Heatherington!' he exclaimed. 'What a delightful surprise!'

'I do hope you weren't about to start interviewing my clients before I'd had a chance to speak to them?'

'Let me guess, you're here to represent Andrew and Richard Priestly?'

'How very astute of you.'

'May I ask what happened to their previous solicitor, the one with the lunch box and sensible shoes?'

'I've no idea. All I know is that they're my clients now, and that they've been arrested for drink driving and assault.'

'Only one was arrested for the drink driving. I'm not sure about the assault.'

'Addressing the former to begin with, do you know when the breathalysing equipment was last calibrated?'

'Surprisingly, no, I don't.'

'Or if the arresting officer had completed the relevant training course for its correct usage?'

Tanner turned to look at Vicky, only to hear the solicitor continue.

'I'd also like to see the report concerning the alleged assault. My client has been very clear that *he* was the one who was assaulted, not the other way round.

'He's also suggested that the only reason they were arrested was because you've developed some sort of personal dislike for them, and that you'd already accused them of abducting an individual by the name of Vincent O'Riley, without providing one single piece of evidence to support such a malicious claim.

'Furthermore, I've also been told that evidence proving, with categorical certainty, that neither of my clients could have been anywhere near Fenside Prison at the time the abduction took place, has already been emailed to you.'

'I must admit to have just this second received such alleged video evidence,' Tanner confirmed, 'however, we've yet to ascertain if the footage has been manipulated in any way.'

'Is there any reason for you to think that it has?'

'Because it was sent to us by someone by the name of George Elliston.'

'You mean, the Right Honourable George Elliston, the MP of Norfolk?'

'Sorry, of course. For a moment there, I'd forgotten you were BFFs.'

'Anyway, Mr Tanner,' Heatherington continued, 'unless you're able to provide me with the breathalysing equipment's calibration results, the date the tests were made, a certificate proving the arresting officer has received the training for its correct usage, a statement from a third-party witness, saying that my client was responsible for instigating the assault, and police forensic evidence proving that the CCTV footage taken of my clients entering and leaving Norfolk County Council offices at the time of

Vincent O'Riley's alleged abduction has been artificially altered in some way, I'd like to formally request that they are both released without hesitation.'

'I'm not letting them go until I've spoken to them!' Tanner exclaimed, holding the solicitors gaze with stubborn intent.

'Well, I'd love to know what you're intending to speak to them about. Assuming it's concerning Mr O'Riley's alleged abduction, then I hope you know that you're going to have to arrest them for it before doing so. To do that, you're going to need at least *some* sort of evidence. At the moment, all you have is what would appear to be a fairly concrete alibi. Bearing all that in mind, I'd like to offer you the chance of doing the right thing, before I'm forced to contact your superior. I believe your line manager is someone by the name of Superintendent Forrester?' she continued, returning to her tablet. 'Is that correct?'

Tanner remained glaring at her for a moment longer, before slowly turning to look at Vicky. 'You heard what Ms Heatherington said. Tell DS Taylor to have them released.'

'Can't we at least wait to see what comes back from digital forensics?'

'Unfortunately,' Tanner sighed, searching his wrist for his watch, 'I've had enough. If forensics does manage to find something, no doubt they'll call. In the meantime, I've got a home to go to.'

Turning back to find the solicitor tucking her tablet under her arm with a particularly smug expression, Tanner caught her eye to ask, 'Are we happy, now?'

'Very happy, thank you, Mr Tanner. I'll be sure to tell Mr Elliston how cooperative you've been. No doubt he'll be able to find some way of showing his appreciation.'

'Not by murdering someone else, I hope?'

The solicitor gave him an odd sort of look, before marching away, only for Tanner to find himself staring into the hesitant eyes of DC Sally Beach.

'Yes, Sally,' he sighed, 'how can I help?'

'Sorry to bother you, boss. I know it's late, and everything, but... there's been a call.'

'Please God, don't tell me it's another body?'

'It's from someone by the name of Yvonne Rose,' she replied, shaking her head.

'Is the name supposed to mean something to me?'

'She says there's some sort of disturbance going on inside the house next door.'

Tanner exhaled with relief. 'OK, well, there's no need to tell me. Just have a squad car sent over.'

'Yes, sorry, I know. It's just that... when I heard the person's name, the one who lives next door, I thought I'd better tell you.'

'And who's name is that?'

'Leonard Burton, boss. The system says you were at his house earlier this evening.'

- CHAPTER THIRTY THREE -

WITH VICKY SITTING beside him, Tanner sped back to the red bricked terraced house they'd left just two hours before to find a squad car already there, parked directly outside.

Reassured to see the door to Mr Burton's house was firmly closed, just as it had been when they'd left, he found a space to park a few cars down for them to climb quickly out.

Making their way back to find a uniformed constable managing a small group of on-lookers, and another speaking to a silver-haired old lady on the doorstep of the house next door, Tanner elbowed his way through the crowd.

Nodding at the first constable he passed, he left Vicky behind to march up the path to where the old lady stood.

With the back of the second constable facing him, he cleared his throat to help garner his attention. 'Would someone mind telling me what's going on?'

As the constable turned with a start, he pulled himself up straight. 'The old lady – sorry, Mrs Rose,' he began, glancing around. 'She said she heard a disturbance from the house next door.'

'It wasn't *just* a disturbance!' the old lady stated, her fragile body shaking with nerves. 'It sounded like someone was being murdered! I'm really worried that something's happened to poor Mr Burton. He's normally so quiet. Half the time, I don't even know he's there.'

'I assume you've tried the door?' Tanner continued, directing the question back to the constable.

'Yes, boss, but there's no answer. It doesn't look like anyone's forced their way in, either.'

'Do you know if there's a key, anywhere?' he asked, glancing back at the woman. 'Under the doormat, perhaps?'

'We've already looked,' the constable replied.

Tanner turned to stare at the door in question. 'OK, then we need to break it down.'

'Er... shouldn't we try knocking again first?' the constable queried, staring at Tanner as if he'd completely lost his mind. 'I mean, it's probably just a domestic.'

'I'm not telling you again. Break it down, and do it now!'

'Yes, of course,' he replied, nudging past to sprint back to his car.

Waiting for him to return, Tanner stepped over the low brick wall that separated the two properties to bash hard on the door. 'Mr Burton!' he yelled. 'Are you in there?'

With no response, he crouched down to peer through the letterbox, looking for some sort of a sign to help justify his concern. But the house appeared undisturbed, at least nothing had been knocked over in the hall to indicate someone had forced their way in.

He was just beginning to question if anyone had, or if the owner was simply out, when he heard the muffled, urgent sound of someone inside.

As the constable came running up behind him, Tanner turned to see a heavy black battering ram being held between his large, sweaty hands.

Standing to one side, he watched him rest its blunted end against the door's painted surface before swinging it back.

The moment the door gave way, Tanner leapt through the opening to charge down the hall.

'Mr Burton?' he called, diving his head into each room that he passed. 'Are you in here?'

When a whimpering sound came from a door at the end, Tanner burst through to find a man tied to a chair, a thin plastic shopping bag resting loosely over his head.

Whipping the bag off, he found himself staring into the terrified, tear-stained eyes of the man he'd last seen gazing anxiously at him from behind his front door, a piece of black gaffer tape flattened over his trembling mouth.

'Are you alright?' Tanner demanded, staring down the length of his body, only to wince when he saw the raw, melted skin on his forearms.

Remembering the tape, he wrenched it off to watch the man gasp desperately at the air.

'Help me – please!' the man was eventually able to say, his pale, strained face trying to look at the patio doors behind him.

Seeing the constable appear at his side, Tanner said, 'Call an ambulance,' to begin tearing at the gaffer tape binding the victim's wrists to the chair. 'Don't worry, Mr Burton. You're safe now.'

'B-but what if they c-come back?'

'What if *who* come back?' Tanner questioned, freeing one wrist to begin working on the other.

'I don't know.'

'Were they the same men as before? The one's from the National Gallery?'

'They could have been, but this time they said they were from the gas board – that there'd been a leak, and were evacuating everyone from the street. But when I opened the door, to see if anyone was actually leaving, they barged in, demanding to know where the painting was.'

'Did you see their faces?' Tanner urged, fixing the man's eyes.

'Not when they were outside,' he replied, shaking his head, 'and when they came in, they both had masks on.'

-CHAPTER THIRTY FOUR -

'IS HE GOING to be alright?' Vicky queried, as Tanner met her in the hall.

'The paramedics seemed to think so,' he replied, leading her out, 'from a physical perspective, at least. Mentally, however, I'm not so sure. He was paranoid enough before!'

'And where does this leave us with the investigation?'

'Well, it couldn't have been the Priestly brothers, I know that much. Not when they were locked inside a holding cell at the time, which unfortunately means I was wrong about them.'

'I wouldn't say you were wrong, exactly,' Vicky replied, offering him a charitable smile.

'Don't worry. I wasn't beating myself up too badly about it, especially when I know that *something's* going on between them and our local MP.'

'Did he say anything about his attackers?' Vicky continued. 'Were they the same men who've been going around telling everyone that they're museum curators?'

'He didn't seem to know.'

'OK, well, whilst you were inside, I've been on the phone to Sally. She's been speaking to the National Gallery about them.'

'And...?'

'They've confirmed that both Edward Phillips and Thomas Ward are employed by them, one as a senior curator, the other as his assistant.'

Tanner's shoulders slumped in frustrated despondency. 'So, it's not them, either!'

'No, it isn't,' Vicky confirmed, in a light, cheerful tone.

'What are you so happy about?' Tanner demanded, turning to face her.

'Because, as you said, it isn't them.'

'And that's a cause for celebration, is it?'

'The real Edward Phillips and Thomas Ward are attending a conference in Barcelona. They've been there all week!'

Tanner's face cracked into a broad, triumphant grin. 'Good work, Vicky. I always knew there was something odd about those two. I'm fairly sure that even museum curators don't go around wearing bow ties anymore. But that does beg the question; if they aren't who they've been saying they are, then who the hell are they?'

'Just a couple of crooks, desperate to get their hands on the missing painting?' posed Vicky.

'Desperate enough to torture and kill?'

'Whoever they are, I think it's far more likely to be them than the O'Riley brothers, don't you think?'

'If it wasn't for the fact that the O'Riley brothers were the only suspects who heard their father utter the name Leonard Burton, then I'd have to agree with you.'

'Then they must have found out from someone else. I mean, it's not as if the O'Riley brothers are the only ones who know. Virtually everyone at Wroxham Police Station does, as well.'

'There's only one way to find out. We're going to have to get hold of their prints and DNA, to see if anything matches those found at the crime scenes. And as there's no point seeing if they're on the police database, being that we don't have a single clue as to who they actually are, we're just going to have to find them.'

'That shouldn't be difficult,' Vicky mused, 'not with what they're wearing, and that they seem happy enough to go around telling everyone they meet that they're curators for the National Gallery.'

'That's if they haven't been tipped off to the fact that we're after them, possibly by the same person who gave them the name Leonard Burton.'

'You think someone at the station is feeding them information?'

'I think it would be a mistake for us to rule it out. Either way, we need to find them, preferably before whoever's behind all this abducts someone else to start torturing with a blowtorch.'

- CHAPTER THIRTY FIVE -

Thursday, 17ᵗʰ August

TANNER RUBBED AT his tired, bloodshot eyes, before staring once again at his computer screen, and the forensics report he'd been attempting to read for what felt like the tenth time that morning.

Glancing at the time to see it was only eleven o'clock, he shook his head in an effort to wake himself up.

Two days had passed since he'd found Leonard Burton, tortured almost to death inside his home. Since then, there hadn't been a single, solitary sign of the men who'd been posing as curators for the National Gallery.

Tanner closed the document in exhausted frustration. Reading forensics reports over and over again wasn't going to help find them, not when he didn't have a single clue as to who they were. The fact that he didn't have a sample of either their fingerprints or DNA wasn't helping, either. All he had was a description that he himself had provided to one of their sketch artists, which he knew wasn't very good. The only thing he could really remember about them was the ridiculous bow tie that one of them had been wearing, which meant that all he'd have to do to pull off a cunning disguise would be to take it off.

Jumping to the sound of his desk phone ringing, he stifled a yawn before lifting the receiver.

'Tanner speaking.'

'Ah, Tanner!' came the unmistakable sound of Forrester's voice. 'You're at your desk, for a change.'

'I've actually been here for the last two days,' Tanner replied. 'I'm not even sure I've moved.'

'I assume that means there's still been no sign of them?'

'Not so much as a discarded bow tie, sir.'

'OK, well, try not to worry. If it remains their intention to find that painting, no doubt they'll show up at some point. I suppose there hasn't been anything more from forensics?'

'I've just been reading their latest report, from inside Leonard Burton's house, but it's not proving to be of much use, not when we don't know who we're supposed to be looking for.'

'No, I suppose not. Anyway, I was actually calling to tell you that Vincent O'Riley's funeral is taking place this afternoon. I thought it might be an idea for you to go, just in case our new suspects decide to make an appearance. Even if they don't, it could be useful to see who does.'

'What time does it start?' Tanner queried, picking up a pen.

'Two o'clock. I thought the location might be of interest, as well.'

'Which is...?'

'The church at Stokesby, where all this started.'

'And that's where he chose to be buried?' asked Tanner, in a rhetorical tone, writing the name down to add a question mark at the end.

'Apparently so, which I think is another reason why I think you should go, to see if anyone knows why.'

'Makes sense,' Tanner replied, 'I'll see if I can drop by after lunch.'

A knock at the door had Tanner glancing up to see Vicky's face appear with an urgent, expectant frown.

Holding a silencing hand up to her, Tanner returned to his call. 'Sorry, sir, but I've got to go.'

'Yes, of course. Maybe you could call me afterwards, to let me know how you get on?'

'Absolutely!' Tanner replied, knowing he wouldn't.

Ending the call, he raised an enquiring eyebrow at Vicky.

'Sorry to bother you, boss,' she began, stepping inside to close the door, 'but something's come up.'

'Let me guess. Another mutilated body?'

'Thankfully not,' she grimaced, 'but it may be the location where one of them was tortured.'

- CHAPTER THIRTY SIX -

NURSING HIS XJS down a potholed, single track road near Tunstall, Tanner rounded a corner to see a dilapidated farmhouse ahead, parked in front of which was an estate agent's heavily branded, olive green Mini.

As he pulled up alongside it, an attractive man in his mid to late twenties stepped lightly out.

'Are you the police?' he called, adjusting a burgundy tie to bound enthusiastically over.

'DCI Tanner,' Tanner replied, climbing out to present his ID, 'and my colleague, DI Gilbert. We understand you've found something you thought might be of interest?'

'I can't say I normally call the police whilst previewing a property,' he nodded, 'but then again, it's not often I find myself inside a house that looks more like something out of a horror film than a characterful three bedroom farmhouse, in need of modernisation.'

'Do you mind showing us what you found?'

'Of course,' he replied, presenting Tanner with a congenial smile. 'Would you like the full tour, or just to see the room in question?'

'The room in question would be fine, thank you.'

'No probs,' he cheerfully responded, turning to lead the way.

Following him through the front door, Tanner led Vicky inside a dark, mouldy hallway, the carpet of which seemed to move underfoot in the most peculiar manner.

'It's down here,' the estate agent commented, coming to a halt at the end.

Stopping to glance about, unsure where "down here" was, Tanner watched him stoop down to open a cleverly disguised secret door, built into the staircase's dark wooden panelling.

'It leads down to what I'd normally describe as a cellar,' the man continued, reaching inside to turn on a light, 'but in this particular instance, I think an abattoir would be a better name, or maybe even a Sixteenth Century torture chamber.'

As Tanner and Vicky exchanged a curious glance, the estate agent rubbed his hands together. 'Shall I go first?'

'By all means,' Tanner replied, waiting for him to disappear under the stairs before leading Vicky through.

'You'll find a handrail on the left,' came the estate agent's detached voice, echoing up the stairwell towards them. 'And I apologise for the smell. Oh, and there's a step missing, near the top.'

'Good to know,' Tanner muttered, his eyes becoming drawn to the stairs, creaking beneath him as he began inching his way down.

Stepping carefully over the one that was missing, it was only when he reached the relative safety of the cellar's concrete floor that he dared to glance about.

'As I said, more like an abattoir than a cellar,' the estate agent repeated, gazing about at dozens-upon-dozens of rusty old tools, each one hanging from a chain drilled into the ceiling. 'I've got no idea why anyone would need quite so many,' he added, 'nor why they'd choose to hang them from the ceiling in such a macabre fashion, but that wasn't why I called you.'

'It wasn't?' Tanner replied, leaning forward to examine a particularly lethal looking hacksaw in an attempt to determine what was covering its leading edge; dried up blood, or flaking rust.

Hearing nothing in response, Tanner glanced about to see the estate agent, gesturing at the shadows behind him.

Following his gaze, he turned to see what appeared to be a Victorian electric chair, with thick brown leather straps around the arms and legs, and something that looked like a round kitchen sieve, hovering at the top.

'What I thought was most disturbing,' he heard the estate agent continue, 'was that it looks like it's actually been used.'

Gagging at the sudden stench of urine, wafting up from its stained wooden seat, Tanner looked away to ask, 'I assume you haven't touched anything?'

'Not a chance!'

'And may I ask how you knew the cellar was here, given the hidden nature of its entrance?'

'It was mentioned in the instructions, provided by the person selling it.'

'And who is that?'

'Yes, of course,' the estate agent nodded, slipping a tablet out from under his arm. 'A certain Mr Jason Armstrong.'

Tanner raised a curious eyebrow at Vicky, before turning back. 'Have you met this Jason Armstrong, face-to-face?'

'He gave me the keys this morning.'

'Was he a tall, thin, elderly man, wearing a bow tie?'

'Er... not exactly.'

'How, not exactly?'

'Well, instead of tall and thin, I'd describe him more as being short and fat. He also didn't have a bow tie, just a good old fashioned normal one.'

- CHAPTER THIRTY SEVEN -

'WHO'S JASON ARMSTRONG?' Vicky quietly asked, as she reached the top of the cellar's steps.

'The person who owns the farmhouse, presumably,' mused Tanner, following her out.

'Any idea where he fits into all this?'

'You're assuming the cellar was used to torture Vincent O'Riley.'

'I must admit, I was, but realistically, there can't be two Medieval styled torture chambers in the local area.'

'You never know. I mean, this *is* Norfolk!'

'I didn't know we had a reputation for torturing people, unless they were suspected of practicing witchcraft, of course.'

'Whether you do, or not, I don't think there's much point speculating as to whether we have yet another suspect, not until we've established if Vincent O'Riley was the last person strapped to that rather uncomfortable-looking chair,' Tanner commented, stepping outside, 'especially when the owner could have easily been blissfully unaware of what his cellar was being used for. That means our first priority is to speak to him.'

'I'll ask the estate agent for his contact details,' Vicky nodded, turning back.

'Don't worry, I'll do it. I'd rather you called the office. We need a forensics unit sent over, preferably before someone realises that they may have left some rather damning evidence behind.'

Watching Vicky spin away to dig out her phone, Tanner turned to see the estate agent, ambling out of the door behind them.

'So, what do you think?' the man asked, joining Tanner to gaze back at the farmhouse. 'I'm not sure what the price is going to be, but it's yours if you want it.'

'I'll take it if you can throw in the electric chair.'

'I'd have to ask the owner, but I'm sure we'd be able to come to some sort of an arrangement.'

'Speaking of the owner, I don't suppose you could provide us with his contact details?'

'I can, of course, although, you should probably know that he's in the process of leaving the country.'

'Not permanently, I hope!'

'He emigrated to Australia last year. He only came back to put the house on the market.'

'I don't suppose you know when he's leaving?'

'He was heading to the airport after dropping the keys off.'

'And what time was that?'

'Just after eight this morning, so – what – about five hours ago?'

Taking his client's contact details, Tanner thanked him for his time to immediately call the number, only to hear it click through to voicemail.

Trying again, only for the same thing to happen, Tanner left him a message, asking him to call as soon as he could, preferably before he climbed on board an aircraft to begin a journey to the other side of the world.

Ending the call to see Vicky approach, he put his phone away to face her. 'Any luck with forensics?'

'A unit should be over in about twenty minutes.'

Wondering if they should wait, just in case someone showed up with a petrol can, Tanner remembered Vincent O'Riley's funeral, the one Forrester had asked him to attend.

'I don't suppose you'd mind sticking around on your own for a while, just until forensics gets here?'

'You mean, in case someone shows up with some matches?'

'Something like that.'

'I don't mind,' she shrugged, her eyes drifting over to the estate agent, busily chatting to someone on the phone. 'Were you able to get hold of the property's owner?'

'Apparently, he's on his way to Australia.'

'Not permanently, I hope?'

'It would appear so. I've left him a message, which reminds me. Whilst you're waiting here, I don't suppose you could find out where he's flying out from, and at what time? If he's already left, then I suppose we'll just have to wait until he's landed.'

'No problem,' she smiled, delving into her handbag.

'Meanwhile,' Tanner continued, glancing down at his watch, 'I've got a funeral to attend.'

'Anyone close?'

'Vincent O'Riley,' he replied. 'So no, not exactly. Forrester asked me to go, just in case anyone interesting shows up.'

- CHAPTER THIRTY EIGHT -

THINKING HE MUST have been late, Tanner reached the picturesque village of Stokesby to find the place virtually deserted.

Unable to see anything that looked even remotely like a church, nor anyone to ask where it may have been, he spent a frustrating few minutes driving aimlessly around, when a gleaming black hearse crept slowly into view. With a dozen or so cars following behind, he pulled over to let them pass, before turning around to eventually tag onto the end of the slowly moving procession.

Seeing a robust church tower, hovering in the distance, he continued to follow, eventually finding himself being led up a narrow, single track lane.

With the church looming up ahead, it wasn't long before the procession reached its base, leaving the cars searching for somewhere to park.

Watching the hearse come wallowing to a halt, Tanner parked under a nearby tree to begin staring curiously about. When the doors of a familiar black Mercedes began opening ahead, he leaned forward to see the O'Riley brothers climb solemnly out.

As they made their way around to the car's boot, he sat with interest as they lifted out a collapsable wheelchair, the same one he'd seen when their father had been released from prison.

With the appearance of the daughter, Rebecca, stepping out from another car to open one of the Mercedes' rear passenger doors, he climbed out to watch Mrs O'Riley being helped down into the assembled wheelchair, a heavy black veil helping to conceal the bandages covering her face.

As her husband's ornately decorated coffin was slid gently out from the back of the hearse, Tanner remained where he was to watch the O'Riley brothers help two other unknown men to lift the casket onto their shoulders.

Waiting for the congregation to follow Mrs O'Riley, her wheelchair being pushed over a path by Rebecca, Tanner took a moment to gaze about.

Unable to recognise anyone else, he was about to join them when he heard the sound of another car, rumbling down the lane towards them. With the vague hope that it was the men supposedly from the National Gallery, he held back to see a light grey Audi Q3 creep slowly into view.

Disappointed to see it contained a very normal looking family, with three fidgeting children stuffed into the back, he continued forward, eventually finding himself walking amidst the tombstones of an ancient graveyard.

Positioning himself discreetly under the branches of a sprawling oak tree, he spent an uneventful half-hour listening to the service. When the casket was eventually lowered into the ground, he watched the congregation begin filing past the grieving widow and her family, each taking a moment to pay their respects.

Relieved that the event had taken place without incident, before heading back to his car, he decided to join the back of the queue, in part to pay his own respects, but mainly for the opportunity to speak to Mrs O'Riley again.

When he eventually found himself standing before her, he nervously cleared his throat. 'Mrs O'Riley, it's John Tanner, Norfolk Police.'

'I know who you are, Mr Tanner,' she declared, her unbandaged eye glaring at him from underneath her veil. 'What I fail to understand is what you're doing here?'

'I just wanted to make sure your husband had a peaceful send off.'

'Then I suppose I should thank you.'

'I also wanted to make sure you were OK. The last time I saw you, the doctor said it was touch and go if you were going to make it.'

'I'm stronger than I look, Mr Tanner.'

'Yes, of course,' Tanner replied, looking up to see her sons, glaring over at him with hostile menace, whilst shaking the hands of their last remaining guests. 'I know this is hardly the time,' he continued, lowering his voice, 'but, if I may, I'd like to arrange a time to talk to you again, about what happened the night of your attack.'

'You can talk to me now, if you like?'

'Excuse me!' came her eldest son's harsh, stern voice, 'but you were right the first time. This *isn't* the time! Nor is it the place!'

'It's alright, darling,' his mother replied. 'I'm fairly sure your father wouldn't mind.'

'That's hardly the point, Mother!'

'He's right,' Tanner responded, pulling himself up straight. 'This is neither the time, nor the place.'

'He wasn't even invited!' Michael continued, stepping forward, as his brother appeared behind him.

'He came to pay his respects, Michael. Please don't make a scene.'

'I shouldn't be here,' Tanner muttered, with apologetic remorse. 'I came to make sure the service was a quiet, respectful affair. My presence here is only hindering that endeavour.'

'Don't be silly!' came Mrs O'Riley's chiding reply. 'Now, why don't you help push me to my car. You can tell me how your investigation has been going on the way.'

'If you're sure?'

'I wouldn't have said so if I wasn't.'

Obediently taking hold of the wheelchair's handles, Tanner pivoted her around, only to find Michael, blocking their way.

'Please stand aside, Michael. The Chief Inspector is trying to help.'

With him remaining stubbornly where he was, she took a more compassionate tone. 'Don't you want to find out who killed your father?'

Michael glowered at Tanner for a moment longer, before turning on his heel to march away, dragging his younger brother along with him.

'You must forgive my sons,' she commented. 'They can be a little over-protective at times.'

'As they should be,' Tanner remarked, pushing her over a cracked, concrete path.

'So,' she continued, leaving her daughter staring wistfully away, 'now that we have a little privacy, how's the investigation been going?'

'We're making progress,' came Tanner's guarded response.

'Is that really all you can tell me?'

Tanner took a breath to consider what he could, or more pertinently *should* be telling her. 'At this early stage, Mrs O'Riley, all I can say is that the people we're looking for are particularly dangerous individuals.'

'Please, Chief Inspector, call me Sarah.'

'Please, Mrs O'Riley, call me John,' Tanner retorted.

'Very well, John,' she laughed, 'have you managed to identify any suspects?'

'One or two,' he replied.

'Anyone I know?'

Again, Tanner took a moment to consider what he should be telling her. 'I don't suppose you've seen a couple of men lurking around your house recently,' he eventually began, 'possibly asking about the missing painting? They may have said they were from the National Gallery?'

'The only people I can remember coming around recently were a couple of Jehovah's Witnesses, but it couldn't have been them. For a start, they seemed more interested in finding out what I knew about Jesus, than a long-lost Turner. And they weren't two men, either, being that they were both attractive young women.'

'Then perhaps you've heard of someone by the name of Leonard Burton?'

She paused for a moment. 'The name doesn't ring a bell.'

'Your husband never mentioned him to you before?'

'Not that I can remember, but that doesn't mean he didn't.'

'How about a Mr Jason Armstrong?'

'Again, I don't think so.'

'He owns a small farmhouse near Tunstall, if that helps. We don't know for sure, but at the moment we think it's where you husband was taken, after he was abducted.'

With her saying nothing in response, Tanner continued by asking, 'Can you remember anything more about the night you were attacked? Something that may help us identify those responsible?'

'I'm sorry, I can't,' she replied, dropping her head. 'As I think I said before, they were wearing masks.'

'What about their voices?'

'Only that I thought they were a little peculiar.'

'Peculiar, as in...?'

'As in they didn't seem natural.'

'You thought they were putting on some sort of an accent?'

'More that they seemed electronic, as if they'd been generated by some sort of computer. But then again, I could be wrong. Thankfully, the whole affair has become a bit of a blur. I'm really not sure that my memory can be relied upon, certainly not as a witness for the prosecution, should that time ever come.'

'Don't worry, Mrs O'Riley, that time *will* come, you have my word on that! Until then, I must advise you to be careful, especially now that you're out of hospital.'

'I sincerely hope you don't expect me to remain locked inside my own home?'

'Well, no, but I would recommend that you have someone take a look at your security. And when you do go out, to make sure you're not alone. We're fairly certain that the men who attacked you and your husband have killed someone else.'

'If my husband hadn't taken that stupid painting,' he heard her mutter, in a brooding, indignant tone, 'none of this would have ever happened.'

Unable to think of a suitable response, Tanner continued steering her around the church. When they reached its humble entrance, he manoeuvred the wheelchair to face her awaiting Mercedes, and her sons talking quietly beside it, when another car appeared, inching slowly down the lane towards them.

Thinking nothing of it, Tanner focussed his mind on pivoting the wheelchair off the path, onto the gravel-lined carpark a few inches below. It was only when he glanced up did he notice the O'Riley brothers' conversation had come to an end. Instead of talking, they were now glaring at the arriving vehicle with hostile looks of menacing animosity.

Curious to know what had caused such an intense reaction, Tanner returned his attention to the car, to see none other than the Priestly brothers, climbing their way slowly out.

'This isn't going to end well,' he muttered to himself, bringing the wheelchair to a gradual halt.

'What the fuck are you doing here?' he heard Michael call out, leading his brother forward.

'We just wanted to pay our respects,' came Andrew Priestly's grinning response.

'You're too late. The service is over. So you can climb back into that sad little car of yours, and fuck off.'

'But... we brought flowers,' he replied, presenting the O'Riley brothers with a goading smirk.

'Really? That's strange. I don't see any.'

Straightening his face, Andrew reached inside his suit. 'That's because they're in here,' he continued, tugging out what was left of three bedraggled tulips. 'I know they're not much, but to be honest, they're more than your father deserved. We were actually hoping to be able to place them on his grave, before my brother relieves himself on it. He's been desperate to go since we left home.'

'Boys!' came the chiding sound of Mrs O'Riley's voice. 'No fighting! Not here!'

'Don't worry, Mother,' came Michael's pacifying response, his eyes remaining doggedly fixed on Andrew's, 'they're leaving.'

'Yes, of course,' Andrew replied. 'The last thing we want to do is cause a scene. If you could just point us in the direction of your father's grave, I'll be able to leave the flowers. Then my brother will be able to piss all over it.'

'That's it,' Michael snarled, lowering his head to charge suddenly forward.

With his brother steaming in behind him, a full blown fist fight erupted within the blink of an eye.

Hearing their mother, screaming for them to stop, Tanner surged forward, determined to make them do just that.

As Michael launched a fist at Andrew's head, Tanner grabbed hold of his collar to haul him back, only for the misdirected punch to slam hard into the side of his face.

As a blinding white pain exploded inside Tanner's head, for one long, drawn out moment, he had a sense of floating in the air, just inches above the ground. But then white turned to black, and he felt nothing at all, nothing but the slowly diminishing pulse of his rhythmically beating heart.

- CHAPTER THIRTY NINE -

BLINKING HIS EYES open, Tanner found himself lying in what he instantly knew was the back of an ambulance, staring into the all too familiar face of a female paramedic. Her face was so familiar, he could even remember her name.

'Hello, Melicia,' he grinned. 'What a pleasant surprise!'

'Detective Chief Inspector Tanner,' she grimaced back. 'If I may, I'd like to make a formal complaint.'

'What... now?'

'Someone would appear to be stalking me.'

'Oh, right,' he laughed.

'It's no laughing matter, Chief Inspector. No matter where I go, I always find him lying in the back of my ambulance, grinning at me like some sort of deranged lunatic.'

'I don't look that bad, do I?'

'You've looked worse, I suppose,' she shrugged. 'Anyway, what have you been up to this time?'

Tanner's mind took him back to the scene. 'If I remember correctly, I was trying to break up a fight.'

'If that's true, then why were you the only one who was injured?'

'Presumably, because I was successful.'

'Or there wasn't a fight at all, and you just fell over.'

'I'm not in the habit of falling over for no particular reason.'

'But you are in the habit of frequenting the back of my ambulance?'

'Not by choice, I can assure you. So anyway, what's the damage this time?'

'Nothing major. You have a slight cut to the back of your head, a swollen left eye, mild concussion, and your teeth are covered in blood.'

'I was wondering what that taste was,' Tanner replied, examining his mouth with his tongue. 'I don't suppose you have some mouthwash I could borrow?'

'You mean, you'd be able to give it back?'

'Was that a yes?'

'You'll probably find some at the hospital.'

'But – I thought you said I was OK!'

'I said, nothing major. Anyone who's sustained a head injury has to go to hospital, I'm afraid.'

'Good luck with that,' Tanner grumbled, pushing himself off the makeshift bed to feel a jarring pain in the back of his head. 'There's no way I'm spending another five hours hanging about at A&E for some sadistic lunatic to take far too much pleasure in stapling my head back together.'

'Don't worry, I doubt you'll need stitches. Not this time.'

'Then why do I have to go?'

'Well, you'll need a cat scan, for a start.'

'Honestly, I'm fine, besides, I'm not a cat. I don't need a scan to tell me.'

'It may also be an idea to have that sense of humour looked at, whilst you're there.'

'Well, *I* thought it was funny.'

'That's what worries me.'

'OK, look, I'll grudgingly agree to go to hospital, but not in the back of an ambulance.'

'Then how else do you propose to get there?'

'I'll drive myself.'

'Not with a concussion, you won't!'

'You said it was mild.'

'That's not the point. Besides, if I let you drive, how can I trust you to go?'

'Because I'm an extremely honest person. I'm also a senior police officer.'

'Sorry, but which one of those is supposed to alleviate my concerns?'

'You don't trust me?'

'Not to drive yourself. Not when you clearly don't want to go.'

'The only reason I don't want to go is because I have remarkably little interest in spending the next five hours of my life hanging about in some hospital waiting room, only to be told that there's nothing wrong with me.'

'Them's the rules, I'm afraid.'

'Tell you what, how about I get someone else to drive me?'

'Unfortunately, I think everyone else has gone.'

'I haven't,' he moaned.

'Sorry, I meant everyone apart from you.'

A knock on the ambulance's open back door had Tanner glancing around to see the arrestingly beautiful face of Rebecca O'Riley.

'How's the patient doing?' she enquired, gazing at the paramedic, before offering Tanner a concerned frown.

'You see!' he responded, staring back at Melicia. 'Not everyone's gone.'

Ignoring him, the paramedic caught Rebecca's eye. 'The patient you're enquiring about doesn't appear to be too keen to go to hospital.'

'Can you blame me?' Tanner muttered.

'I don't suppose you'd be able to give him a lift?'

'Who, me?' Rebecca questioned.

'Well, he can't drive himself, not after he's been concussed. And for some reason, he doesn't want us to take him.'

'I actually only came to thank him for breaking up the fight my brothers started.'

'Ah-ha!' Tanner exclaimed, once again staring around at the paramedic. 'I told you I'd been trying to break up a fight.'

'An honest policeman. Now, there's a first.'

'I'd be happy to give your patient a lift to the hospital, if you think it would help.'

'We were going that way anyway, so it would be more for the patient's benefit, than ours.'

'I'd be happy to accept your kind offer of a lift,' Tanner smiled at Rebecca, pushing himself unsteadily to his feet to begin clawing his way out. 'Anything's better than being stuck with a paramedic who not only doesn't trust me, but seems intent on following me around, waiting for the very next time I bang my head, simply for the opportunity to drag me back to that bloody hospital again. I wouldn't be surprised if the next time I see them, they're trying to reverse over me.'

'Until then,' Melicia responded, presenting Tanner with a supercilious smile, as he held onto the door to step carefully down.

- CHAPTER FORTY -

W ITHOUT BEING GIVEN the chance to respond, the paramedic heaved the door closed to disappear inside.

'I take it she's a friend of yours,' commented Rebecca, as the engine rumbled into life.

'I wouldn't say we were friends, exactly. More like casual acquaintances.'

Seeing the ambulance's reverse lights come suddenly on, Tanner leapt instinctively back, only to see the reflection of Melicia's face, grinning at him in the passenger's side mirror.

Shaking his head at her with a look of stern reproach, he watched the lights flicker off for it to begin trundling slowly forward.

'At least they have a sense of humour,' mused Rebecca.

'Who said they were joking!' came Tanner's earnest response.

'Anyway, I do want to thank you for breaking up my brother's fight.'

'I didn't know I had.'

'When they saw what happened to you, they thankfully came to their senses.'

'They probably thought I was dead.'

'I must admit, the thought did cross our minds. Fortunately, however, we were able to find a pulse, even if it did take a while.'

'Good to know!' he laughed, reaching for his wrist, as if to make sure.

'My brother wanted to apologise to you in person, but they had to escort my mother to the wake. He did ask me to explain that he had no intention of hitting you. His intended target had been Andrew Priestly.'

'Don't worry, I won't be pressing charges. Besides, it was my fault, at least in part. I should have anticipated that there could be trouble, and had a police squad car at the scene.'

'Well, I'm pleased you didn't. My father would have hated to have uniformed police officers attending his funeral.'

'How about a humble Detective Chief Inspector?' Tanner replied, finding himself gazing into her mesmerising blue eyes.

'No doubt he'd have preferred it if you hadn't been here either, but I'm grateful that you were. My mother was, as well.'

'To be honest, the only reason I came was because my boss told me to.'

'Presumably, to see who showed up, in case one of them was the person you're looking for?'

'I suppose that was the idea.'

'Do you think they did?'

Tanner took a moment to study her hopeful expression. 'I assume you're referring to the Priestly brothers?'

'Well, the thought had crossed our minds,' she replied, looking away, 'but considering what our father did to theirs, I'm not sure you can blame us.'

'To be honest, we had been thinking along similar lines. That was until someone provided them with a seemingly bullet-proof alibi.'

'Which was?'

'I'm sorry, I'm unable to say.'

'Is there anything that you *can* tell me about the investigation?'

'Only that everything appears to be centred around the missing painting.'

'The one my father always said he never had?'

'Did you believe him?'

Rebecca tilted her head to stare at him with indignant hostility. 'You're not seriously standing there, asking if I believed my own father?'

Tanner felt his skin burn with acute embarrassment. 'Sorry, that was unforgivable, especially given the circumstances.'

She continued scowling at him for a moment longer, before her face cracked into a broad, perfect grin. 'I'm winding you up, Chief Inspector. Of course I didn't trust my father. You seem to be forgetting that he was a convicted criminal.'

'Does that mean you think he *did* hide the painting?'

'Oh, I don't know about that.'

'Did he ever mention it?'

'Not once,' she replied, shaking her head, 'but I was very young when he was arrested.'

'Didn't you see him afterwards?'

'Not very often.'

'But – when you did, he didn't say anything about it?'

'We never discussed what he'd been imprisoned for, for good reason.'

'May I ask what that reason was?'

'Because we never knew who was listening!' she laughed.

'Fair enough,' Tanner replied, smiling back.

'Saying that, if he had wanted to tell us, he'd have found a way, which makes me think he didn't know. Why else would he have kept it a secret?'

'Because he didn't want to get you into trouble. After all, receiving stolen property is a crime in and of itself.'

'I'm not sure that's relevant. If he had told us, we'd have simply handed it in. Unlike him, we weren't brought up to be criminals.'

'Does the same thing go for your brothers?'

Rebecca cast a stern eye at him. 'They may allow themselves to be goaded into the occasional fight, but that doesn't make them criminals.'

'Sorry, of course. Forgive me. It's my job to speculate about such matters, but that doesn't mean I have to do it out loud.'

'Does that mean my brothers are suspects?'

'As are you, I'm afraid. Your mother, as well.'

Tanner's response was met by an indignant snort of laughter.

'Sorry, Chief Inspector, I wasn't laughing at you. But the idea of either myself, or my mother, being some sort of criminal mastermind, was rather amusing.'

'It's nothing personal, I can assure you. Family members are always treated as suspects during such investigations.'

'I thought everyone was supposed to be innocent until proven guilty?'

'Well, it's a nice idea, in theory, at least. Actually, whilst we're on the subject, you wouldn't mind telling me where you were, the night your mother was attacked? I did ask your brothers, but they said they didn't know.'

'What – really?'

'I'm afraid so.'

Rebecca shook her head to begin fishing around inside her Louis Vuitton handbag. 'I'm fairly sure I was out with friends,' she eventually replied, pulling out her phone.

With her attention focussed on the screen, Tanner took a voyeuristic moment to study her face. She really was a remarkably attractive woman, someone who men could easily find themselves falling head-over-heels in love with.

Determined not to be one of them, Tanner redirected his attention to her phone. 'Any luck?'

'I was out with Catherine and Sarah. They're friends from university. We went out to a restaurant together.'

'How about on Tuesday afternoon, between three o'clock and five?' Tanner continued, digging out his notebook.

'Why, what happened then?'

'Unfortunately, another body was found. We believe his attackers were the same as those who abducted your father.'

'I'm sorry, I'd no idea!'

'There's no reason for you to have. So far, we've been able to keep it out of the press.'

'Tuesday, between three and five, did you say?'

'Uh-huh.'

'I was in a meeting.'

'A meeting regarding what?'

'I'm a fashion journalist.'

'Oh, right. That makes sense, I suppose.'

'And what's that supposed to mean?' she demanded.

'Sorry, I didn't mean anything by that,' Tanner quickly said. 'It's just that – well – you clearly have immaculate taste in clothes. You're also extremely attractive. But you must know that – right?'

Rebecca's stern expression melted instantly away. 'That's kind of you to say,' she replied, blushing slightly, 'but it isn't true, I'm afraid, at least, not in the eyes of the fashion world.'

'I'm sorry, but I find that very hard to believe.'

'It's true, I'm afraid. When I was young, I wanted nothing more than to become a fashion model. Unfortunately, I was rejected at every turn, which is why I was eventually forced to write about clothes, instead of being paid to wear them.'

Realising he'd been inadvertently flirting with her, he brought his attention back to his notebook. 'There's also between the hours of six and seven o'clock in the evening, on the same day.'

'You mean – someone else has been killed?'

'Thankfully, in that particular instance, they survived, but it could have gone either way.'

Looking flustered, Rebecca returned to her phone. 'If it was the same day, then I was in another meeting.'

'Whereabouts was that?'

'Nowhere. It was a Zoom meeting, the same as the other one.'

'So, you were at home?' Tanner queried, glancing up from his notes.

'These days, I normally am.'

'Would anyone be able to vouch for you?'

'The people I was in the meeting with, I suppose, but do they have to?'

'It would help to eliminate you from our enquiries,' Tanner replied.

'You don't really have to speak to them all, do you?'

'We may be able to check your login details instead, but if you could provide us with their names, it would be useful. The details of the friends you went to a restaurant with, as well.'

'At least you're taking this seriously, I suppose,' she shrugged, returning to her phone. 'Do you need them all now?'

'On email would be fine, thank you.'

'And what's your email address?' she enquired, glancing up.

'Here, let me give you my card.'

'And then I'd better give you that lift to the hospital.'

'There's no need,' he continued, handing her one of his business cards.

'But the doctor said.'

'Yes, I know, but she's not a doctor. And as I kept telling her, I'm fine.'

'Are you sure?' she queried, studying his swollen eye.

'Quite sure, thank you.'

'Then let me give you my mobile number, just in case you change your mind.'

Reaching into her handbag, she pulled out her own card, holding it out for him with a flirtatious smile. 'Even if you don't, maybe you could give me a call sometime?'

'Oh – right,' he replied, staring down at it with hesitant indecision. 'You should – er – probably know that I'm married. Happily so, I may add,' he continued, glancing up.

Once again, Rebecca snorted with laughter.

'Sorry,' she apologised, biting her lip, 'but I wasn't asking you out.'

'No, of course.'

'However,' she continued, holding his gaze, 'if you'd like to come over to play with me sometime, then you'd be more than welcome. And there's no need to worry about your wife. If she's even half as attractive as you are, then I'd be more than happy for her to join you.'

- CHAPTER FORTY ONE -

ARRIVING BACK AT his house, Tanner opened the front door to call out, 'Honey, I'm home!' only to be met by an unwelcome, hollow silence.

'Shit,' he cursed, remembering he wasn't supposed to be charging inside, just in case baby Samantha was asleep, or worse, was about to be.

With a dull ache creeping all the way from the back of his skull to the front, he quietly closed the front door to go in search of both painkillers, and his wife and child.

'Not in here,' he muttered, opening the door to the main living area to peer gingerly about.

Spying a bottle of rum with his name on it, apparently waiting for him on the kitchen's breakfast bar, he spent a moment trying to decide which would be more effective, the rum, or some Nurofen.

Deciding to hedge his bets, he made his way through to the kitchen to pry a couple of painkillers out from their foiled wrapper, before pouring himself a glass of rum.

'Bottoms up!' he said to himself, popping the pills inside his mouth before downing the drink.

Already feeling better, he re-charged his glass to begin searching the house for his missing family.

Finding Christine, lying on her back in their darkened bedroom, with Samantha snoring on top of her, he poked his head inside to ask, 'Are you awake?'

'I have been for a while,' she whispered, 'but I don't seem to be able to move. I don't suppose you could pick Samantha up for me?'

'Well, I would, of course, but... wouldn't that mean waking her up?'

'Don't worry, she should be alright, as long as you're gentle.'

'Gentle is my middle name,' he murmured, setting his glass down to lift Samantha slowly up.

'That's funny, I thought Clumsy was your middle name?'

'Only when I'm drunk,' he continued, cradling her in his arms.

'And you're not now?' she asked, seeing the drink he'd left on the bedside table.

'That's for medicinal purposes.'

'Oh, really,' she replied, switching on the bedside light to reach for a glass of water.

'It's for the eye. The back of my head, as well.'

With the glass in her hand, she stood slowly up to stare at his face with motherly concern. 'What on Earth have you been up to?'

'It's not what it looks like.'

'Well, it looks like you've been in a fight.'

'Exactly!'

'Are you saying you have, or you haven't?'

'I was endeavouring to prevent one.'

'That's original.'

'It's true!'

'Uh-huh.'

'Good grief!' he sighed, wincing with pain as Christine dabbed a finger at his swollen eye. 'Why does nobody believe me?'

'Probably because you've been going around with a black eye, telling everyone that you haven't been in a fight, when it looks every bit like you have.'

'As I said, I was trying to prevent one, when I found myself inside an ambulance, all set to take me to hospital.'

'Not again!'

'With the same paramedic as last time,' he added. 'The time before that, as well.'

'Having a bit of a bromance, are you?'

'Actually, he's a woman.'

'Oh, right. Did he used to be a man, but now identifies as a woman, or was he a woman, but now considers himself to be a man?'

'What?'

'Or is he what they call, "gender neutral"?'

'I'm sorry, but I've got no idea what you're talking about.'

'You said he's a woman.'

'Only in the sense that you assumed he was.'

'I assumed he was what?'

'A man.'

'Did I?'

'You did, but don't worry, I won't tell her.'

'And when are you planning on seeing her again?'

'Why do you think I'll be seeing her again?'

'Because you said you wouldn't tell her, leading me to assume you were intending to.'

'Well, I hadn't been, but I probably will, being that she seems intent on following me around, waiting for the next time I get punched in the face.'

'So you did get into a fight, then?'

'As I said, I was trying to break one up.'

'But you did end up in hospital?'

Tanner shook his head. 'Thanks to Vincent O'Riley's daughter, I managed to wriggle my way out of having to go.'

'And what's Vincent O'Riley's daughter got to do with it?'

'I was attending her father's funeral when the fight started. She offered me a lift to the hospital, which I declined, allowing me to drive myself home. And here I am!'

'Then let's just hope you don't have a brain haemorrhage. If you do, you'll probably wake up dead tomorrow.'

'That's certainly something to look forward to. Assuming I'm still alive, I don't suppose I could take a night off from babysitting duty at some stage, to see a friend?'

'Not the paramedic, I hope?'

'It's actually Rebecca.'

'And who the hell's Rebecca?'

'Vincent O'Riley's daughter. I thought I said. She's invited me over to her place.'

'Has she, now!' Christine exclaimed, her nostrils flaring in rather an alarming manner.

'Don't worry, she said it wasn't a date.'

'I assume you told her you were married?'

'Of course!'

'Then why, may I ask, did she invite you over?' Christine continued, taking a sip of water.

'Because she wants to have sex with me.'

Choking, Christine sprayed the contents of her mouth all over baby Samantha's tiny body.

Mortified by what she'd done, she stared down at her with her mouth hanging open.

With Tanner following her stunned, muted gaze, they each held their breath, expecting Samantha to erupt into a torrent of tears at any moment. But to both their relief, and surprise, nothing happened. She just continued to sleep, without so much as batting an eyelid.

'She must be impervious to water,' mused Tanner, glancing up. 'Maybe it's her superpower?'

'Before we continue this conversation, I suggest it may be an idea to put her down. I wouldn't want to hurt her.'

'Does that mean you're going to hurt me?'

'I think that depends.'

'On what?'

'On what you said in response to this Rebecca woman, saying that she wanted to have sex with you, like, for example, "thanks for the offer, but I'm fine".'

'I don't *think* that was it,' Tanner replied, staring pensively up at the ceiling.

'Then dare I ask what you did say?'

'From memory, that I'd have to ask you first.'

'You'd have to ask me *first?*' Christine repeated.

'Well, yes, but only because it was an open invitation.'

'And what's that supposed to mean?'

'She asked if you'd like to come, as well.'

'What?' Christine questioned, staring at him with a look of deranged incomprehension.

'I think she likes girls as well as boys,' Tanner replied, by way of explanation.

'Oh – right,' Christine eventually replied, unable to hold Tanner's gaze.

'So, what do you say?' Tanner enquired, raising an intrigued eyebrow.

'Well, to be completely honest, I wouldn't actually mind. I've always fancied a threesome.'

It was Tanner's turn to stare at Christine with a look of astonished disbelief. 'You mean – seriously?' he eventually managed to say.

'Of course not seriously!' she blurted out. 'Between a new born baby, and a husband with only half a brain, when would I have either the time, or the inclination?'

'No, of course. I wouldn't have wanted to, either.'

With Christine still glaring at him with a particularly ominous expression, Tanner found himself glancing nervously about at the bedroom furniture.

'Anyway,' he eventually said, edging his way around her in the direction of the cot. 'I suppose I'd better put Samantha down.'

'Yes, I suppose you should.'

'Then perhaps I should make us something to eat.'

'That would make a nice change. What did you have in mind?'

'Er... cheese on toast?' Tanner replied, resting the slumbering Samantha gently down into her cot.

'We don't have any cheese.'

'Toast it is, then!'

'Don't worry, it was a nice thought, but I've already got something planned. If you can dab some of that water off Samantha's face, preferably without waking her up, I'll sort something out.'

- CHAPTER FORTY TWO -

Friday, 18th August

BREATHING FAR HARDER than he knew it was safe for him to, Adrian Mallot pedalled his rusty old bicycle along the towpath beside the River Bure. It was barely half-past eight in the morning, but as he was supposed to be at his desk at Crawford's accountancy firm in Horning by nine, he knew he didn't have long. He certainly couldn't risk being late again. Not for what would have been the third day in a row. If he was, and his boss kept his promise, the same one who'd been yelling obscenities at him the morning before, he doubted he'd have had a job when he got back. However, what his boss didn't seem able to understand was that he didn't have a choice. He *had* to make the trip down the River Bure, once in the morning, and again in the evening, every single day, probably until the end of the month.

As President of the Norfolk Birdwatching Society, it was up to him to make sure that the nesting pair of curlews, spotted by one of his society's members the week before, remained undisturbed, a job made far harder than usual by the ridiculous place they'd chosen to nest: at the furthest end of a long public jetty, not far from where he was now.

Thankfully, the jetty in question was one of those little used dilapidated ones, that most tourists would consider to be too dangerous to use. It was also part-hidden from the river by a bed of overgrown reeds.

Unfortunately, however, none of those things meant the nest was going to be safe, certainly not during the summer months, when literally millions of noisy tourists would descend upon the Broads to spend their lives driving ungainly plastic hire boats up and down the miles of meandering rivers, in desperate search of free moorings.

There was also a small public carpark next to it, making it just as likely that someone would park there for a drunken picnic, or to do whatever else people did in remote public carparks.

Of course, they had no legal right to stop anyone from either mooring on the jetty, or using the carpark. The best they could do was to put up signs, warning approaching boats, dog walkers, and car owners having sordid affairs with their co-workers, to keep their distance from the birds nesting nearby. Then they had to keep a close eye on the nest, to make sure people were heeding their urgent request.

Cursing the day he'd failed his driving test, he stood up on the bicycle's pedals to peer ahead. The moment he did, his heart jumped in his throat. In the distance, just above a thick line of trees, was the unmistakable sight of a motorboat's flybridge.

'Shit!' he cursed, loudly to himself, leaning over the handlebars to pedal even harder. 'How long have they been there for?'

Bursting into the carpark to see someone's SUV, parked to one side with its boot left hanging open, he ditched his bicycle on the ground to run down the path to the jetty.

Coming to a breathless standstill to see an enormous motorboat, looming up in front of him, he cursed again before crouching silently down. From where he was, he could just about see the curlew's sprawling nest, perched at the furthest end of the jetty. But as he feared, there was no sign of the parents.

Hoping to God that they'd only been temporarily scared off by the arrival of the monstrously proportioned motorboat, he crept carefully over the jetty's rotting wooden surface towards the hopefully not completely empty nest. When he felt he was quite close enough, he lifted himself onto the balls of his feet to peer gingerly inside.

Seeing four small speckled brown eggs, thankfully lying undisturbed, he let out a controlled sigh of relief. 'At least the eggs haven't been taken,' he muttered, quietly to himself.

Egg theft was something that was always at the back of his mind. Sometimes they were taken by children, as a dare, other times by tourists, looking for a unique souvenir. But when it came to eggs belonging to a pair of rare nesting birds, just occasionally they were targeted by professional egg thieves, looking to sell them to collectors at the most ridiculously inflated prices.

Keen to see if either the female, or the male, were nearby, waiting until it was safe to return, Adrian continued along the jetty, all the way to where the giant boat's aft end had been tied, less than two feet from the nest itself.

'Bloody tourists,' he muttered, seeing the sign he'd personally put up, on the very post the boat had been tied to. There was no way the boat's owners couldn't have seen it.

Stepping over one of the boat's thick black mooring ropes, he leaned forward to peer around its wide, curving aft end.

With the River Bure sparkling gently in the morning's sun, he took a moment to scan the bank on the other side, hoping to see one of the curlew's peering anxiously back. But as he expected, there was no sign. Even if they had been there, it would have been unlikely he'd have been able to see them. Their slim curling beaks, and brown mottled plumage, would have made them virtually invisible.

He was about to give up when a flicker of movement caught his eye to the right.

Focussing his attention on a small clump of reeds, he managed to see one of the curlews twitch its head to the side.

The moment he saw it, he knew it was the female. She was slightly larger than her mating partner. Her beak was also longer, with more of a curve to it.

It was then that he caught sight of the male, just a few feet away, his head twisting around to face his partner's.

With it being all too obvious that they were desperate to return to their freshly laid batch of eggs, Adrian felt a wave of anger surge through his veins. The boat had to move, and it had to move now!

Stepping back over the mooring line, his attention returned to the boat. 'Hello!' he called, as loudly as he dared. 'Can I speak to someone on board, please?'

Knowing they couldn't have been asleep, not with the car having been left with its boot open, he called out again. 'Is anyone there? I really do need to speak to someone!'

With no response, he lifted himself up onto the balls of his feet in an effort to peer through one of the windows. But with the reflection from the sun, all he could see was his own fat, stupid-looking face, staring back.

'Hello!' he called out again, reaching a hand through the railings to rap his knuckles against the glass. 'Can someone please come out? It really is rather urgent!'

Hearing the haunting cry of the curlews from the other side of the river, as if pleading for his help, he set his jaw firm.

'Whoever's inside, you need to move your boat. You've clearly decided to ignore the signs about the nesting birds. You certainly couldn't have missed them. If you're not prepared to,' he heard himself continue, 'then I'm just going to have to move it for you!'

Surprised by what he'd said, he remained resolutely where he was, waiting for the owner to charge out to tell him to f-off. But there wasn't a single sound from inside. It was as if both the boat and the car had been abandoned.

'I mean it!' he eventually added, wondering if he actually did. It was a colossal boat to move. Even with someone's help, he'd still have thought twice before doing so.

Coming to the conclusion that the owners were leaving him with little choice, he took a step back to cast his eyes along its length. All he had to do was drag it down to the other end of the jetty. It shouldn't be too difficult. It should also be enough for the curlews to feel it safe to return.

Still unsure if he should take the risk, he returned to the back of the boat, to check the state of the river. The water was flowing at what he considered to be a manageable pace. Even the wind was blowing in his favour. It also wouldn't have been the first boat he'd had to move. It was a long time ago, but he'd had a summer job as a student, cleaning boats, something that often involved having to manoeuvre them around without the use of their engines.

Hearing the curlews' call again, he made up his mind. If the owner wasn't prepared to move it, then he was just going to have to do it himself. As long as he wasn't caught, he should be alright. It wasn't as if it was against the law, or anything; at least, he didn't think it was. 'As long as I don't put a hole in it,' he said to himself, 'it will be fine. They probably won't even realise it's been moved.'

Having made up his mind, he took a moment to consider the safest, fastest way to do so. If he first untied the mooring line at the back, before running to undo the line at the front, he risked the boat's aft end being swept out into the middle of the river. If that happened to a boat this size, it would quickly become impossible to control. It could also leave him unable to reach the stern line, to haul it back in. Worse would be if he reached the line at the front, only to find himself unable to untie it.

No, the safest thing to do was to loosen the line at the front first, making sure it would be easy to untie. He could then undo the one at the back, before returning to the front, preferably keeping hold of the aft end's line as he did. That would allow him to drag the boat slowly down the jetty without having to let go of either the front, or the back.

With the decision made, he hurried down to the boat's imposing front end.

Reaching the cleat around which the mooring line had been tied, he stooped down to wrestle with the knot. The moment he began, he congratulated himself with his decision. Whoever had tied it had clearly no idea what they were doing. Instead of simply wrapping it around the cleat in a series of figure-of-eights, they'd used what appeared to be some sort of a bizarre combination of a reef knot and a bowline.

Eventually able to untie it, he looped the rope back around the cleat, just enough to keep it in place. He then ran to the line at the back, only to find they'd used the same ham-fisted knot there as well. How they'd have been able to untie them in an emergency, he'd no idea.

With the knot finally undone, he stood up to take a firm hold of the line.

Making sure to keep it taut, he began feeding it through his hands to begin walking backwards towards the cleat at the bow.

Eventually reaching it, he crouched down to slip the rope off the cleat to end up standing with the boat's forward line in one hand, and the aft end line in the other.

'OK,' he said to himself, taking a calming breath. 'That was the easy part.' Now he had to pull the entire boat all the way to the other end, making sure the aft end wasn't dragged out by the river's current as he did.

Glancing over his shoulder, he made a mental note of where the other mooring cleats were. If the river did pull the boat out, all he'd need to do was to hook the aft end line around one of them to either tie it off, or to use it as a make-shift pulley to drag the boat back in.

'Right, here we go,' he muttered, taking up the slack on both lines to begin hauling the one leading to the back.

Wondering if he was even going to be able to move it, with the help of both the river's natural flow, and the summer's warm gentle breeze, the boat eventually began creeping forward.

Making sure to keep enough tension on the bow line, so it didn't steer itself away from the jetty, he began walking steadily backwards, dragging the mammoth boat with him as he went.

'It's easier than I thought,' he soon said to himself, even allowing a smile to play over his lopsided mouth.

Glancing again over his shoulder, to see how far he had to go, something caught his eye from the top of the flybridge.

Curious to know what it was, he lifted his gaze to see a small, red, star-shaped object, hanging over its side. 'What on Earth is that?' he asked himself, tilting his head as he continued to walk steadily backwards.

When another one, almost exactly the same, appeared beside it, he found himself transfixed by the strange, alien-like objects.

It was only when a moon-like entity began rising slowly between them, did it dawn on him that that they weren't the alien-like crabs he'd first thought, but were instead a pair of human hands, each covered in a thick layer of glistening blood. If that was true, then the object hovering between them must have been a human head, but where one of its eyes should have been, was nothing but a gaping black hole.

As the head rotated slowly around to glare dementedly down at him, all he could do was to stare straight back, his mouth hanging open as he struggled to look away.

Failing to keep an eye on where he was going, he stepped back onto one of the jetty's cleats, his ankle instantly twisting under his body's considerable weight.

Yelping out in pain, he first stumbled, then fell backwards, the ropes slipping through his hands as the back of his head cracked against another cleat behind him.

As a blinding white pain exploded inside his skull, he blinked his eyes open to see the gigantic motorboat begin slipping slowly past, its two untethered mooring lines being dragged along the jetty behind it like the tails of a kite.

Cursing with panic as the boat drifted further away, he forced himself up to his feet, only for his brain to spin madly inside his pain-filled skull.

As he fell back to the jetty's damp wooden surface, all he could do was to watch in hopeless agony, as the deformed one-eyed head seemed to be laughing at him, as if it had made him fall over on purpose, just to see the look on his face when the boat he'd only wanted to move a few feet was swept uncontrollably away, ready to plough into whatever happened to be lying in its way.

- CHAPTER FORTY THREE -

STUCK IN WHAT was becoming an all too familiar line of traffic over Wroxham bridge, Tanner glanced down at the clock on his Jag's wood veneered dashboard to see that he was far later than he'd realised.

As he ground to a halt on the crest of the bridge, he took a reflective moment to stare out over the River Bure.

Thinking he may as well use the time to let someone know he was going to be late, he reached for his phone, only for it to spring to life in his hands.

Jumping with a start, the phone slipped through his fingers, leaving it falling between his knees to end up ringing relentlessly on the floor.

With an irritated curse, he reached down to find it had somehow managed to lodge itself underneath the seat.

Eventually being able to prise it out with his fingers, he took a firm hold of it to answer the call, when it suddenly stopped.

Glaring down at the screen to see it had been the office calling, he was about to return the call, when the cars ahead began inching forward.

'I suppose it can wait,' he muttered, ditching it on the seat opposite to place both hands on the steering wheel.

Hearing it spring to life again, he rolled his eyes to reach over and answer it.

'Tanner speaking!'

'Hi boss, it's Vicky.'

'Yes, Vicky, I know I'm late. The traffic over Wroxham bridge is an absolute bloody nightmare!'

'Actually, I wasn't calling about that.'

'Dare I ask why you were?'

'I don't suppose you've had a chance to check your email recently?'

'Not since leaving home.'

'OK, well, a preliminary report has just come through from forensics, regarding the cellar with the electric chair.'

'Go on,' Tanner replied, holding his breath.

'They were only able to find three clear sets of fingerprints and DNA, one of which belonged to the person we suspected of being tortured there.'

'Vincent O'Riley?'

'Uh-huh.'

'Then at least we know where he was taken. I suppose his abductors must have known the farmhouse's owner, but weren't expecting him back in the country. I don't suppose they were able to find a match for the others?'

'They did.'

'Let me guess, the Priestly brothers, which means our friend, Mr Elliston, was lying about them having a meeting at the time of O'Riley's abduction.'

'Would you like to try again?'

'Well, it can't be those two con artists, the ones going around telling everyone they're from the National Gallery. For a start, we've got no idea who they actually are.'

'You're right, it isn't them.'

'But – that only leaves...'

'Michael and Jonathan O'Riley,' continued Vicky, 'which means they must have tortured their father and mother, presumably in an effort to find the missing painting.'

'Having told us that they had no interest in finding it?'

'Then they must have been lying.'

'Not exactly the first time, I suppose,' Tanner replied, taking a reflective moment to allow the implications of what she'd told him to sink in.

'Are you still there?'

'Yes, sorry. I'm still here.'

'So, what do you want to do?'

'For a start, I'd like to read the report for myself. It's not that I don't believe you, I'm just struggling to get my head around the idea that it was them. If it had been, then surely their parents would have recognised them.'

'Not if they were wearing masks.'

'Maybe not their faces, but they must have recognised their voices, unless...'

'Unless, what?'

'Nothing,' Tanner replied, his mind harking back to something Mrs O'Riley had told him, when he'd spoken to her after her husband's funeral. 'I don't suppose anyone knows where they are?'

'At work, presumably. Unless they're off torturing some other poor soul.'

'Do me a favour, will you? Can you give their office a call? Find out if they're there. Then we can make a decision as to what to do next.'

'You mean, apart from arresting them?'

'I was thinking that it may be an idea to have a chat with them first, if for no other reason than to see their reaction, after telling them what we've found. I wouldn't mind speaking to the Priestly brothers about it, as well, just in case they had the foresight to plant their fingerprints and DNA. Then there's those two from the National Gallery. I don't suppose they've turned up anywhere?'

'Not that I'm aware of. I assume they didn't show up at Vincent O'Riley's funeral?'

'Sadly, only the Priestly brothers put in an appearance.'

'I bet that went down well.'

'A fight broke out about thirty seconds later.'

'Did anyone get hurt?'

'Yes, me!'

'You?'

'Only because I was the one stupid enough to try and break it up.'

'Don't tell me you spent another night in A&E?'

'Fortunately I was saved by a knight with a shiny Louis Vuitton handbag.'

'Huh?'

'Rebecca O'Riley came to my rescue.'

'Oh, right. May I ask how she did that?'

'She offered me a lift, before asking if I'd like to have sex with her.'

'I beg your pardon?'

'Don't worry, I told her I was married.'

'I should hope you did!'

'But then she invited Christine to join us, which led to a rather interesting discussion at home. After that, we had to call Rebecca, to put something in her diary.'

'Please tell me you're joking?'

'Why would I be joking? Doesn't everyone arrange sex parties with their wives and potential murder suspects over dinner?'

'Then, thankfully, I must be missing out.'

'Anyway, the traffic's moving. I'll tell you more about it when I get in.'

'Please don't.'

'Then perhaps you can find out if the O'Riley brothers are at work. We'd then be able to head straight over there to have a preliminary chat with them, before doing so with a little more formality down at the station.'

CHAPTER FORTY FOUR

FINALLY ABLE TO fight his way through Wroxham's rush-hour traffic, Tanner arrived at the police station to make a beeline for his office. There, he made himself a much needed coffee, before slumping down behind his desk to open his email.

With a hand clasped around his mug, he spent a few quiet moments speedreading his way through the forensics report that Vicky had alerted him to, before sitting back in his chair. The report had told him nothing Vicky hadn't already. The O'Riley brothers' fingerprints and DNA had been found all over the farmhouse cellar, including the antique electric chair, as well as the various tools found hanging from the ceiling. Apart from the victim's, nobody else's had been, at least nothing that had been left there recently, making it far less likely that they'd been planted.

He was about to call Vicky's direct line, to see if she'd had any luck tracking the O'Riley brothers down, when a knock at the door was followed by her lightly freckled face, gazing at him with an anxious frown.

'Let me guess. You can't find them?'

'Sorry, boss. I spoke to their secretary. She said they were due to come in for a meeting early this morning, but never showed up. I then tried their mobiles, but there was no reply.'

'How about their home numbers?'

'They both rang through to voicemail. Do you think it's possible that they know we're after them, and have done a runner?'

'I don't see how. We only found out ourselves about five minutes ago.'

'Unless they've been in contact with that guy selling the farmhouse, who just happened to tell them that we'd been there.'

'Shit!' Tanner cursed, glancing away with a frustrated grimace. 'I hadn't thought of that.'

Leaning forward in his chair, he planted his elbows down on is desk. 'OK, we're going to have to get an All Ports Warning out for them. Then we need to plug their cars' numberplates into the ANPR. If that doesn't come up with anything, we're going to have to ask their mother and sister, to see if they know.'

'Would they tell us if they did?'

'Probably not, but it would be worth a shot.'

With a nod, Vicky turned to head out, only for DC Henderson to appear in her place.

'Sorry boss,' the tall, lanky DC began. 'Is – er – now a good time?'

'I suppose that depends if you're at the front of a queue,' Tanner replied, leaning over to see if there was anyone standing behind him.

'It's just me, I think,' he replied, following Tanner's gaze.

'OK, but make it quick. If you hadn't noticed, we're in the middle of a double murder investigation.'

'Yes, of course. It's just that we've had a call.'

'About anything in particular?'

'A boat's been found floating down the River Bure. I think someone may have deliberately untied it.'

'Was that it?' Tanner demanded, in an exasperated tone.

'Was that – er – what, boss?'

'Was that what you came in here to tell me?'

'Well, yes. That and the fact that two bodies have been found on board.'

'Sorry – but – what did you say?'

'That two bodies have been found on board. At least, that's what the caller said.'

'OK, yes, I understand. What I don't is why you didn't start with that, instead of standing there for half-an-hour, telling me about the boat they were found on.'

'Well, boss, they were found on board the boat, so I thought that's where I should start.'

Shaking his head in dismay, Tanner reached for his desk phone. 'I don't suppose you know where this boat currently is?' he asked, glancing up.

'It's being towed into the marina, just below Horning.'

'And have you told anyone else?'

Henderson shook his head. 'I came straight here, after taking the call.'

'Then perhaps you could let our medical examiner know. Our forensics department, as well.'

'Yes, boss. Right away!'

'And close the door on the way out, there's a good chap.'

Waiting for him to do so, Tanner snatched up his desk phone's receiver.

'Vicky, it's Tanner!' he said, the moment she answered. 'Whatever you're doing, get someone else to do it, although preferably not Henderson. The guy's at least three sandwiches short of a picnic. Once you've done that, meet me out in the carpark.'

'Why, what's up?'

'After much deliberation, Henderson has finally managed to tell me that no less than two bodies have been found onboard a boat, one that some kind soul would appear to have deliberately let loose from its moorings.'

- CHAPTER FORTY FIVE -

ARRIVING AT THE marina some twenty minutes later, Tanner saw what they were looking for long before he found anywhere to park. It was an enormous motorboat with a huge flybridge, on top of which could be seen two overall-clad police forensics officers, each examining a body draped precariously over its side.

Surprised to see Dr Johnstone's boxy old Volvo Estate was already there, Tanner parked behind it to lead Vicky over to where its owner stood, leaning up against the boat, just the other side of a line of blue and white tape.

Approaching, Tanner raised a hand to call out, 'Morning Johnstone! Have you had a chance to take a look?'

'Only briefly.'

'Anything interesting?'

Johnstone pushed himself off the boat to gaze behind him. 'It would appear to be a rather expensive motorboat,' he began, nudging his glasses up the ridge of his nose, 'one that has no less than two dead people on board. I don't know if they came with it, or if they were added on later. Either way, they certainly make for an intriguing accessory.'

'I was actually hoping for something a little more detailed,' Tanner replied, stopping in front of the tape to stare up at the boat, 'and relevant.'

'Sorry, yes, of course. According to the harbour master, it's a fifty-two foot Fairline Squadron, one that's far too big to navigate the Broads, at least not without running aground at every turn.'

'And the dead people?' Tanner prompted, pointing up to the one on the flybridge.

'Oh, right! Well, there are two of them.'

'So I've been told.'

'Both male.'

'Uh-huh.'

'One's on the flybridge, as you can see. The other's underneath, in the saloon.'

'Anything else?'

'They were both shot at point-blank range.'

Tanner returned to look at Johnstone. 'I don't suppose there's any chance it was a murder / suicide? It would certainly make my job easier, if it was.'

'Being that they were both shot through the back of the head, unfortunately, I think that's a little unlikely.'

Tanner raised an eyebrow at Vicky, before turning back. 'Any idea about the weapon used?'

'Judging by the entry wound, it must have been something relatively small, like a low calibre handgun, for example.'

'And the time of death?'

'The body in the saloon was probably about two, maybe three hours ago.'

'Not the one on the flybridge?' Tanner queried, glancing up.

Johnstone shook his head. 'I'd say he died about an hour later.'

'So, they were killed at different times?'

'They died at different times,' Johnstone corrected. 'Had the chap up there received immediate medical attention, he may have even lived to fight another day.'

'I'm sorry, but didn't you say he was shot at point-blank range through the back of the head?'

'I need to take a closer look, but from what I can tell, it looks like the bullet may have tracked around the inside of his cranium, before exiting through the left eye's orbit. It may have even managed to miss his brain entirely!'

'Is that possible?'

'If the gun was fired at an angle to the skull, then it isn't uncommon, especially if a low calibre weapon was used.'

'How about their identities?'

'We've yet to find any IDs.'

'OK. Let me know if you do.'

'Yes, of course.'

'And when can we expect your post mortem report?'

Johnstone let out a world-weary sigh to stare down at his watch. 'Had there been just the one body, then I'd have said by end of play today. But with two of them...!'

'How about the one up there by the end of the day, and the other by lunchtime tomorrow?'

'OK, well, I'll do the best I can, but I can't promise anything.'

Watching him climb back on board, Tanner called after him. 'Sorry, one more thing. I don't suppose you know who found them, or where the boat had been moored previously?'

'I've no idea about the first. It's probably worth asking the Broads Authority about the second. If they know, then they should also be able to tell you who it belongs to.'

'And I presume it's OK if we take a look?'

'By all means!' Johnstone replied, stepping to one side to invite him on board.

Nodding, Tanner turned to look at Vicky, only to find she wasn't there.

With no idea where she'd gone, he began staring around the marina, to eventually see her deep in conversation with a large red-face man, standing astride a decrepit old bicycle.

'Let me just grab Vicky,' he quickly said, pivoting himself around.

'OK, but don't be long. If you want both post mortem reports by lunchtime tomorrow, then I'm going to have to start thinking about moving the bodies.'

- CHAPTER FORTY SIX -

WITH NO IDEA who Vicky was talking to, Tanner remained where he was, waiting for her to finish, when she glanced up from her notebook to beckon him over.

'Mr Mallot,' she began, as Tanner approached, 'this is Detective Chief Inspector Tanner. Perhaps you could tell him what you've just been telling me?'

'Yes, of course,' the sweaty, red-faced man replied. 'I was just saying that I have a confession to make.'

'Go on,' Tanner prompted, offering Vicky an inquisitive frown.

'It's just that – well – I'm the President of the Norfolk Birdwatching Society. Perhaps you've heard of us?'

'I'm sorry, Mr Mallot,' Tanner interrupted, 'but do you think you could get to the point?'

'Actually, I was, or at least I was trying to. You see, there's a pair of curlews. They're nesting on a pontoon, on a bend in the River Bure.'

'I thought you said you were getting to the point?'

'That's where I discovered the boat that's behind you. Despite all the signs we'd put up, warning people not to stop there, someone had moored it right next to them.'

'Is any of this in the least bit relevant?' Tanner demanded, his gaze switching between Vicky and the dithering man.

'He untied the boat from its moorings,' Vicky stated, in an accusatory tone.

'You did what?'

'I didn't have any choice!' the man exclaimed. 'The boat had already scared the birds away. If I hadn't moved it, it's unlikely they'd have returned, and what with curlews being an endangered species, and everything, I felt it was my civic duty to.'

'To untie a boat of this size, leaving it to drift aimlessly down the river?'

'I didn't set it adrift, at least, that wasn't my intention. I was simply trying to move it to the other end of the pontoon – away from the nest – when I saw that – that – man – staring at me,' he continued, gesturing up at the boat's flybridge, where the body could still be seen. 'That's when I must have tripped over one of the mooring cleats.'

After glaring at him with a disapproving scowl, Tanner turned to look at the boat. 'When you say the victim was looking at you, I assume that means he was alive at the time?'

'Possibly. Unless, of course, I imagined it.'

'Is that likely?'

'I don't think so, but then again, I could have sworn he was laughing at me, so I may have done. To be honest, I found the whole affair to be all rather upsetting.'

'But not as upsetting as the victim must have.'

'No – of course. I didn't mean...'

'What time was this?'

'It was around half-past eight. I was checking the nest, before going to work.'

'Did you step on board the boat, when you were moving it?'

Mallot shook his head.

'Not even to see if anyone was on board?'

'I called out a number of times, but there was no response. To be honest, the only reason I thought there may have been was because of the car.'

'The car?'

'The one left in the carpark.'

'You think it belongs to the boat's owner?'

'Well, yes, but only because the boot had been left open.'

- CHAPTER FORTY SEVEN -

MAKING SURE THAT they had Mallot's contact details, and the location of where he'd discovered the boat, Tanner thanked him for his time before leading Vicky away.

'We need to get someone over there,' he began, 'preferably before anyone else shows up to further contaminate the scene. If they're not doing anything, perhaps you could ask Townsend and Henderson? Another forensics unit, as well.'

'What about the nesting curlews?'

'What about them?' Tanner replied, in a curt, irritable tone.

'Shouldn't we warn them that they're there, to make sure they keep clear?'

'Yes, of course. What was I thinking. Tell whoever gets there first to immediately cordon off the nesting area with Police Do Not Cross tape.'

'Oh, right.'

'Then contact the RSPB. Ask if they have some sort of an armed endangered bird protection unit they could send over, just in case someone tries to cross it.'

'I see. You're joking.'

'Only in part. Perhaps you could call the Broads Authority instead. With any luck, they'll be able to tell us who owns the boat.'

'I assume that means that we don't know who the victims are?'

'Not yet, which is why identifying the bodies has to be a priority.'

With Vicky digging around for her phone, Tanner glanced behind him to see Dr Johnstone, staring down at them from the top of the flybridge, his arms planted firmly down on his hips.

Raising a hand in acknowledgment, he turned to look back at Vicky. 'As soon as you've done that, you'd better join me on board. From what I can tell, it looks like our medical examiner is waiting, somewhat impatiently, for us to join him.'

- CHAPTER FORTY EIGHT -

STEPPING UP INTO the cockpit to take first a pair of shoe coverings, then some latex gloves from off a particularly youthful looking PC, Tanner took an annoying moment to put them all on whilst waiting for Vicky to join him.

With the sound of Dr Johnstone, on the phone to someone above, he decided to kill time by having a quick look inside the saloon.

Making his way through a pair of open patio doors, he found himself inside a wide, spacious room, where two large, unopened holdalls could be seen resting on a table to the side. It was only when he turned to the right did he see the body, its head resting awkwardly against a thick black leather steering wheel.

Unable to see any signs of injury, he inched his way closer, to eventually find himself staring into a person's face, or at least what was left of it. What remained was grossly deformed, with ruptured skin hanging limply from its fractured cheek bones.

Averting his gaze from what appeared to be its brain, scattered in clumps over a wood veneered instrument panel, he turned on his heel to head quickly out.

Taking a much needed breath of fresh country air, he stepped back into the cockpit to look for Vicky. When he saw she was still in the carpark, pacing up and down with her phone glued to her ear, he thought he may as well make his way up to the flybridge, to see if Johnstone was free.

'Sorry about that,' Tanner apologised, finding him sitting on a plastic moulded seat, swiping at his tablet's screen with a finger. 'I was taking a look at the body downstairs, whilst waiting for Vicky.'

'Is she coming?' the medical examiner asked, standing up.

'She's on the phone, but you may as well carry on,' Tanner replied, taking in the second body, its arms and head draped over the flybridge's curving plastic side, like a blood-stained bedsheet being hung out to dry. 'I can update her later.'

'OK, well, as you can see, it's a man, probably in his mid to late twenties.'

'I don't suppose you've been able to find any identification?'

'I've had a quick look, but there doesn't seem to be anything.'

'Not even a wallet?'

'Not even a phone!' Johnstone exclaimed. 'I know it's not my job to speculate, but I think it's possible that whoever killed them was hoping to keep their identities hidden, at least in the short term. That could be why they targeted the backs of their heads, knowing the exit wound was likely to make their faces virtually unrecognisable. If that was the case, then I think they failed, at least they did with regards to the victim here. As you can see,' he continued, leading Tanner over, 'apart from the fact that he's missing an eye, you wouldn't have known there was anything wrong with him.'

As Tanner found himself staring unblinkingly down into the victim's face, he heard Vicky's breathless voice behind him.

'Sorry I took so long,' she began, 'I've just come off the phone to the Broads Authority. They said that this boat was registered less than three weeks ago. They've also given me the name of the person it belongs to.'

'Let me guess, Michael O'Riley, or maybe his brother, Jonathan?'

'It was actually Michael,' Vicky replied, in a surprised tone. 'How did you know?'

'Because, if I'm not very much mistaken, I'm currently staring into what's left of his face, which to be completely honest, is rather annoying.'

'Forgive me,' interrupted Johnstone, 'but why is it annoying to know their identities?'

'Because...' Vicky began, on Tanner's behalf, 'we were on our way to arrest them for the murder of their father, when we got the call to come here instead.'

'I suppose that could be considered somewhat irksome,' he nodded, in a rueful, sagacious manner.

'It also doesn't make any sense,' Tanner continued. 'If they had tortured and killed their father, presumably to make him tell them where the missing painting was, then why would someone else feel it necessary to come on board their brand new boat to assassinate them?'

'Maybe they knew that they'd found the painting,' proposed Vicky, 'and were about to make a run for it? That would explain the car being left with its boot open. They must have been all set to cross the channel, when someone came on board with the intention of stopping them.'

'That theory would only work if they, too, were looking for the painting. But from what I can tell, it doesn't look like the boat's been searched, at least not with any conviction. Nor does it appear that anything's been taken. For example, there are two large holdalls downstairs, neither of which have even been opened.'

'Then the painting must have been left in plain sight.'

'Would they really have left a priceless Turner, lying around for anyone to see?'

'They might have done if they weren't expecting visitors.'

'Perhaps,' Tanner mused, 'although, had their assassin's intention been to take the painting, it doesn't explain the apparent absence of the victim's identification.'

'Didn't you say there were two bags downstairs that haven't been opened?'

Tanner cast a questioning eye over at Johnstone.

'Don't look at me!' he replied. 'I'm responsible for bodies. I leave unopened bags to forensics.'

Hearing his phone ring from the depths of his sailing jacket, Tanner dug it out to answer, 'Tanner speaking!'

'Hi, boss, it's Townsend.'

'Yes, Townsend, how can I help?'

'Henderson and I have arrived at the location Vicky directed us to, the one where the nesting curlews are.'

'That was quick!'

'Yes, well, we were – er – out buying coffee, you see.'

'You do know that you're not paid to wander around Norfolk, buying coffee, don't you?'

'Sorry, boss. It's just that we've run out of the good stuff.'

'Fair enough, I suppose.'

'Anyway, we don't seem to be able to gain access.'

'Access to where?'

'The carpark, where the rare birds are supposed to be.'

'Why on Earth not?'

'There are some people there from the Norfolk Bird Watching Society. They're telling us that we're not allowed to go any further, because of the nesting curlews.'

'Please, God, tell me you're joking?'

'I'm afraid not, boss.'

'I assume you've told them who you are?'

'Repeatedly.'

'And...?'

'They still won't let us through.'

'Then you'll just have to force your way past.'

'Yes, boss.'

'Actually, better still, you have my permission to arrest them for obstruction.'

'Er... thank you, boss,' came Townsend's unenthusiastic response.

'Well...?' Tanner demanded, realising he was still on the line.

'It's just that they're women, boss. Quite old, as well.'

'What's that got to do with it?'

'There're also both somewhat on the large side. Each one is probably bigger than Henderson and I put together!'

Picturing the rather disturbing image of Townsend and Henderson having been put together by some sort of futuristic DNA splicing machine, Tanner found himself praying to God for patience, as well as some more manly detective constables.

When he heard a voice to his side, he opened his eyes to find Vicky, staring at him with a quizzical expression.

'Sorry,' he said, 'for a moment there, I thought you were an angelic being, sent from Heaven to offer me psychological counselling.'

'Only me, I'm afraid,' she smiled. 'What's going on?'

'Just Townsend being Townsend.'

'Are you still there, boss,' came the young DC's voice.

'Unfortunately, yes, I am.'

'So... what do you want us to do?'

'Well, I'd hate for you to get beaten up by a couple of old ladies.'

'I suppose we could always call for backup.'

'No need. Stay where you are. We're on our way.'

- CHAPTER FORTY NINE -

WITH VICKY BACK beside him in the passenger seat, Tanner drove to where they'd been told Michael O'Riley's motorboat had originally been moored to find Townsend and Henderson, waiting for them at a public carpark's entrance.

Observing two large, elderly women, chatting together at the carpark's furthest end, Tanner pulled up beside his junior detectives to wind his window down.

'Are you two alright?' he enquired, offering them each a look of earnest concern. 'Those two mean-looking old ladies didn't hurt you, did they?'

'They're tougher than they look,' came Townsend's defensive response.

'I find that very hard to believe.'

'Then may I suggest that *you* go and talk to them?'

Glancing back at the women in question, only to see one of them fold her tree trunk-like arms to start glaring over at them, Tanner leaned his head out of the window to whisper, 'You know, you might be right. Maybe we should send Vicky in first? Being that they're the same gender – and everything – should mean that they'd be less inclined to hurt her.'

'I'm right here!' he heard Vicky exclaim, opening her door to begin clambering out.

'You heard that, did you?' Tanner enquired, climbing out after her.

'I don't mind talking to them,' she continued, making her way around the car, 'that's assuming you lot are all too scared?'

With Townsend and Henderson staring nervously around at each other, Tanner straightened his tie. 'Tell you what, why don't we all go?'

'To be honest,' began Townsend, 'if you don't mind, I think I'd rather stay here, just to be on the safe side.'

'Me too!' exclaimed Henderson, nodding enthusiastically beside him.

'Good grief,' muttered Vicky, taking her police ID in one hand to give Tanner her handbag with the other. 'Hold my beer, will you?'

'Er... sorry, Vicky,' Tanner replied, 'but this isn't a refreshing alcoholic beverage. It looks more like a Gucci handbag. Not a real one, either.'

'It's a Tommy Hilfiger, you moron.'

Tanner stared over at her, blinking repeatedly as he did. 'I'm sorry, but did you just call me a moron?'

'Only figuratively,' she replied, offering him a sheepish smile.

'Oh, right. That's OK, then.'

'Anyway,' she continued, glancing away, 'I suppose I'd better have a chat to them. We can't have them standing there all day, now, can we.'

'No, I suppose we can't.'

Struggling to believe that he'd let her get away with calling him a moron, he watched her begin ambling her way over to where the two women obstinately remained.

'Who thinks she's going to get punched in the face?' he heard Towsend enquire, as the three women began talking together.

'Apparently not,' Tanner soon found himself saying, as they watched them share some sort of hilarious joke.

As they continued to stare in curious surprise, Vicky escorted the women over to what must have been their car, before signalling that it was safe to proceed.

Offering both Townsend and Henderson a mystified shrug, Tanner led them over to where Vicky was waiting.

'What did you say to them?' he eventually asked, as the women climbed slowly into their car.

'I said I'd give each of their phone numbers to Townsend and Henderson, with the promise that they'd call. They're on their way home now, to wait by their phones.'

'Please tell me you're joking?' pleaded Townsend, his face becoming visibly pale.

'I actually said that the three of you were scared of them, which they both found rather amusing. I then promised that the curlews' nest would be cordoned off, and that we'd be as quiet as possible, at which point they were happy to leave. But I have made a note of their phone numbers, just in case any of you do fancy a hot date.'

With the three men gazing curiously around at each other, Townsend slowly raised his hand. 'Go on then, but only if you promise to keep it between the four of us.'

Shaking his head, Tanner turned back to find Vicky had transferred her attention to a black Range Rover, left to one side of the carpark with its boot hanging open.

'I assume that belongs to either Michael or Jonathan O'Riley?' she enquired, gesturing towards it.

'It looks like the one I saw Michael driving, when I first met them,' Tanner replied, making his way over, 'but I suggest we check, just to make sure.'

'And these bicycle tracks,' she continued. 'They must belong to that guy who found the boat.'

'I assume so,' Tanner replied, cupping his hands to gaze through the Range Rover's windows.

'What about these?'

'These what?' he asked, glancing back to find her pointing at the ground.

'There are more tyre tracks.'

'Someone else with a bicycle, presumably,' he shrugged, returning his attention to the car. 'I'm fairly sure he's not the only person in Norfolk who has one.'

'That maybe so, but they weren't left there by a bicycle.'

'They look like bicycle tracks to me,' commented Townsend, standing beside her.

'Not when they're running parallel to each other like that,' Vicky continued, 'unless they were held together by some sort of strange, mystical force.'

'What did you say?' Tanner demanded, staring back.

'I was telling Townsend that they can't be bicycle tracks, not when they're running parallel to each other like that. If you ask me, they look more like they've been left there by a wheelchair.'

Hearing the word, Tanner span around to join them.

'I'd say there was someone pushing it, as well,' Vicky added.

'Someone wearing stilettoes,' mused Tanner, following the tracks from the abandoned car, all the way to where the River Bure could be heard running gracefully past. 'I don't suppose anyone knows where

249

Mrs O'Riley is, by any chance? Her daughter, Rebecca, as well?'

'You don't really think it was...?'

'I'm not saying it was anyone, but I'd certainly be interested in having a chat with them about it.'

'Well, I'd have thought Mrs O'Riley would be at home. Not sure about her daughter, though.'

Tanner lifted his gaze to see a thick bank of clouds, rolling ominously over the gently undulating landscape towards them.

'Townsend and Henderson,' he began, his eyes still studying the sky, 'I need this whole carpark cordoned off. No one else is allowed in, not even if they're concerned members of the Royal Family, helicoptered in by the RSPB. Is that understood?'

'Yes, boss,' Townsend replied, with Henderson nodding beside him.

'And when forensics gets here, tell them that we need plaster casts taken of these tyre tracks. The shoe prints between them, as well, preferably before it starts raining. Then they need to look for the same tracks down by the river, where Michael O'Riley's boat had previously been moored.'

'What about me?' enquired Vicky, with an expectant look.

'Remember that All Ports Warning you put out, the one for the O'Riley brothers?'

'What about it?'

'It needs to be for their mother and sister instead, but you can do that with me in the car.'

'And where are we going again?'

'To their house, of course. Where else?'

- CHAPTER FIFTY -

S PEEDING TOWARDS THE O'Riley estate, Tanner was half-listening to Vicky's phone conversation whilst thinking about the investigation, in particular the reason why Mrs O'Riley and her daughter had been at the carpark where Michael and Jonathan's bodies had been found. It was, of course, more than possible that they'd been there to simply wave them off, to wherever it was that they'd been going. If that had been the case, then there was a chance, albeit a slim one, that they'd seen the person who'd gone on to execute them in such a cold, calculating manner. But if they'd only wanted to say goodbye, why wouldn't they have done so at home, instead of driving all the way to some little used carpark in the middle of nowhere?

Rapidly approaching a junction, he was brought screeching to a halt by a set of traffic lights, changing from amber to red directly in front of him.

Being forced to wait as a seemingly endless stream of cars, vans, and trucks began rumbling past, he glanced around to talk to Vicky to find she was still on the phone.

The sound of someone beeping rudely behind him, snapped his attention back to the lights, only to find they'd changed from red to green.

'That was quick,' he mumbled to himself, fumbling with the Jag's chrome gear selector.

Lurching forward, he raised both his eyes and an apologetic hand up to the driver behind, only to see the glint of another car, charging straight at him from the road to his right.

Tanner jumped on the brakes to be flung hard against the seat belt as the car blasted past, missing his front bumper by what must have been inches.

'Jesus Christ!' he cursed, glaring madly after them. 'That guy nearly killed us!'

'Didn't you see who that was?' Vicky queried, following his gaze.

'Didn't I see who what was?'

'The driver?' she continued, turning to face him.

With Tanner staring back at her with a blank expression, Vicky was left to continue. 'Rebecca O'Riley! I think that was her mum in the back, as well!'

'Are you sure?' Tanner questioned, watching it disappear into a sea of traffic.

'It was definitely Rebecca,' she confirmed, 'and there was *someone* in the back.'

With the sound of horns blaring impatiently at him from behind, Tanner steered his XJS around in the opposite direction to wheelspin away, leaving the line of cars behind them, languishing in a cloud of burnt rubber as the traffic lights changed again, this time from green to red.

- CHAPTER FIFTY ONE -

'CAN YOU SEE them?' Tanner questioned, weaving his way between the various cars in front.

'Not anymore,' Vicky replied, staring ahead, 'but I'm hardly surprised, judging by how fast they were going.'

'Do we have any idea where this road might be taking them?'

In an effort to orientate herself, Vicky sat up in her seat to start glancing about. 'It just goes back to Wroxham, doesn't it?'

'OK, so, what's at Wroxham that they could be in such a hurry to get to?'

'Not a clue, although I think Roy's might have a sale on.'

'I'm fairly sure they're not shopping.'

'Unless they ran out of milk, and the vicar's expected for a nice cup of tea.'

Tightening his grip on the steering wheel, Tanner shot her a distinctly unamused glance. 'I don't suppose there's any chance that you could be taking this a little more seriously?'

'Well, I could, of course, but as we've only just escaped being T-boned by a three-tonne Mercedes, that was doing at least seventy miles an hour, I find myself enjoying a rare sense of euphoria. Anyway, apart from a sale, I can't think of anything else there that's worth going that fast for. Unless, of course, they have a train to catch.'

'That must be it,' mused Tanner, further increasing his speed. 'Do me a favour, will you? Call the office. Ask for a squad car to meet us there.'

'You think they're going to the station?' Vicky replied, digging out her phone.

'I can't see where else they'd be going. As you said yourself, apart from a sale, there's nothing else at Wroxham that's worth going that fast for.'

- CHAPTER FIFTY TWO -

L ESS THAN TEN minutes later, Tanner was turning his car into Wroxham train station's modest carpark to see what appeared to be the car that had nearly driven into them, parked in one of the few spaces available.

'Is that theirs?' he asked, bringing his to an ungainly halt.

Glancing fitfully about, Vicky replied, 'I think so.'

'Any sign of them?'

'There!' she exclaimed, pointing through the windscreen towards the station's entrance, where a tall, elegant woman could be seen pushing someone in a wheelchair up a series of gently sloping ramps.

Seeing them, Tanner opened his door to call out, 'Mrs O'Riley!'

The moment the words left his mouth, he saw the couple stop where they were to squint over at them with hesitant uncertainty.

As Tanner climbed to his feet, he watched them confer for a moment, before they nodded in apparent agreement to continue on.

'Did they see who we were?' Vicky questioned, climbing out from the other side, as the odd-looking couple made their way past a station guard to disappear. 'Did they know it was us?'

'Oh, they knew it was us, alright,' Tanner stated, surging suddenly forward to begin pelting towards the entrance.

With Vicky forced to chase after him, Tanner reached the first of three pedestrian ramps, each one running parallel to the other, to begin charging his way up.

Turning sharply at the end of each, he reached the barrier to present his formal ID to the station guard standing beside it. 'DCI Tanner, Norfolk Police,' he announced, peering into the shadows beyond. 'Is it alright if we go through?'

'By all means,' the man replied, taking Vicky in as she came to a breathless halt beside Tanner. 'I assume you both have a ticket?'

'She's with me,' Tanner responded, watching Vicky dive into her handbag to pull out her own ID.

'Does that mean you do?' he questioned, glancing down at their proffered IDs with uninterested disdain.

'That's just my point,' Tanner continued. 'We're both from Norfolk Police. Neither of us have a ticket.'

'And may I ask where you're heading?'

'Nowhere. We just need to go through.'

'I'm sorry, but you must be going somewhere. This is a train station, after all.'

The grinding sound of an approaching train's brakes, pulling slowly into the platform, had Tanner fighting to remain calm. 'If you must know, the couple you just allowed through – the ones with the wheelchair – we need to speak to them as a matter of urgency.'

'I assume it's a matter of life and death?' the man queried, presenting Tanner with a supercilious frown.

'You could say that.'

'Then you won't mind buying a ticket,' he added, his face cracking into a derisive smirk.

Hearing the clunk of train doors opening, followed by the murmur of disembarking passengers, Tanner fixed the man's eyes. 'Listen, if you don't let us through, I'll be forced to arrest you for obstruction of justice.'

'And if you refuse to buy a ticket, like everyone else, I'll be forced to call my superior.'

'You're not being serious?'

'I'm just doing my job, sir.'

'As am I!' Tanner stated, shoving him back to catapult himself over the barrier.

'OI!' he heard the man bellow after him. 'You can't do that!'

'Sorry, mate,' muttered Tanner, glancing back to see Vicky, helping the guard to his feet, 'I thought I just did.'

- CHAPTER FIFTY THREE -

LEAVING VICKY TO dust the guard down, Tanner forged ahead, only to come face-to-face with a barrage of commuters, pouring out from the station in the opposite direction.

Feeling like a beleaguered dinghy, beating to windward in a stiff breeze, he elbowed his way through to eventually burst out onto the now seemingly deserted platform, only to see the train pull gradually away.

'Shit!' he cursed, jumping into a run to chase after it, before realising the futility of such an endeavour.

Coming to a grudging halt, he shoved his hands despondently down into his pockets to watch it clunk slowly away.

'Are we too late?' came Vicky's still breathless voice behind him.

'By about thirty seconds,' he muttered, 'which was about the same time we spent arguing with that bloody ticket collector!'

'Then who are those two, down there?'

Whipping his head around, Tanner followed her gaze to see the same people they'd seen enter the station, apparently still waiting for a train at the platform's opposite end.

'Looks like it's our lucky day!' he chirped, removing his hands from his pockets to begin marching towards them.

As Mrs O'Riley, and her daughter, Rebecca, came gradually into view, Tanner raised a welcoming hand. 'Imagine meeting you two here!' he eventually called out, drifting to a stop in front of them.

'Detective Chief Inspector Tanner!' came Mrs O'Riley's surprised reply, gazing at him from over the top of a pair of large black sunglasses. 'What are you doing here?'

'I was about to ask you the same question!'

'My daughter is taking me away for a few days,' she replied, glancing back to offer her a benevolent smile.

'No suitcases?' he reflected, staring curiously about.

'We like to travel light. Besides, we have all we need in here,' she added, her skeletal-like hands resting on a vintage carpet bag, sitting squarely on her lap.

'And where are you off to?'

'We're actually going to Kew Gardens,' she beamed, with an excited glint in her eye. 'I have a friend giving a piano recital down there.'

'Oh, right!'

'We managed to get hold of some tickets at the very last minute, so we thought we'd make a weekend of it!'

'Well, lucky you. I can't say that I've ever been.'

'Then you should go! It really is quite magical at this time of year.'

'I'm sure it is,' he remarked, taking a moment to study her face. 'Good to see you've had your bandages removed.'

'I took them off myself this morning, to replace them with at least two inches of foundation, as well as these,' she added, taking her glasses off to rotate between her fingers, 'what I think might just be the largest sunglasses in the world.'

'You look remarkably well, all things considered.'

'That's kind of you to say, thank you! And where are you two off to?' she queried, taking Vicky in.

'We actually came to see you.'

'Me?'

'Both of you, really,' Tanner added, offering them each an affable smile. 'You just happened to drive past us, about ten minutes ago. You were going rather fast at the time, so fast, in fact, that you nearly drove straight into us.'

'That was my fault,' admitted Rebecca, presenting Tanner with an apologetic grimace. 'I sped up, hoping to make the lights.'

'As they were green on our side, I can only assume you didn't.'

'We thought we were late for our train,' she continued. 'Fortunately for us, it's been delayed.'

'That's hardly an excuse for driving through a red light, though, is it?'

'It was stupid of me, I know.'

'If there's a fine to pay,' interjected her mother, 'then I'd be more than happy to cover it. After all, it was as much my fault as it was Rebecca's. I'm the one who told her to ignore them.'

'Unless there were cameras, I doubt it will come to that. Anyway, we didn't come to talk to you about driving through a red light.'

'Then may I ask why you did?'

'Well, we *were* hoping to have a quiet word with your sons,' Tanner replied, glancing vacantly about.

'I'm sorry to disappoint, but as you can see, they're not here.'

'I don't suppose you know where they are?'

'On board their boat, I think. Exactly where, I don't know.'

'Can you tell me when you saw them last?'

'Yesterday evening, wasn't it?' she enquired, glancing up again at her daughter.

'It was just after dinner,' Rebecca replied. 'If you remember, they were telling us about their intended trip to France.'

'So they were! You must forgive me, Chief Inspector, but my memory isn't what it used to be.'

'You didn't see them off?'

'It would have been nice, but unfortunately, we were too busy planning our own little adventure.'

'Do you at least know where they were leaving from?'

'I've no idea, I'm afraid. May I ask what you wanted to talk to them about?'

Tanner continued to cast a roaming eye around at the still empty platform. 'A man came to see us this morning,' he eventually began, 'telling us about a boat he'd inadvertently let loose from its moorings. According to him, it had been moored up alongside a pair of nesting curlews, a rare wading bird, apparently registered as an endangered species.'

'And that's what you wanted to ask them about?'

'Not exactly.'

'Then what, exactly?'

'It's with regret that I have to tell you this,' he replied, returning his attention to her, 'but we've found evidence to suggest that they may have had a hand in what happened to your husband.'

'I beg your pardon?'

'Yourself, as well, I'm afraid.'

'I'm sorry, but what are you talking about?'

'We can only presume it was because they thought your husband must have told you where the missing painting was.'

'I can assure you, Chief Inspector,' she began, her eyes darting erratically between his, 'that they have absolutely no interest in finding that bloody painting!'

Scrutinising her face, Tanner drew in a pondering breath. 'Why do I get the feeling that you knew it was them?'

'What?'

'The men who tortured you. You knew it was them, didn't you? Which means you must have known that they tortured and killed your husband, as well?'

'I'm sorry, but what possible reason do you have for thinking they would have wanted to hurt not only me, their own mother, but their father, as well?'

'Because their fingerprints and DNA were found at the scene where we believe your husband was taken. But as I said before, you'd already figured that one out for yourself, hadn't you?'

'If you *really* think they could have done something quite so horrific, then why are you standing there, telling me about it, instead of being out there, trying to find them? I've already told you that they're not here, which must be fairly obvious, given the fact that we're the only ones who are.'

'Forgive me, Mrs O'Riley, but I must admit, I haven't been completely honest with you.'

Her razor sharp eyes narrowed to stare suspiciously up into his. 'About what, may I ask?'

'It did take us a few minutes to identify them, but we actually know where your sons are. Their bodies were discovered on board their boat, having each been shot at point-blank range through the back of the head.'

With both the mother and daughter gawping at him with apparent horror, Tanner let out an impatient sigh. 'You can drop the amateur dramatics. I may not know which one of you pulled the trigger, but I do know that you were both at the scene, being that you rather foolishly forgot about your wheelchair, and the rather unique tread patterns such contraptions leave behind.'

'Surely you mean that you've discovered the tyre marks of *someone's* wheelchair?' Mrs O'Riley enquired, returning to Tanner a look of self-satisfied conceit.

'Imprints from your daughter's shoes as well, all of which we'll be able to match, once we've taken you into custody. That's before forensics have finished examining your sons' boat with a fine toothcomb. So, unless whichever one of you it was who climbed on board had the foresight to wear overalls, gloves, shoe coverings, and a hairnet, I think it's unlikely that they won't be able to find some sort of a trace that you'd been there.

'Then there's the gun, of course. Even if you'd had the good sense to throw it into the river, before heading home to plan your escape, there will be gunshot residue on your skin, leaving me with only two questions. The first being what could have possibly made you want to execute your own children, and the second,' he continued, switching his attention to Rebecca, 'which one of you pulled the trigger? From a purely practical perspective, I'm assuming it was you, being that your brothers' boat doesn't have wheelchair access, certainly not all the way up to the flybridge, where Michael's body was found. But we can sort that out later. For now, I'm afraid you're going to have to cancel your little weekend away to accompany me down to Wroxham Police Station.'

Tanner watched them exchange a brief but emotionally charged glance, before Mrs O'Riley placed her hands on her wheelchair's rims.

Pivoting herself away from her daughter, she lifted her head to look Tanner square in the eye. 'There's no need to involve Rebecca in any of this. I'm the one you need to talk to.'

'You're willing to confess to their murder?' Tanner queried, glancing curiously around at Vicky.

'I am!' she stated, lifting her chin with proud disdain.

'Whilst at the same time trying to convince me that Rebecca had nothing to do with it?'

'Correct again. I even have the gun I used, in my coat pocket.'

'That's all well and good, Mrs O'Riley, but given your condition, and everything, I'm sorry, but... well, it just doesn't seem very likely.'

'I'm not an invalid, Chief Inspector. My wheelchair is to help me get around, that's all.'

'Forgive me,' Tanner began, feeling a little awkward, 'but you're telling me that you can walk?'

'Of course I can walk!'

With both Tanner and Vicky staring at her with a look of doubtful expectation, she let out an indignant sigh.

Heaving the carpet bag off her lap, she raised a hand up to her daughter. 'Hand me my stick, will you? There's a good girl.'

Unhooking an elegant walking stick from off the back of the wheelchair, Rebecca placed its worn ivory handle into her mother's fragile hand, before skirting around to offer her assistance.

'I don't need your help!' she barked, placing the stick's rubber tip firmly down onto the ground.

Fixing Tanner's eyes with a look of dogged determination, her face grimaced in pain as she heaved herself up.

'There, you see!' she exclaimed, standing triumphantly before him. 'I'm quite capable of walking. I'm also more than capable of exacting revenge for my husband's murder.'

'By executing your own children?' Tanner questioned, watching her walking stick tremble under her weight.

'They didn't leave me with much choice. The moment they broke into my house, I knew it was them. Wearing ridiculous-looking masks, and attempting to disguise their voices with silly electronic contraptions, made little difference. Any mother worth her salt would have been able to recognise her own children. Apart from their basic mannerisms, and their distinct body odour, the way they talked to each other was enough of a giveaway.'

'But to have taken the lives of your own flesh and blood?' Tanner found himself repeating, his mind still struggling to comprehend the act she was admitting to.

'I couldn't agree with you more,' she replied, holding his eyes with stoic indifference, 'but then again, they weren't my children.'

'I'm sorry?'

'Their real parents died in a car crash, when they were small. At the time, the doctors said we couldn't have any of our own, so we rather foolishly decided to adopt them. Then, completely out of the blue, our darling Rebecca arrived, something which our two so-called sons never seemed able to forgive us for. The moment their father was carted off to prison, they made my life a living hell. Rebecca's, as well. When they broke into my house to set about torturing me, having already done something similar to my husband, the man I loved with all my heart, I drew a line in the sand.

'So, there you have it!' she proclaimed. 'My full, unabridged confession. I'll even write it all down for you, in front of a lawyer, on the sole condition that you let my Rebecca go.'

'I'm sorry, Mrs O'Riley, but for now, at least, you'll both need to accompany me to the station. Whether we'll be able to let either of you go will depend on what forensics finds on board your sons' boat. Your clothes, as well.'

'But I just told you what happened!' she stated, her eyes glinting with earnest desperation. 'What more do you need?'

'The truth!' came Tanner's forceful reply.

'I told you the truth! Rebecca had nothing to do with it!'

'It's alright, Mother,' came her daughter's pacifying response. 'I don't mind coming with you.'

'That won't be necessary, my dear,' her mother replied. 'The Chief Inspector, here, is going to accept my offer.'

'As previously stated,' Tanner continued, lifting his voice above the clatter of the incoming train, 'I'd only be willing to let her go if the evidence proves her to be innocent.'

'I appreciate that, Mr Tanner, but you've yet to see all my cards.'

'OK, well, I'm not sure how anything else you could say would make any difference.'

'It's nothing I have to say,' she added, reaching into the folds of her heavy black coat. 'It's something I have to show you.'

'Which is?' he enquired, with curious intrigue.

'The gun I used to kill them,' she replied, drawing out a small silver revolver to point directly at his chest.

'Please, Mother!' Rebecca protested. 'I've already said that I don't mind coming with you.'

'Mrs O'Riley,' Tanner began, his eyes becoming transfixed by the gun. 'I think you need to listen to your daughter.'

Holding it steady, she turned her head to say, 'I'm sorry, darling, but I can't let you go with them.'

'But I did everything you said,' Rebecca whispered, her voice barely audible over the slowly approaching train. *'They'd never be able to prove it was me.'*

Mrs O'Riley turned back to look first at Vicky, then at Tanner. 'Unfortunately, even if they can't prove it, they'd still be able to charge you as an accessory.'

'Then I'll just have to take my chances.'

'No, you'll just have to get on board the train!'

'And what about you?'

'It doesn't matter about me. Whether I spend my last few years stuck in an old people's home, or locked up inside a prison cell, will make very little difference. But you, on the other hand, still have your best years ahead of you.'

'Excuse me,' interrupted Tanner, clearing his throat, 'but as I said before, neither of you are getting on board that train.'

'Please don't think for a single minute that I'm not prepared to shoot you, Detective Inspector. This is, after all, my daughter's life we're talking about.'

'I know you won't, Mrs O'Riley, because, thankfully, you're not the sort of person who could kill someone in such a cold, dispassionate manner.'

'Oh, really,' she smiled, lifting the gun high in the air to pull the trigger.

As a deafening crack tore through the air, Tanner and Vicky instinctively ducked, leaving the gunshot to echo harmlessly away.

Lifting his gaze to find the revolver pointing back at him, Tanner raised his hands in a show of surrender. 'You do realise that if you do decide to shoot me, you'll have the entire British Police Force out looking for you. Bearing that in mind, I sincerely doubt you'd make it to the end of the day before finding yourself stuffed in the back of a police car. Your daughter, as well.'

'Maybe / maybe not,' she mused, as the train pulled into the station behind her. 'However, if you force me to, then neither yourself, nor your attractive red-headed colleague, would be around to find out.'

As the train came grinding to a halt, leaving dozens of people to start squeezing themselves between the opening doors, Mrs O'Riley hid the gun within the folds of her coat.

'On you get, my dear,' she muttered, glancing around at Rebecca. 'Don't worry about Mr Tanner and his friend. They won't be foolish enough to try and stop you.'

'I'm sorry, mother, but I'm not leaving without you.'

'Don't be silly! I'll be perfectly fine! Now, on you get, before the doors close.'

Taking hold of the empty wheelchair's handles, Rebecca hauled it back towards the awaiting train. 'As I said,' she stated, fixing her mother's eyes, 'I'm not leaving without you!'

'Why do you always have to be so difficult?'

'I'm not being difficult,' she retorted, holding a hand out for her. 'I'm trying to save you from having to spend the rest of your life in prison.'

'You're both wasting your time,' interjected Tanner, seeing the gun re-emerge from the folds of her coat. 'Wherever this train is heading, we'll have an armed police unit waiting.'

'You're more than welcome to let them know its final destination,' Mrs O'Riley said, stepping carefully back as Rebecca lifted her wheelchair into the carriage, 'but before you do, you should probably know that there are at least twenty stops between here and there. So, unless you're planning on having an armed police unit waiting at each of them, then I suspect they'd be wasting their time.'

'Then we'd simply arrange to have the train stopped and boarded.'

'You mean, the one that's about to leave?' she enquired, stopping on the platform's edge to offer Tanner a thin, calculating smile.

With her gun pointing directly at him again, Tanner watched her pivot herself around to step over the gap between the platform's edge and the awaiting train.

The moment she lowered the gun, he leapt forward, just as the doors emitted a series of short, intermittent beeps.

Reaching inside, he grabbed hold of her coat to heave her back, straight into the path of the closing doors.

As they slammed hard into her shoulders, a muffled explosion rang out from inside the carriage, followed by a long, deathly silence.

With a morbid sense of dread, Tanner let go of the coat to see Rebecca's pale, elegant face, staring at him from inside the train, her mesmerising blue eyes holding his with a look of bewildered desperation.

As her focus drifted towards her mother, where her gun could be seen, smoking in her still outstretched hand, a sliver of blood appeared between her barely parted lips.

'Mother?' she enquired, as if speaking to her from beyond the grave, 'I think I've been...'

'Rebecca?' the old lady questioned, watching her daughter take a faltering step, before collapsing to the floor.

As a pool of blood began spreading out from underneath her limp, sprawled out body, Mrs O'Riley remained staring down, as if unable to comprehend what her eyes were telling her.

As she gazed down at her gun with the same expression of curious incomprehension, Tanner glanced around to see Vicky step slowly back from the platform's edge, pulling out her phone to press hard against her ear.

'This is DI Gilbert, Norfolk Police,' she eventually began, staring at Tanner with a look of mortified disbelief. 'We need an ambulance. Wroxham train station. It's urgent!'

- CHAPTER FIFTY FOUR -

Monday, 21st August

CLUTCHING NERVOUSLY AT a posy of brightly coloured flowers, Tanner left his XJS behind a line of neatly parked cars to amble his way up a narrow lane towards Stokesby Church, its rectangular stone tower floating above a thick line of trees ahead.

Pulling at the collar of a new office shirt, he glanced down at his watch. It was the morning of the funeral for not only Rebecca O'Riley, but her brothers as well, and he was having second thoughts about being there. He certainly didn't want to arrive when everyone else was supposed to. Unlike Vincent O'Riley's funeral, nobody had asked him to attend. The only reason he was there was because of a deep-seated sense of guilt for what had happened four days before, when he'd tried to stop their mother from boarding that train. Despite what everyone had told him since, that she was the one holding the gun, not him, it was a feeling he'd been unable to shake, leaving him staring at the ceiling in bed, unable to stop replaying the moment endlessly inside his constantly aching head.

Reaching the church to hear the vicar's voice, drifting over the air from somewhere near the back, he followed the path to find a large crowd of mourners, gathered around the same plot where the children's father had been buried the week before.

Coming to an eventual standstill, he spent a respectful moment listening to the vicar's solemn words, whilst glancing curiously about. At first, he wasn't able to recognise a single person in attendance, but then he caught sight of a policewoman's uniform, her hands resting on the handles of an NHS wheelchair.

A half step to the side revealed the person slumped inside, the deceased children's mother, a thick black veil obscuring all but the outline of her battered, inconsolable face.

Movement from under the trees to his right had him gazing about to see the shadowy figure of someone he knew all too well. What he failed to understand was what she was doing there. From the voicemail she'd left him that morning, before he'd snuck out of the office to drive there himself, he thought she was lying in bed with a migraine.

Creeping up behind her, he cleared his throat to say, 'Hello Vicky!'

Taking sadistic pleasure in watching her jump with a start, he met her reddening face with an amused shrug. 'Sorry, I didn't mean to startle you.'

'*What are you doing here?*' she whispered, glancing furtively back at the mourners, as if expecting each and every one of them to be glaring over at them.

'I could ask the same thing of you?'

'Yes, of course, well, um...'

'You were feeling better, so you thought you'd drag yourself out of bed to attend a nearby funeral?'

Vicky's eyes fell to the ground. 'Sorry, boss. I didn't think you'd have given me permission to come.'

'I don't think it's a question of whether or not you should have, but more why you'd want to?'

'I'm not sure, really,' she shrugged. 'I suppose I've been feeling guilty about what happened.'

'What on Earth do *you* have to feel guilty about?' Tanner demanded. 'I was the one stupid enough to try and stop Mrs O'Riley from boarding that train, something that hasn't escaped the attention of the powers that be, either.'

'What do you mean?' she asked, her expression changing from embarrassed guilt to motherly concern.

'Professional Standards have opened an investigation into what happened. They've scheduled a meeting with me next week, to discuss my involvement.'

'They're not blaming you, are they?'

'Not yet, but assuming they will, I think they have every right to. I should never have tried to stop her, not when I knew she was holding a loaded gun.'

'The same loaded gun she'd been pointing at you, less than a minute before?'

'She wasn't pointing it at me at the time, though, and if I hadn't grabbed her coat, Rebecca would still be alive today. That much I'm certain!'

'What about Forrester?'

'What about him?'

'Has he said anything about it?'

'He's the one who told me about the investigation.'

'I assume he's going to stand by you?'

'Well, yes, at least, he said he would. But if they conclude that I was to blame, I'm not sure what he'd be able to do about it.'

'And what would happen if they did?'

'I'd be kicked off the Force to face criminal charges.' Tanner replied, in a matter-of-fact tone of voice.

'OK, well I'm sure that won't happen. All you did was try to arrest someone for murder, the same person who'd been resisting arrest by threatening to shoot you, just moments before.'

'We'll have to see, but it's not exactly going to help when they read my report; that only Rebecca's DNA was discovered on board her brother's boat, meaning that her mother was most likely to have been innocent.'

'I assume you included the fact that gunshot residue was found on both of them?'

'I did,' he nodded, 'but I also told them that Mrs O'Riley had fired a shot in the air, when we were on the station platform, and that she'd used the same gun to shoot Rebecca, of course.'

'Either way,' Vicky continued, 'I don't see how it makes much difference. Even if she didn't kill her sons with her own hand, she was complicit in every other way. She'd also just confessed to having murdered them, so I'm not sure how you were supposed to have known that she hadn't. And it's not as if you tried dragging her off the train, knowing what was about to happen.'

'Anyway,' Tanner muttered, glancing away with a capitulating sigh, 'it's out of my hands.'

'What do you mean, it's out of your hands?' Vicky demanded, taking hold of his arm to glare into his eyes. 'You're going to sit down and tell them that it wasn't your fault! Then you're going to make sure Forrester does, as well!'

'I'm only prepared to tell them the truth, Vicky. It will be up to them to decide what to do about it.'

'Then I'm just going to have to have a word with them myself.'

'Have you been asked to?'

'Not yet, but don't worry,' she huffed. 'I will, whether they want me to or not.'

The sound of the funeral service, drawing to a respectful close, had Tanner turning to watch the mourners begin drifting away.

'We never did find that missing painting,' Vicky mused, following his gaze.

'And I doubt we ever will.'

'I don't suppose you've seen any sign of those two con artists, the ones saying they were from the National Gallery?'

'Not that I've seen,' Tanner replied, craning his neck as the crowd made their way back to their cars. 'Apart from you, the only person I've been able to recognise is Mrs O'Riley,' he added, pointing her out with his chin.

'I'm surprised she was even allowed to attend!'

'I was asked if she could.'

'Oh, right,' Vicky replied, in a questioning tone.

Tanner glanced around to see her disagreeably shaking her head. 'She may have been complicit in her sons' execution, but don't forget, the poor woman lost her entire family in less than a week.'

With Vicky remaining silent, keen to change the subject, he glanced down at his flowers. 'Do you think anyone would mind if I paid my respects to Rebecca?'

'I don't see why,' she replied, crouching down to pick up a posy of her own, hidden at the base of one of the overhanging trees. 'I was hoping to do something similar myself.'

Waiting for the last of the mourners to sidle their way past, they made their way over the neatly cut grass to eventually find themselves standing in front of four polished marble headstones, marking an equal number of graves, three of which were waiting to be filled.

Placing his flowers gently down beside an abundance of others, Tanner stepped back to bow his head, leaving Vicky to rest hers next to his.

As he took a reflective moment to read the inscription, carved into Rebecca O'Riley's headstone, he took in the others before resting his eyes on the rectangular mound of freshly filled-in earth, underneath where her father's body lay.

Hearing the distant song of a blackbird, lifting and falling in the warm summer's breeze, he stared up at the cobalt blue sky above. 'What a pointless waste of life,' he sighed, bringing his eyes back to the graves. 'Even more so when you think that they'd all be alive today if it wasn't for that bloody painting.'

'After all these years,' Vicky murmured, glancing absently around at the dozens of surrounding gravestones, 'it's hard to be believe that it still hasn't been found.'

'Maybe it was never lost?' Tanner mused.

'You think Vincent sold it, before he was arrested?'

'It would seem the most likely answer. I can't think of any other reason why he wouldn't have told at least one person where it was, unless, of course, he did.'

'But he didn't, though,' Vicky stated. 'The last person he said anything to was Michael, and that was simply to tell him the name of some random person.'

'Then perhaps it wasn't as random as we thought.'

'Haven't we been down this road before?' she enquired, catching his eye.

'Well, yes,' Tanner replied, 'but only in relation to persons living.'

'What do you mean, "persons living"?

'I was thinking that maybe he'd meant someone who was already dead. Possibly someone who'd died a few days before he was arrested.'

'I'm sorry, boss, I'm not with you.'

'The person's name he mentioned to Michael,' Tanner continued, gazing over Vicky's shoulder. 'Leonard Burton, wasn't it?'

'It was,' she nodded.

'And when was Vincent O'Riley arrested?'

'The eighth of July, 1994,' Vicky replied. 'Do you think it's important?'

Surprised she knew the exact date, Tanner glanced around to find her pulling out her notebook.

'Because there's someone else who shares the name Leonard Burton, who just happens to be buried directly behind you,' he continued, directing her attention towards a lopsided weather-worn headstone, only a few feet away. 'And according to the inscription, he died only a few days before Vincent was arrested. The fifth of July, to be precise.'

Vicky took a moment to read the date for herself. 'Do you think...?' she eventually asked, turning to look at him with a questioning frown.

'Do me a favour, will you?' Tanner replied, searching the pockets of his suit. 'Take a picture of that headstone, and then send it to me?'

'Yes, of course,' she replied, pulling out her phone. 'What are you going to do?'

Finding his own, he began jabbing a finger at the screen. 'I'm going to call Forrester,' he eventually said, lifting it to his ear, 'just in case I need written permission to send Henderson out to buy a shovel.'

- CHAPTER FIFTY FIVE -

S PINNING AWAY, TANNER pressed the phone to his ear, impatiently waiting for his call to be answered.

'Forrester, sir, it's Tanner,' he eventually said, grateful not to have to leave some sort of convoluted message.

'Dare I ask what the occasion is?' came his superior's curious response.

'The occasion, sir?'

'For you to have called me? I assume someone else has turned up dead?'

'Well, yes, at least, sort of.'

'What do you mean, "sort of"?'

'We think we've found Leonard Burton, sir.'

'Who?'

'Leonard Burton?' Tanner repeated. 'If you remember, it's the name Vincent O'Riley said to his son, a few moments before he died.'

'Of course I remember, Tanner, being that it was also the name of that man you found nearly tortured to death inside his own home.'

'Yes, of course.'

'I sincerely hope you're not calling to tell me that you've found the body of yet another Leonard Burton?'

'Actually, I am, although probably not in the way that you're thinking.'

'You do realise that you're not making any sense.'

'His body is lying a few feet away from where Vincent O'Riley was buried.'

'What?'

'He died on the fifth of July, 1994, which, if I'm not mistaken, was only a few days before Vincent O'Riley was caught.'

'What are you getting at, Tanner?'

'I think I know where that painting is,' he continued, 'the one Vincent stole, all those years ago, the same one that everyone's been so desperate to find ever since.

'You think it's somewhere near the grave?'

'No, sir. I think it's hidden at the bottom of one. If Leonard Burton died three days before Vincent was arrested, then I'd have thought it would have been likely that his grave would have already been dug. It would therefore have been a relatively simple task for Vincent to have hidden it underneath some earth at the bottom, expecting a casket to be lowered on top of it. That would explain why nobody's been able to find it after all these years. It would also explain why Vincent used his last dying breath to tell his son the name of the person whose body its hidden under.'

'Are you sure about this, Tanner? It's going to be a hell of a job trying to get permission to have someone's body exhumed.'

'I'm about as sure as I can be, sir.'

'Then for your sake, I hope you're right. If the press finds out that you ordered a grave to be desecrated for no apparent reason, only a week after you'd been implicated in the death of a murder suspect, I can see them asking for your head, and I'm not entirely sure I'd be able to stop HQ from giving it to them.'

- CHAPTER FIFTY SIX -

Thursday, 24th August

THE MACABRE SIGHT of some slimy green rotting wood, hanging precariously from the end of a mechanical digger's arm as it lurched out from what was left of Leonard Burton's grave, had Forrester shuddering besides Tanner.

'I don't like this,' the superintendent muttered, barely loud enough for Tanner to hear.

'So you've said, sir,' he replied, exchanging a glance with Vicky beside him.

'I mean, I *really* don't like this,' Forrester repeated, as a broken piece of bone appeared between the digger's crooked, rusting teeth. 'It feels like we're breaking one of God's laws.'

'If it's any consolation, I don't recall any of the Ten Commandments saying, "Thou shalt not dig up thy neighbour's grave". I'm fairly sure I'd have remembered if there had been.'

Glaring acrimoniously at him, Forrester began glancing nervously about. 'If someone's told the newspapers we're here, desecrating someone's grave with a mechanical digger, and there's a photographer taking pictures of us doing so, I dread to think what the headlines will say in tomorrow's newspapers.'

'Dead People Dug Up for Loitering?' posed Tanner, offering Vicky a rueful smile.

'This isn't funny, Tanner!'

'Forgive me, sir, but I really don't see what harm we're doing. I mean, the guy is dead, after all.'

'But his family aren't, though!'

'That maybe so, but we did ask their permission, which they seemed happy enough to give.'

'After we'd promised to treat his body with the utmost respect. Had they known we were going to claw him out, one piece at a time, with something as unceremonious as a mechanical digger, I doubt if they'd have been quite so amenable.'

Tanner was about to respond when he saw one of the workmen by the side of the grave, lifting a hand up to the digger's driver.

As the engine came spluttering to a halt, the workman peered down into the grave's gloomy depths.

'Have you found something?' Forrester called out, stepping forward as he did.

'There's something down there,' the man replied, glancing up. 'It looks like some sort of a bag.'

- CHAPTER FIFTY SEVEN -

A S THE WORKMAN clambered down the muddy incline left by the mechanical digger's jagged claw, Tanner and Vicky joined Forrester to peer down into its shadow-filled depths.

'It's a bag, alright,' the workman called up, scraping away at a layer of mud.

'Is there anything inside?' Forrester asked, the inflexion of his voice lifting with excitement.

'No idea, mate. Why? Is there supposed to be?'

Forrester glanced uncertainly around at Tanner.

'We're – er – not sure,' Tanner replied, on Forrester's behalf, 'but if you could lift it out for us – carefully – it would be appreciated.'

Staring up at him with a pair of ever-widening eyes, the workman stepped suddenly back. 'Look, mate, if there's some poor bastard's head in there, then I don't want nuff'n to do with it.'

'It's nothing like that.'

'What – you mean – you think it's a bomb?' he enquired, his face becoming visibly pale.

'We don't *think* it is,' Tanner responded, amused by the man's panic stricken face.

'Anyways,' the workman continued, staring fitfully around at the surrounding walls, 'we've dug the hole for you. I think you can do the rest.'

Watching him scamper quickly out, Tanner found himself wishing he'd kept his mouth shut.

With it looking likely that he was going to have to climb down himself, he had a better idea.

As the workman ambled away with the digger's driver, he turned to offer Vicky an inviting smile.

'Don't even think about it!' came her clairvoyant response.

'Think about what?'

'Me, climbing into a six-foot deep hole, the same one where some poor sod's decomposing body had been less than five minutes ago.'

'I wasn't going to!'

'Oh, really!' she replied, with doubtful suspicion.

'I was going to ask Henderson,' Tanner continued, his eyes drifting towards the carpark.

'You sent him off to get some coffee, if you remember?'

'Oh, yes, so I did.'

Bringing his attention back to the grave, and the bag they could see buried at the bottom, Tanner let out a petulant sigh.

'May I offer another suggestion?' he heard Vicky say, gazing into the hole whilst standing beside him.

'By all means!' Tanner replied, glancing eagerly around.

'That you lead by example, and pull it out yourself?' she smiled.

'Fair enough,' he shrugged, reluctantly taking his jacket off. 'Would you mind looking after this for me?' he asked, holding it out.

'Not at all,' she smiled, hooking it over her arm as Tanner rolled his shirt sleeves up.

As Vicky and Forrester watched from above, Tanner climbed to the bottom, to eventually stand over what appeared to be a large holdall.

With most of it embedded firmly in the ground, he crouched down to begin scooping away at the mud, until eventually able to prise it out. Using both hands, he then carried it up the steep incline to place gently down on the grass.

As they all took a moment to gaze silently down, Forrester eventually clasped his hands together. 'Well, we can't just stare at it all day,' he stated, glancing around at Tanner. 'Someone's got to open it.'

'I thought maybe you'd like to, sir,' Tanner offered.

'In this particular instance, I'm more than happy for you to do the honours,' Forrester replied. 'Besides, there's no point in us both getting our hands dirty.

'What if it *is* a bomb?' Vicky queried, her eyes still fixed on the mud-encrusted holdall.

'Then it would have gone off by now,' came Tanner's factual response.

Kneeling cautiously beside it, he took a gentle hold of the zipper's tab to begin inching it along. When it stopped at the end, he gradually prised it open to reveal a faded orange plastic bag.

With Forrester offering him an encouraging nod, Tanner delved inside to lift the plastic bag carefully out.

Placing it next to the holdall, he gradually peeled open the top to peer inside.

'What can you see?' Vicky queried, leaning inquisitively forward.

'A shed load of cash,' came Tanner's excited response, 'and this,' he added, lifting out a rolled up tube of canvass.

'My God!' came Forrester's astonished response. 'It's the painting!'

- CHAPTER FIFTY EIGHT -

THE SOUND OF two metallic clicks, one after the other, had them staring around to see a couple of vaguely familiar men, both dressed in jeans and a t-shirt, and both pointing a sawn-off shotgun directly at them.

'We'll be taking that, thank you very much,' said the older of the two, raising the barrels of his gun to aim directly at Tanner's head.

'I was wondering when you two were going to show up,' Tanner muttered, taking them in. 'Mr Edward Phillips and Mr Thomas Ward, isn't it?'

'Something like that,' the old man replied.

'How's life treating you at the National Gallery?'

'We don't work for the National Gallery.'

'You don't say?'

'We work for ourselves. We always have done.'

'I assume your names aren't Edward Phillips and Thomas Ward, either, being that they were attending a conference in Barcelona when we were first introduced.'

'If you say so,' the old man replied. 'Now, if you don't mind handing me the painting, the cash as well, we'll be on our way.'

'Yes, of course,' Tanner smiled, stepping forward before stopping again. 'Actually, before I do, may I be so bold as to ask who you really are?'

'There's no reason for you to know. All that's important is the painting, the money, and the fact that there are no less than two shotguns pointing directly at your head.'

'Then I'm going to have to assume that you're Vincent O'Riley's partner in crime, Coby Morgan?'

Hearing Vicky mutter something unintelligible under her breath, Tanner continued to hold the old man's eye.

'At your service,' Coby eventually replied, offering Tanner a subservient nod.

'And I assume that means the person standing next to you is your son?'

'He is, although I fail to see what difference it makes. You're still going to give us that painting. The money, as well.'

'Or else, what? You're going to kill us?'

'I've waited far too long to get my hands on that painting. So yes, if I have to.'

'And what about your son?'

'What about him?'

'If you murder me, in cold blood I may add, he'd be treated as an accessory during the fact. Even if he doesn't pull the trigger, a court of law would consider him to be equally responsible. Do you really want him to spend the rest of his life in prison?'

As Coby's son sent a concerned look up at his father, Coby kept his eyes firmly fixed on Tanner's. 'Don't worry, son. If it does come to that, we're not going to get caught.'

'Are you sure about that?' Tanner enquired. 'I mean, there are two squad cars in the carpark behind you, and there's another one on the way.'

Seeing a glimmer of doubt linger over Coby's eyes, Tanner pulled in a breath. 'Listen, as far as I'm concerned, up until this point, neither of you have done anything wrong. You're only guilty of pretending to be a couple of curators from the National Gallery, which I'm not even sure is a crime.'

'You seem to be forgetting about Deborah Clarke,' Coby muttered.

With Tanner returning to him a look of bewildered incomprehension, Coby re-opened his mouth. 'She was the policewoman I shot, when we were caught, or at least when Vincent was. So you could say that I've got nothing to lose if I *do* shoot you.'

'But your son didn't have anything to do with that, which means we have nothing to charge him with – unless, of course, you do pull that trigger.'

With his eyes flickering with hesitant indecision, Coby took them off Tanner to look at his son.

Anticipating the moment, Tanner was about to leap forward to grab hold of his gun, when as if from nowhere, Vicky shoved her way past to hurl herself at him with a primordial scream.

Taken completely by surprise, Tanner was left to watch her tackle him to the ground to instantly begin clawing at his face, like a crazed, demented lunatic.

As both Tanner and Forrester sprang forward to drag her off, a shotgun's explosion brought them skidding to a halt.

With the sound of the gunshot reverberating around the graveyard, they looked on in horror as Vicky's body rolled off the terrified old man to end up lying on her back, her eyes staring unblinkingly up at the cloudless sky above.

As they stared down in incredulous horror to see a widening circle of blood creep slowly over the front of her white cotton blouse, a cold, numbing silence fell over the group.

Staring down at the shotgun, still clasped in his pale, slab-like hands, Coby's uncomprehending eyes gazed slowly up into Tanner's. 'I – I didn't do it!'

As Tanner watched the man's son inch gradually back, before spinning around to sprint suddenly away, he took a slow, deliberate step forward.

'Looks like your son's deserted you,' he muttered, snatching the shotgun from out of the old man's trembling hands.

'But – I – I d-didn't do it!' Coby repeated, tilting his head to stare dementedly at Vicky, her body lying unnaturally still beside him.

'I can't think who else it was,' Tanner replied, lifting the gun's butt to his shoulder. 'Any final words?'

'But I just said – I didn't do it!' came Coby's terrified reply, his eyes staring desperately up into the barrels of his own still smoking shotgun.

Resting a finger on the trigger, Tanner closed an eye to take careful aim at the old man's head. 'Sorry, but I beg to differ.'

'Stop it, Tanner!' came the berating sound of Forrester's commanding voice.

Turning to see his superintendent, kneeling besides Vicky's lifeless body, Tanner directed his revenge filled rage back to his intended victim. 'Give me one good reason why I shouldn't?'

'Because she's still breathing!'

'What?'

'She's still breathing, Tanner!' Forrester repeated, pressing a finger against her neck. 'She's not dead!'

- EPILOGUE -

Sunday, 27ᵗʰ August

CARRYING AN UNWIELDY bouquet of flowers, Tanner eased his head around the door of a dimly lit private room to see Vicky, propped up in a hospital bed with her eyes closed.

Assuming her to be asleep, he inched his way inside to rotate slowly around, searching for somewhere to leave the flowers.

With the cabinet behind the door already bustling with other people's, he wondered if he'd be able to leave them on her bedside table, only to find there was even less space there.

Glancing around again, he heard Vicky stir behind him, leaving him turning to stare down into her pale, lightly freckled face.

As her eyes flickered open to gaze up at him, her mouth cracked into a fragile smile. 'Morning, boss.'

'Sorry, Vicky, I didn't mean to wake you.'

'That's OK. I was only dozing.'

'I just wanted to stop by to say hello,' Tanner continued, feeling a little awkward, 'and to see how you were doing, of course.'

'Not bad, all things considered.'

'By all things considered, I assume you mean because you were shot at point-blank range by a 12-gauge double-barrelled shotgun?'

'Something like that,' she grimaced.

'Anyway, the doctor says you'll be back on your feet in no time.'

'Oh, really? That's a shame. I was kind of hoping to have some more time off.'

'Which you can have, of course! Take as long as you need!'

'Paid?' she enquired.

'Ah, now that could be a little more difficult.'

'Don't worry, boss. I was only joking. To be completely honest, I'm becoming increasingly desperate to get back to work. I'm not exactly the type to enjoy lying around all day with nothing to do.'

Unsure what to say next, Tanner glanced down to see a local newspaper, lying on the bedside table.

Seeing a photograph of none other than Superintendent Forrester, standing in full uniform in front of the Turner they'd unearthed just three days before, he reached down to pick it up.

'I assume you heard about the painting?' he enquired, casting his eyes over the article.

'You mean about it being sold to a Canadian collector for over a million pounds?'

'1.2 million, to be precise.'

'I did,' she nodded. 'It actually led me to wonder if we were going to see any of it, being that we were the ones who actually found it.'

'There's talk of a donation being made to the Police Benevolent Fund.'

'So that's a no, then,' she lamented.

'If it's any consolation, your name was mentioned.'

'Well, yes, at least it would have been if they hadn't spelt it wrong.'

'Did they?' Tanner enquired, studying the article with renewed interest.

'It's supposed to be Gilbert, spelt G I L B E R T.'

'What did they write?'

'Giblet, which is something completely different.'

'So they did!' Tanner laughed. 'How funny!'

'Yes, hilarious,' Vicky replied, offering him a distinctly unamused expression.

Turning the newspaper over, to see if there was anything interesting on the back, Tanner asked, 'Did you hear we charged Coby Morgan with attempted manslaughter, for inadvertently shooting you?'

'Gina mentioned something about it. Do you think it will stick?'

'Probably not, so we charged him with the murder of that police woman instead. I know it's somewhat late in the day, but at least he'll now have to serve time for it.'

'What about his son?'

'We were thinking of charging him with being in possession of an illegal firearm.'

'I assume you didn't?'

'It turned out to be his father's,' Tanner replied, returning the newspaper to the table, only to remember the flowers. 'Oh, I nearly forgot. I brought these for you,' he said, holding them out.

'Thanks, boss,' she smiled, taking them from him. 'You didn't have to.'

'I know, but I thought it was the least I could do.'

'You're making it sound like the whole thing was your fault.'

'Well, it wouldn't have happened if I'd been able to stop you.'

'And how were you supposed to have done that?'

'By disarming him first.'

'Maybe so, but I wasn't trying to disarm him.'

'If you don't mind me asking, what *were* you trying to do?'

Looking vacantly away, a heavy shadow passed over her eyes. 'I'm not sure, really, but I wasn't trying to disarm him, I know that much.'

Realising he'd stayed far longer than he'd intended to, Tanner glanced briefly around at the door. 'Anyway, I'd better let you get some more rest. Now remember, there's absolutely no rush for you to come back to work. Take as long as you need.'

Leaving her with an affectionate smile, he heard her call out behind him.

'Before you go, do you mind if I ask you something?'

'Yes, of course!' he exclaimed, spinning back.

'It may seem a little out of the blue, but I'm just curious, really.'

'About what?'

'Why you joined the police?'

'Why I joined the police?' he repeated, the question taking him completely by surprise. 'Well, I'm – er – not sure really,' he eventually replied.

'I signed up because of my mother,' Vicky stated, her deep blue eyes filling with tears. 'She joined straight out of school.'

'Oh, right. I'd no idea!'

'There's no reason for you to have known. It's something I've kept to myself, I think mainly because I've always wanted to be judged on my own merits. She also used her maiden name, so it's unlikely you'd have recognised it.'

'And what does she do now?' Tanner enquired, more interested to know the reason she'd so suddenly brought up the subject of her mother.

'Nothing,' Vicky replied, staring despondently down at her hands. 'She died when I was only two.'

'I'm sorry to hear that.'

'There's no need to be. It was a long time ago.'

'Even so, it must still be difficult.'

Vicky replied by wiping away at an escaping tear.

'May I ask her name?' Tanner continued, in a quiet, respectful tone.

'Constable Clarke,' Vicky replied, smiling to herself.

'Clarke?' Tanner repeated, the name jarring in his unconscious mind.

Vicky gazed up at him with an anxious frown. 'Her first name was Deborah. She was the policewoman Coby Morgan killed, back in 1994.'

'Jesus Christ!' Tanner exclaimed.

Vicky looked shamefully away. 'I know I should have told you before, probably when Vincent O'Riley was abducted, certainly when Coby Morgan's name first came up. And I did mean to – it's just that – well – if I had, you would have taken me off the investigation.'

'No kidding!' Tanner exclaimed, stunned by her extraordinary revelation. 'And for good reason. Do you have any idea how close you came to being killed?'

'So, anyway,' she grimaced, 'I thought I should apologise to you, personally. I also wanted to say that I fully understand if you feel it necessary to take disciplinary action against me.'

'Why on Earth would I want to do that?'

'Because, by launching myself at Coby Morgan, I didn't only put my life in danger, but yours and Superintendent Forrester's, as well.'

Tanner took a moment to draw in a contemplative breath. 'OK, well, first of all, I'm not going to recommend disciplinary action. Quite the opposite, in fact.'

Tanner waited for Vicky to look back at him before continuing. 'I'm actually putting your name forward for the King's Police Medal for bravery.'

'I'm sorry?' she replied, her mouth hanging open. 'Why would you want to do that?'

'Because you risked your life to protect your fellow officers.'

'But, I didn't, though. At least, that wasn't my intention.'

'That's not what my report says.'

As Vicky's lips trembled into a tearful smile, Tanner returned to her a stoic frown. 'However, the main reason I'm not recommending disciplinary action to be taken against you, even though you were stupid enough to charge at someone with a loaded double-barrelled shotgun, is far more selfish, I'm afraid.'

With Vicky gazing up at him with an expectant look, Tanner cleared his throat. 'It may be difficult for you to believe,' he eventually continued, offering her a sheepish smile, 'but I was about to do the exact same thing myself.'

*DCI John Tanner
will return in
The Bastwick Testament*

- ABOUT THE AUTHOR -

David Blake is a No. 1 International Bestselling Author who lives in North London. At time of going to print he has written twenty-five books, along with a collection of short stories. When not writing, David likes to spend his time mucking about in boats, often in the Norfolk Broads, where his crime fiction books are based.